THE BOOKSTORE AT RIVERS END

PHILLIPA NEFRI CLARK

Storm

Ebook ISBN: 978-1-80508-306-1
Paperback ISBN: 978-1-80508-308-5

Cover design: Eileen Carey
Cover images: Shutterstock

Published by Storm Publishing.
For further information, visit:
www.stormpublishing.co

ALSO BY PHILLIPA NEFRI CLARK

Temple River

The Cottage at Whisper Lake

The Bookstore at Rivers End

Rivers End Romantic Women's Fiction

The Stationmaster's Cottage

Jasmine Sea

The Secrets of Palmerston House

The Christmas Key

Taming the Wind

Martha

Bindarra Creek Rural Fiction

A Perfect Danger

Tangled by Tinsel

Maple Gardens Matchmakers

The Heart Match

The Christmas Match

The Menu Match

Detective Liz Moorland Series

Lest We Forgive

Lest Bridges Burn

Last Known Contact

ONE

It was a beautiful space, this shop here on the corner of the main street. If she chose the right moment, when there was no traffic on the road and the footpath was quiet, Harriet could imagine a gentler time. Vintage cars trundling by. Pedestrians dressed up to go shopping or take tea – perhaps on the opposite corner where the existing café might once have been a fancy tearoom. Or even further into history with the clip-clopping of horses harnessed to drays and small carriages on cobblestones. The madness of today's frantic lifestyle with its technology and noise of people wanting more, more, more... it was intrusive and exhausting.

Harriet's phone beeped. Intrusively.

'Well, bother.'

'What's wrong, Mum?'

Olive carried two folding chairs from the back room and set them up at the card table in the middle of the shop. The table had multiple uses depending upon the needs of the moment. This moment was lunch.

'Nothing, honey. But I might get you to turn off the notifications on the phone once we've eaten.'

'Then you'll miss messages from the shopfitters and suppliers and signwriters and who knows who else. But sure, I'll turn them off.' Olive plonked herself onto one chair and picked up her mother's phone. 'Oh.'

Reluctantly turning from one of the huge windows, Harriet stepped around and over shopfittings in various stages of construction to join her daughter. At twenty, Olive knew everything about technology and social media and little about what she wanted from life. But she'd give anything a go and not complain too much. Even uproot herself from her life in the city for a sea change thrust upon them both.

'Oh?' Harriet prompted.

Olive tapped on the phone without responding.

Harriet opened the paper bags Olive had left on the table a few minutes earlier. Freshly made pies from the café – which had an in-house bakery – and didn't they smell good. The neighbouring café had become a firm favourite for quick and delicious lunches since they'd begun the big job of converting an old real-estate agency into a bookstore. Three weeks down and at least another three to go on the fittings and fixtures alone.

Raising the phone above her head, Olive took a few photographs of the shop then tapped away on the phone. She put it down, the WhatsApp screen fading to black.

'What was that about?' Harriet pointed at the pies. 'Which do you want?'

Olive helped herself to the closest one. 'I turned off notifications so you need to remember to check now and then. Like, every hour, Mum. Not once a week. And it was just Dad. He wanted to know how we're going.'

Somehow Harriet stopped the rush of unfiltered words before they left her lips. The ones which were true and vented her frustration and anger but would hurt Olive. And Olive was the only good thing to have come from her now-finished marriage to Jason Main. Instead, she took a big bite of pie. It was too hot and burnt the back of her mouth when she swallowed but it was better than speaking her mind.

'I told him we're working long hours and hired a handyman to help.'

'You didn't.'

'A handsome handyman, recently divorced and looking for love.' Olive smirked and shoved a strip of pastry into her mouth.

'Olive... you'd better be teasing me. He'll get the wrong idea.' Harriet wiped her fingers on a napkin and reached for her phone. There was no such message. Olive had only said she was replying because her mother had her hands full with a million jobs and he could see for himself from the photos how much there was to do. 'Okay. You were teasing me.'

'You're easy to tease, Mum, and besides, if he thinks you're moving on then he'll realise what he's losing.'

'Lost, honey.'

'Nothing is ever really lost.' Olive's eyes were wide, bright. 'Something precious might be misplaced but there's always a chance it will turn up.'

'I think in this case there's no chance. Divorce is kind of final. And it looks as if the shopfitters have arrived and are parking out the front.' Harriet stood. 'I'll let them in.'

'Mum?' Olive's voice was plaintive. 'How about with a map?'

'Huh?'

'A treasure map. We can find what was lost.'

Harriet went around the table and kissed the top of Olive's head. 'Not too many treasure maps these days. Besides, the only precious thing in my life is you, my sweet child and I'm not about to misplace an entire human.'

'But we're talking about you and Dad. Not me.'

A tap on the door saved Harriet from responding. This wasn't a discussion with any kind of happy ending. No map was going to lead her back to Jason nor he to her. The only map she needed was one to make it clear how on earth she would transform the existing mess of boxes, paint cans, unbuilt bookshelves, and a computer system she was avoiding, into a thriving bookstore in their new town of Rivers End.

Understanding the computer system was easy – according to Olive.

Almost six weeks had passed since they'd begun the fitout and now that they were close to the point of ordering the first shipments of stock, there was no more putting off learning the software.

'I don't know why we can't find a nice old cash register and a beautifully bound orders book instead of this thing.' Harriet gazed at the wide screen connected to the computer which was housed beneath the counter. 'We can't use this if the power goes out.'

Olive rolled a second stool over and sat. 'Are you ninety or something? Who on earth writes up orders by hand?'

'George Campbell does.'

'And he *is* about ninety.'

'That's a terrible thing to say.'

'Truth, Mum. And you taught me to be honest. Besides, as nice as Mr Campbell's jewellery shop is, I doubt he'd sell dozens of items a day, if not more. And isn't a lot of his inventory handmade? Not the same as dealing with sales representatives and online ordering.'

Harriet glanced through the window to their left. The jewellery shop was a very old and established family business that had remained housed in its original building since the early nineteen hundreds. She and Olive had already met the delightful owner and been given a brief rundown of the history of the beautiful shop.

On the corner to her right was the café, and diagonally

across the intersection was Rivers End Real Estate with its bright flower planters beneath the windows.

Until a few months ago, this building had been a second real-estate agency. One of the ladies at the café had been happy to chat about how nice it was to now have four different businesses on the intersection. What they didn't know was that Jason had purchased the building quite a while ago and given the tenants notice at the time of the divorce.

Poor people. I'm so sorry.

'You're not even listening, are you?' Olive sighed dramatically. 'All that money spent on good schools and providing every advantage and you still don't know what you want to do.'

'I have never said anything like that.'

'But you've thought it. Anyway, the point is that I can teach you how to do all of this and I *know* you are smart enough to learn. As long as you apply yourself.' Olive's lips twitched and all it took was a gentle dig in her ribs from Harriet and she burst into laughter.

'Teach me, oracle,' Harriet said with a grin. 'Then tonight I will take you out for dinner and you can even have dessert.'

'Gee, that sounds... actually, it sounds good. Now, are you paying attention?'

After an hour of clicking and scrolling and practising ordering, Harriet had to admit it was straightforward. She wasn't entirely useless with computers and software systems after working as a school librarian for the past few years but this was different. She was the boss and the bookstore would thrive or fail based on how well she managed it. Knowing how every moving part worked was a steep learning curve but one she was willing to climb.

Olive stood and stretched. 'I might go for a run before we have dinner. Is that okay?'

'On the beach?'

'Probably. I'm sitting too much.'

'Sorry, honey. And thanks for this. For helping me, because it makes it easier.'

'Well, you're not a bad pupil.'

'And you are not a bad teacher,' Harriet said with a smile.

And today has been good. You seem happier.

Olive should have still been at university, studying law. She could be living on campus and enjoying being a young, independent woman. But the abrupt departure from her course after only two semesters had left Olive subdued and unwilling to explain. At first, Harriet had put it down to the upset of the divorce but eventually Olive had shared enough of what had happened to break Harriet's heart.

A group of older ladies, one with a cute dog on a lead, stopped outside and peered through the window. Olive waved and with smiles, the ladies waved back, before continuing on. 'There you go. Customers, for sure.'

A small flame lit in Harriet's heart. She'd dreamed of owning a bookstore from the first time she stepped into one as a child and now it was a reality. Not the way she'd expected – as part of a divorce settlement – and she still hadn't come to terms with Jason owning the building for so long without telling her. Regardless, this dream was coming true and with Olive at her side it was an adventure to meet head-on.

'And now I'm going. See you later.' Olive waved over her shoulder.

'Enjoy the run.'

Although Olive insisted the daily runs were for fitness, Harriet suspected it was as much to have time alone and hopefully be healing. And wearing her 'mother hat', she sometimes worried about long runs on an often deserted beach or along lonely backroads.

For a while after Olive left, Harriet made some notes to remind herself how to access the ordering side of things and the inventory once they had one. Then she closed the computer for the day and took their cups and empty teapot to the kitchen.

This room was the first part of the building she'd set up, figuring a kitchen was the heart of a home, so just as important for a business. The round table and chairs, which had only arrived yesterday and were a welcome change from the card table, could seat four. A small but modern fridge and freezer were housed below a built-in microwave and there was a narrow pantry filled with staples. A new sink was installed along with drawers for cutlery and a cupboard for crockery. With the coffee machine Harriet had splashed out on, the kitchen was a welcoming space.

She turned off the lights and collected her handbag and briefcase from the counter. At the glass door she paused to look back, as she did most days. There was such satisfaction in working so hard for their future... hers and Olive's. This bookstore was every bit as much for her daughter and hopefully would give Olive some breathing space and a chance to consider her future without pressure to find a job somewhere else.

Bookshelves lined almost every inch of every wall and rows of standalone shelving would invite the shopper to browse – once they were filled with books. They had the makings of a cute and functional kids' area and would host reading days each week. There were tables among armchairs and several quiet nooks to relax or read in. Harriet's intention was to have a pile of books always available as read-only options for those who weren't ready to buy.

The town didn't have a public library. The closest was in Green Bay, more than twenty minutes away, so replicating some spaces found in libraries made sense. If she listened carefully she could almost hear hushed voices and children's laughter. On a whim, she took a photograph and sent it to Jason with a message:

Not long now.

Now why did I do that?

She frowned as she stared at the message. Sent. Too late.

Outside the air was warm. Nothing compared to an early summer evening in Rivers End as a light breeze carried a hint of sea air. She should follow her daughter's lead and be down on the beach. As tempted as she was, the paperwork was piling up and if she hurried home she could pay some bills before dinner. That was a better use of her time.

The cottage they were renting was adorable. Built from sandstone blocks with a dark green metal roof, it sat on a quarter-acre block on Temple Road, which ran between the beach and township. It took Harriet less than five minutes to get there, cutting across the parkland behind the bookstore, and even though they'd only been here a few weeks, unlocking the stained-glass and timber door was like coming home to a long-loved house.

Inside was just as inviting with polished floorboards, pastel colours, and comfortable furnishings throughout. With just two bedrooms it was ideal for now. Once the bookstore started to support itself then Harriet would consider buying something a fraction larger.

When the family home sold – the one she and Jason had built all those years ago in a leafy eastern suburb of Melbourne – all the furniture sold as well. Apart from a few treasured pieces, she wasn't attached to keeping tables and chairs and beds and Jason intended to travel for the next few years. Just as well, given the difference in space between her two-level home of so many years and this little cottage.

Harriet had emptied the mailbox on the way in and added

several bills to the pile on the kitchen table. Among them was a postcard.

Ignoring it, she unzipped her briefcase and removed the laptop. She'd done a crash course in basic financial management before the move because even though she had an accountant, Harriet was determined to understand the business inside and out. Keeping a close eye on the financial side of the bookstore was as important as the day-to-day management and she'd surprised herself by having an aptitude for numbers. Not bad for an ex-librarian who would prefer to have lived in a time before technology.

She was finishing the last payment when Olive arrived, puffing and sweating as she jogged on the spot.

'I need a shower. You need to stop working for the day.'

'Well, you're right about the first part.'

Olive laughed and jogged to her room. 'You work too hard, Mum.'

Is there any other way?

When she heard the shower turn on, Harriet packed the laptop away and tossed the paid bills into a file to take to work. She had a lockable filing cabinet there for everything to do with the bookstore but until the place was fully furnished it was just more comfortable doing some things at home.

She picked up the postcard. The picture on the front was of the city of Darwin. The note was typically brief.

Last week on Aussie soil. Got a sweet ride by boat to the next stop... wherever that is. Love you both. Jason/Dad.

So he was almost gone.

Her stomach tightened in anticipation of angry butterflies battering her from the inside. They came, taunting her that she was no longer married to her university sweetheart. No longer secure in a long-term relationship with no debt and a nearly perfect life.

Three years ago they'd been the happiest family in the world – until Jason had a health scare which almost took him from them. Against the odds he'd recovered from a brain tumour, but he was a changed man, no longer interested in his career as a corporate accountant and willing to give up almost every part of his carefully built life in a desire to pursue his new idea of happiness. To his credit he'd hung around long enough to help sort out the house and finances but the day the divorce was final – less than six months ago – he was off to follow his dream of slow travelling the world, starting by hitchhiking around Australia.

Without us.

Reeling from the shock of the breakdown of her marriage, Harriet had withdrawn into herself. She'd needed to protect herself but by doing so, had missed any subtle signs there might have been from Olive about the terrible situation she was in. Both became experts at keeping to themselves and Jason was far too excited about his wonderful future to notice. Or care.

Harriet pushed away the bitterness.

Olive was singing at the top of her lungs and Harriet burst into laughter.

Jason could travel far and wide but he'd lost more than he yet realised. She'd only lost a husband but he'd lost a wife and a daughter – at least until he sorted himself out, if he ever did. She left the postcard where Olive would see it and went to get ready for dinner.

TWO

Olive had barely touched her nachos and absently ran a finger around the rim of her still-full glass of mango juice. She'd been quiet since they'd headed out and left the choice of venue to Harriet. Once seated in the bistro, she'd politely smiled at the server and ordered before sinking back into her own thoughts.

'Are you tired, honey?'

'Hm?' Olive's eyes focused as she looked at Harriet. 'Not really. Are you?'

'To the bone.'

'I'm sorry, we should have stayed home.'

'Not a chance. I promised you dessert but I don't know how you'll have room after eating so much.'

Olive glanced at her meal. 'Oh.'

'It looks nice.'

'It is. Actually, it is outstanding. How's yours?'

'You know I'm a sucker for good fish and chips and this one is delicious.'

With a nod, Olive took a few sips of her juice. She gazed out at people wandering past, heading off to eat or just walking in the almost darkness, many with a dog or two. 'We should have opened a dog shop. You know, grooming and snazzy jumpers and treats and supplies.'

'I don't really know anything about that kind of business.'

Olive picked up a nachos chip. 'Don't really know about running a bookstore... but I guess you were a librarian. And we've never had a dog so it isn't like we could have had that experience. Why haven't we ever had a dog?'

What on earth is going on with you?

'You know why.'

'Dad's allergies.'

'It's not like we didn't want one. And your dad loves dogs but—'

'Yeah, yeah. I remember. His needs came first. Are all men that way? Just like...' Olive bit her lip.

'Oh, honey.'

'Did you read the postcard, Mum?' Olive dropped the chip and wiped her fingers on a napkin. 'Once he gets on this boat then we lose track of him. Even *he* doesn't know where he's going so how are *we* supposed to know he's safe?'

Harriet mentally kicked herself for not picking up on Olive's worry earlier.

'I thought the same when I read the postcard. Off on a boat to a new adventure but to where? Will he be safe? How long until we hear from him next... so many thoughts. But then it occurred to me that your father is a capable and intelligent man. He's lived more than fifty years and before we married, he back-packed across South America.'

'Well, yeah, but he was young then.'

Afraid she was going to laugh at an inappropriate moment, Harriet drank some of the crisp light beer she'd chosen. It paired well with the locally caught fish.

'Are you not worried about Dad?'

'I guess I always will worry, to a degree. But I believe he

knows what he's doing and won't take risks. There may be times you don't get a call or text for a while but it doesn't mean he's in danger or that anything is wrong. When did you last speak with him?'

'I don't remember. Ages. And it doesn't matter. You're right. He's a grown man and one who wants to follow his dreams.'

So much emotion under the surface, honey.

'You should call him.'

Olive shrugged and finally began eating.

Harriet checked her phone. Jason hadn't responded to the photo she'd sent so she added a message.

> Olive is worrying about you. We're out at dinner but if you get this before you leave, give her a call. Please.

The response was almost immediate.

> I can phone in an hour. Is anything wrong?

'Who's that?'

'Dad. He wants to know if he can call in an hour.'

With a sudden smile, Olive nodded. 'You said yes?'

'Sure did.'

> She just wants to know you're going to be safe.

After sending the final message, Harriet put the phone face down. Olive was eating with gusto and in minutes pushed an almost empty plate away.

'Ready for dessert?' Their server appeared. 'I'm sure I heard my name called.' She was a friendly faced woman in her forties, with *Tessa* emblazoned on her apron. 'Here's the new menu and I'll run off with your plates and give you both a moment.'

'Oh, yum. Oh, and that one.' Olive pored over the menu.

Harriet had the same issue of too many delicious choices. In the end they elected to share a trio of gelato and a strawberry cheesecake. When Tessa brought the desserts, Harriet and Olive both made sounds of appreciation. The presentation was above normal pub standards and the fruit smelled divine.

Tessa laughed. 'Our little kitchen team love making things pretty.'

'All the food has been beautiful,' Harriet said. 'On a par with the best in Melbourne.'

'Is that where you've come from? That is a mighty nice compliment.'

'Well deserved, and yes, we are recent transplants from the city.'

'And when is the grand opening of the bookstore?' Tessa chuckled again. 'Don't look so surprised. Rivers End is buzzing with the news. We can't wait.'

After a moment or two chatting about the bookstore, Tessa tended another table and Harriet dived into the gelato. 'Mmm.'

'She has a point, Mum.' Olive slid a large spoonful of cheesecake into her mouth and closed her eyes.

They stopped talking until the plates were empty and the bill paid. The bistro was getting busier when they stepped out onto the pavement and wandered to look through the windows of the bookstore.

'We do need a grand opening. Maybe not on the first day or even week, but we could do a soft opening and then once everything is going perfectly, have a special day or weekend. Invite local papers and politicians.' Olive hooked her arm through Harriet's. 'We need to get home.'

It was dark now but the air was still warm and the moon lit the path across the park.

'Ooh, I like it, let's put some time aside tomorrow to make a plan.'

'Not tomorrow.'

Harriet frowned, trying to remember why not tomorrow.

'Book buying, Mum.'

'Of course. I knew that.'

Olive rolled her eyes. 'I'd put reminders in your phone but you never look at it. Do you have the addresses of where we're going or should I find them again?'

'Cheeky. I do have them. Our first appointment is in Driftwood Cove, at ten.'

'Very good.'

They turned onto Temple Road and almost made it to the door of the cottage when Olive's phone began to ring. 'It's Daddy.'

Harriet opened the door and Olive answered the phone as she rushed in first. Her excited chatter made Harriet smile. If only all things were as easily fixed as hooking up Jason and Olive for a phone call.

'I like it here.' Olive stared out of the window of the car as Harriet drove along the road to Driftwood Cove. 'The scenery changes all the time. And last night?' She turned to smile at Harriet. 'After you went to bed I remembered to take the bin out. Collection day today. Anyway, I saw an owl!'

'You did?'

'In the tree out the front. It was watching me and wasn't the least bit afraid. Owls are supposed to be a good omen. Though I did read somewhere that they can bring bad luck and I hope that's not true. Bit over bad stuff. Oh, sometimes when I'm at the beach there are dolphins a little way out. And I read up about how this region is perfect for whale watching in winter.'

This was better. Olive's mood had lightened after talking to Jason for ages last night. She'd said little about the conversation but Jason had texted Harriet later with a quick message.

Thank you. For everything. Live the dream.

Whether he was referring to him living his, or the bookstore, Harriet wasn't about to guess. Neither was truly her dream without him at her side.

'That's the turn-off we just went past.'

Harriet pulled over when it was safe and U-turned. 'Sorry about that. Can you navigate to our first stop?'

'Like a pirate? Ahoy, me hearty, there be rocks ahead.'

Today was part exploring and part acquiring. Harriet was keen to create a corner in the bookstore for rare and out-of-print books. After putting a small ad in the local paper a few times, she'd received a number of invitations to look at collections. Most sounded more suited for an op-shop but it was worth looking. There were always gems to be found among the rubble.

'Scrub the decks then heave-to.'

Harriet chuckled. 'Can we heave-to this address?'

'If we must. We go all the way to the end of this road and turn right, then there's a road up a hill. I'll say when.' Olive glanced at the phone on her lap periodically. 'Oh, there's the sea. I thought we'd gone a long way inland.'

'How pretty is this?'

As the car went over a rise the view expanded to a small township nestled between two hills. A row of pines dotted a park between the beach and the road and on the other side, a dozen or so shops made up the hamlet of Driftwood Cove. Harriet slowly drove past the shops and took the road Olive pointed to.

There were occasional houses along the hillside, far back from the road and built for the view.

'These look new. Can we buy one?'

Harriet snorted. 'Are you planning on winning the lottery?'

'Oh. Would they be expensive all the way out here though?'

'You should browse the listings at Rivers End Real Estate. Which driveway, honey?'

The first three appointments only resulted in the purchase of half a dozen books. Harriet had always had a keen interest in old books and over the years had gathered a small collection of her own. After the decision was made to move to Rivers End and open the bookstore, she couldn't resist the idea of adding a small section offering rarer, possibly antique books, if she could find enough, although she'd never part with her personal collection. Olive was just as fascinated with the search and had discovered a few favourite websites where she could check on a particular title if Harriet didn't know it.

They'd stopped for lunch bought from a café in Driftwood Cove, sitting at a table in the park between the beach and the road. Being out of the bookstore was good. Harriet loved what she was creating but in the weeks since they'd arrived she'd barely been outdoors during daylight hours. She'd breathed deeply of the sea air and let her body relax... as much as it would. Her muscles ached and there was a tension which went far beyond a few weeks of emptying out one shop and building another.

Now they were on a twisty, climbing road inland from Rivers End and Harriet was doubting her life choices as bitumen turned to dirt and narrowed. On one side was an alarming drop and she prayed no vehicle would approach head on.

Olive's eyes hadn't left her phone in minutes. 'Okay, on the right in a hundred metres. It is a sharp turn and looks like it goes up even more, but you have to take it because there's not another driveway to turn in for ages.'

A moment later Harriet nosed around an almost hairpin turn and then applied power. It was steep and barely even a track but her car got them to an open gate and the ground abruptly levelled out.

'Good driving, Mum. Glad it was you.'

'Want to drive back?'

'Not a chance.'

The difficult drive was forgotten as a beautiful homestead came into view. With a backdrop of bushland, the house was on about an acre of gardens with tall gums somehow perfect among clusters of roses and deciduous trees. It was built with limestone and timber and sprawled around a circular driveway with a central garden overrun with cottage flowers. The riot of colours and different heights might have been taken from a gardening magazine.

'Wow. I wonder if this place is for sale.'

'Isn't it lovely?'

'Oh look... horses!'

In a paddock to one side, several horses with shining coats galloped toward a post and rail fence, somehow stopping without any incident to watch the newcomers with interest.

Harriet parked at one end of the house. 'Shall we?'

'Do you think I could say hi to the horses?'

'We can ask.'

When she climbed out, a sensation of utter peace cradled Harriet. There was birdsong and a welcoming whinny from one of the horses and the air was crisp and cool, even on a warm day. It had to be the vegetation and altitude.

Armed with a lined book she'd been using to keep track of purchases, Harriet, with Olive following but casting longing glances toward the paddock, made her way to the front door along a path paved with large red bricks. The door was timber with a clear window in the top half, offering a glimpse into a large entry area with hooks along the wall, some holding coats. She tapped.

'Who is it that lives here?' Olive's eyes were wide.

'We're meeting Mr Brock Salisbury.'

'He sounds ancient and very proper,' Olive said. 'I expect a formal suit and a monocle.'

Footsteps approached and the door opened.

The man on the other side was closer to Harriet's age than ancient. And he looked puzzled. A bit over six feet tall, he had broad shoulders and a slim waist, around which was tied a long white apron. The front of his dark green T-shirt had a puff of flour in the middle. Black hair was shoulder-length and a three-day growth accentuated strong features. Strong, handsome features.

Are you the cook?

'May I help? Are you lost?'

'We have an appointment with Mr Salisbury. I'm Harriet Main and this is my daughter Olive.'

Understanding crossed his face and he stepped back. 'Apologies, I'd forgotten. Please come in. Would you mind closing the door? I have to check the oven.'

With that he was gone.

'Mum,' Olive whispered. 'Do you think we should go in?'

'Probably the best way to see the books.'

Olive peered through the door but made no move forward.

Harriet's heart sank. Olive never used to be so wary of people.

'Would you rather wait here?' Harriet slipped off her shoes and left them outside then stepped onto rich timber floorboards. 'It's fine if you do.'

'But what if he's... busy? Cooking?'

'Then we'll be quick.'

Olive followed Harriet, leaving her shoes on the bricks and closing the door behind them both.

'Do you smell the baking?' Harriet sniffed the air.

'It's making me hungry again. We'll need to get afternoon

tea when we leave and I might need to run twice as far a day at this rate,' Olive grumbled.

They reached an open-plan kitchen and dining area and stopped in awe. Olive whispered, 'Told you, he's cooking so we shouldn't interrupt.'

The kitchen was huge, with two wide ovens and a double-size cooktop. Pots and pans hung over a central work station, too high for Harriet to easily reach but obviously suited to the owner. The man in question was removing a tray from one oven and he frowned as steam rose around his face.

'Not right. But closer.' He spoke to the tray.

Between the kitchen and dining room was a long counter with a stainless-steel top. For that matter, all the surfaces in the kitchen were the same. If anything, it was like a small commercial kitchen. On the counter were rows of baked goods on plates. Pies and rolls and pastries and cupcakes. Using his fingers as tongs, Brock transferred half a dozen croissants to a fresh plate and added it to one of the rows. He tore one croissant open, held it to his nostrils and then took a bite. It must have been steaming hot but he didn't react other than to nod his head once.

A large whiteboard on wheels was pushed against a wall and Brock strode to it, picked up a marker, and wrote some notes beside a photograph which was attached with a magnet. Then, rubbing his chin, he stepped back, eyes widening when he noticed Harriet and Olive.

'I am so sorry. Right in the middle of something and multi-tasking is not my friend. Are you hungry?'

'Er, no, we just—'

'What are these?' Olive stepped to the counter and pointed at a plate filled with small, squarish pastries. 'They smell all caramelly and walnutty and something else.'

Brock crossed the room, stopping on the other side of the

counter and gazing at Olive intently. 'Can you identify the something else?'

Harriet joined Olive, a bit surprised by the conversation. The golden brown pastry was folded on itself like a little parcel.

'You'll laugh at me,' Olive said.

'I assure you I will not.' Brock's eyes hadn't left Olive's face. 'What do you smell?'

'Cheese. But not a plain cheese... something with bite.'

He said nothing.

'Okay, you didn't laugh but you think I'm silly.'

'Gorgonzola. You've got a good nose, have you done culinary training? I'm sorry, I don't know your name.'

'Olive. And no, never. So I got it right?' Her face was alight when she looked at Harriet. 'Doesn't it smell nice?'

'It does, honey.'

Brock pushed the plate of parcels closer. 'Please, try one. Both of you. I value feedback.' He crossed his arms. 'They came out of the oven twenty minutes ago.'

Wasting no time, Olive took a parcel and bit into it. When Harriet hesitated, Olive handed one of the treats to her. The pastry was still warm but crisp and golden. Inside was a smooth and crunchy and sticky mix which tasted sugar-sweet and creamy-savoury all at once.

'This is delicious. I've never eaten anything quite like it,' Olive said.

'And what do you think, Mrs Main?'

Caught with her mouth full, Harriet felt herself redden and hurried to swallow. Brock waited with no sign of impatience.

'I don't normally enjoy blue cheeses but the caramel brings out such a richness that it all just works. And please... Harriet, not Mrs Main.'

He nodded and returned to the whiteboard where he made further notes.

Harriet caught Olive's eye and they both smiled.

'I imagine you would like to see the books we discussed.' Brock turned off the oven and removed his apron, suddenly noticing the flour on his T-shirt and brushing at it. 'And after that, perhaps you'd both like to try some of the other baked goods.'

Without another word the man left the kitchen and as Harriet followed, she was certain she heard Olive moan under her breath and mutter something about a diet.

THREE

'My mother has a great love for collecting but she recently decided to downsize and move into the town. While I'd be happy to keep these for her, she isn't one to revisit a book once read so she asked me to find a solution.' Brock offered a wistful smile. 'I saw your advertisement and spoke to Mum about it.'

'And she has no objection?'

He laughed. 'Quite the opposite. She can't wait for your bookstore to open so she can recycle whatever money you might pay today with the purchase of new books.'

I like her already.

They were in a room Harriet could only describe as a reading room.

Along two walls, heavy timber bookcases reached almost to the ten-foot-high ceiling. A lovely small oval table graced the middle of the room with two straight-backed chairs at one end. A bay window had a seat built into it and thick cushions were piled against a wall. Several tub seats and comfy armchairs were around the room, each with a side table.

'Such a gracious room.'

'Both my parents loved it in here and I admit to using it as often as my work permits. I've put the books in question on the main table if you'd like some time to look?'

Brock hesitated.

'Please feel free to stay or else we will be as quick as we can. We don't wish to take up too much of your time,' she said. 'Nothing you'd prefer to keep?'

'Thank you. But these are Mum's and she's keen to sell them. I need to return to the kitchen so just call when you're ready.'

Once he'd left the room, Harriet approached the table and Olive took her phone out, ready to search for information. There were close to fifty books, sorted into eras, which was an interesting approach. The newest books were from the 1970s, going all the way back to the mid-1800s. Every one of them was in pristine condition and there were only a handful which weren't of interest.

'This is the best selection yet, Mum,' Olive said.

Harriet gently opened a leather-bound bible from 1830. Printed in England, it was an edition with coloured illustrations and gold edges and although the condition was good, rather than excellent, she wanted it. Whether she could allocate sufficient cash from her budget for such a find was another thing.

'Look at this, Mum. It must have been a gift.'

Olive had a thin book open and read aloud. *'To my beloved husband Henry, may your birthday be as wonderful as these beautiful poems. Your ever-loving wife, Eleanor 1852.'*

'Oh that is true history. Who is the author?'

'It's a collection of Australian poems. I don't recognise the poets or publisher so perhaps this was a locally or privately published book. Let me see...'

Olive began to search on her phone and Harriet picked up the book. It was beautifully bound but with little information other than the publisher and year of printing. 1852. She was reluctant to flick through the pages, although sorely tempted to.

Better to protect the book by less handling until she owned it. Her heart fluttered a bit with excitement.

What a find!

'Sorry, nothing to report. I might be able to search more at home on the laptop.'

'I'm going to make an offer, Olive. Something about this screams history and it will be a wonderful addition to our collection.'

There was little Harriet didn't want from this wonderful room. This made everything worthwhile, finding little gems which would add interest to her bookstore and perhaps eventually encourage booklovers from further afield to visit.

'Shall I go and find Mr Salisbury?' Olive was already leaving.

Harriet did some calculations. Brock hadn't set a price so she might not be in a position to buy everything she wanted. Keeping within a budget mattered because there were no guarantees that used books would bring the clientele and sales that her market research had shown new books would. This was more about her love of books and desire to create a sustainable business which catered for many tastes.

After a few minutes her daughter hadn't returned so Harriet went in search, stopping short of the kitchen when she heard a conversation underway.

'Initially there will be seven. The first is here in Rivers End.' Brock's voice was conversational. 'Three more in other regional parts of Victoria follow within months plus three in New South Wales. Those are all based on the model here which will open later this year.'

'And you are creating the menus for all the communities? That's a huge job.'

'It is. But I thrive on challenges, Olive.'

'And it's such a good cause.'

Hearing her daughter sound so relaxed and interested was

good. Olive was naturally friendly but had become a bit reluctant to meet new people since her parents separated. Harriet had hoped the move onto campus would help and it had. Until Olive met the wrong kind of man.

It kept Harriet's anger at Jason's choices simmering beneath the surface. Before her mood could deteriorate, she stepped into the kitchen.

Olive was perched on a stool on one side of the long counter while Brock constructed a row of small cake boxes on the other side. They both glanced up.

'Whoops, sorry. Mr Salisbury, Mum would like to make an offer on the books.' Olive grinned. 'Which is why I came in here in the first place.'

'Brock, please. If you have a minute, I'll just pack two of these for you first.' His hands moved swiftly to collect a half dozen or so mixed pastries which were deposited in a box, then repeated in a second one. He closed the lids and held them out to Olive. 'If any are awful then let me know. And why.'

It was unlikely that the man's other creations would be anything other than delicious. The yummy taste of the earlier pastry was still in Harriet's mouth. And she was curious to find out more about the conversation she'd overheard.

'Did you find some interesting books?'

Brock gestured for Harriet and Olive to go through the doorway first.

'The collection is wonderful. Beautiful condition and some real treasures there.'

At the oval table, Harriet opened her purchase book. 'I'm happy to make an offer on the entire collection on the table, or just some. There are several I would love to acquire but depending on your price my budget may not stretch far enough.'

'Mum didn't set a price. She genuinely intends to become a

regular customer of yours and hoped to get a couple of hundred dollars.'

'For all of them?'

Brock nodded.

'Oh goodness, no, I have a more appropriate figure in mind,' Harriet said. She quickly wrote an amount in her book and showed him. It was more than she'd planned for any one purchase but no other stop today had yielded such beauties.

Brock's eyes widened as he read the figure. 'That is a lot more than a couple of hundred dollars. What's so special about these books?'

Olive picked up the poetry collection. 'This has to be a very limited print run and the old message in it must add to the interest. Is that right, Mum?'

'It is. And the Bible is special on several fronts. Are you certain your mother wants to sell it? Most people keep Bibles.'

'I told you earlier, Mum only reads a book once. In this case, possibly never. Her religion is gardening.'

Although his tone was serious, his eyes flickered with amusement and something deep within Harriet's heart stirred. Her own sense of humour had all but left months ago yet this stranger made her feel something. A sudden urge to tease him in return.

'But people read bits of the Bible all the time... oh. I see. That was a joke.'

Over Olive's head, Brock and Harriet exchanged a smile.

'Mum, next appointment is in half an hour.'

'Thank you. So, is the offer suitable?'

'Very. Would you like a box?'

Olive grabbed Harriet's car keys from the table. 'We have some. Be right back.' She dashed out.

The room suddenly felt... different. Harriet was acutely aware of Brock standing only a few feet away. He gazed at her until she didn't know what to do or say. It wasn't unpleasant. More like he was sizing her up.

'Um—'

'She's a smart and kind young woman.'

'Oh. Olive? Light of my life.'

His eyes dropped to Harriet's hands. Her left hand, where she still wore her wedding ring. She loved the ring and what it once represented and even six months after the divorce was a long way from feeling comfortable without it. The front door opened and Olive appeared carrying several sturdy cardboard boxes. The moment was gone, whatever that moment was. Harriet's pulse was going too fast.

'Would you mind packing for me, honey? And Brock, would you prefer cash or else I can do a direct payment by PayPal.'

'Do you normally carry so much cash?' He raised an eyebrow. 'Cash is fine.'

She counted out the agreed sum and handed it to him. 'Only today, to look at stock. Do you mind if I get you to sign my purchase book as confirmation of the sale?'

'And Brock, am I allowed to say hello to the horses?' Olive asked.

A broad smile crossed his face. 'Watch the smaller bay mare. She acts like your best friend then nips, so after she nuzzles you, step back.'

After Olive left again it only took a few minutes to complete the transaction. Brock piled a couple of the boxes on top of each other and lifted them with a small grunt. 'I'll come back for the others but don't forget the pastries.' He headed to the front door and Harriet collected the cake boxes, her book, and handbag and followed. She opened the door for them both and stopped long enough to slip her shoes on.

The boxes went into the boot then they wandered across the garden to where Olive was stroking the soft muzzles of the horses, although she kept out of reach of one who kept extending her neck with her lips flapping.

'Mum, aren't they divine? Are these all yours, Brock?'

'More like me belonging to them,' he said. He rubbed between the ears of the bay, who'd given up on Olive. 'All rescues and here to live out their lives with plenty of food and friends.'

A sudden prickle behind Harriet's eyes threatened to turn into tears as a shiver ran over her body. Who was this man?

'What about other pets?'

'Olive...'

Brock gently pushed the bay away when her teeth came out. 'Until recently I've travelled a lot and worked away from home too much to have a dog. Or several dogs. The horses have been here for years, thanks to my parents, and one of the neighbours cares for them and the place when I'm away. I think I'll be home more now.'

'Then you should get a whole house full of needy dogs.' Olive grinned and leaned her forehead against that of one of the horses. 'I love you, horsey.'

Before her woeful need to weep became a reality, Harriet touched her daughter's shoulder. 'We do have to leave. Would you mind helping with the other boxes?' Not waiting around to risk further emotional battles, Harriet headed to the car.

By the time Brock and Olive – who were again deep in conversation – arrived with the remaining books, Harriet had dabbed her eyes and given herself a mental shake. She managed a smile at Brock.

'Please let your mother know how happy her books have made us and that I look forward to welcoming her into the bookstore soon. And thank you for the pastries.' Those were stowed on the back seat.

He offered his hand and she shook it. Brief, firm, and over in a couple of seconds, it left her skin warm and tingly.

I'm totally losing the plot today.

'Thanks for letting me meet the horses,' Olive said.

'Come and visit them anytime.'

He waved and strode away and Harriet nosed the car onto the driveway. In her rear-vision mirror she saw him standing near the house, watching them leave.

As tired as they both were from the long day of driving and buying, Harriet and Olive were still cataloguing the books after dinner. Tomorrow was promising to be full-on with the final shopfittings going in so there would be little free time to complete this.

'I've almost finished the last of my boxes, Mum, and then I'll make us tea and shall we have more of Brock's pastries?'

'We definitely shouldn't let them get stale,' Harriet said, trying to hide a smile.

'I could eat them all in one go. Do you think he was just being polite about me visiting the horses again?'

'We don't know him, honey.'

Olive picked up another book. 'He's an executive chef and nutritionist who has managed kitchens on cruise ships and now he is formulating meals for the new assisted living centres.'

Harriet straightened. 'Is that what you were discussing earlier? About the one in Rivers End?'

'Yup. Being built now as the flagship, up near the school.'

'You found out a lot in that short time.'

'He's easy to talk to. When I think about how... *other* people have ignored me or talked down to me or tried to tell me how to talk and think... but Brock was interested in my opinion.'

'I'm so sorry you've experienced that, Olive. Your opinion does matter. A lot. Some people can be so condescending.'

'Well, Brock was talking to me like an old friend and I felt safe with him. Hang on... this is a diary, Mum. How did this one slip in?'

'Oh dear. Which box is that from?'

'Um... oh, the last stop.'

They'd arrived later than planned and there'd been no answer when they knocked, but a cardboard box had been left on the verandah with a note that they could take the box for fifty dollars but it had to be everything.

'We only looked at the books at the top and you liked them. This was at the very bottom so I wonder if they meant to put it in?'

'Okay, well put it to one side and we can ring tomorrow and let them know. Unless a diary is of historical importance *and* not one with sensitive personal details, I don't think we could keep it.'

The diary had a worn fabric cover with a lock and no engraving or identification on the outside. Olive jiggled the lock and it clicked open. She gasped and her eyes shot to Harriet's. 'I just want to see if there's a name inside.'

'Go ahead. Neither of us is about to tell someone's secrets to the world.'

When Olive opened the diary, a folded piece of paper fell out onto the floor, so she scooped it up and handed it to Harriet. 'No name inside.' She turned a couple of pages. 'The first entry is in January, 1961.'

The paper was fine and felt fragile as Harriet carefully unfolded it and placed it onto the table. 'Oh, how sweet. It's a hand-drawn map.'

Olive looked over her shoulder. 'Look. Rivers End and a bit along the coast and then inland. Further than we were today.'

The map was far from professionally drawn but it was a good likeness of the region, with some single letters and Roman numerals beside different landmarks. One corner was missing, leaving a ragged edge.

She tilted her face up to see Olive's. 'Ask and you shall receive.'

'Huh?'

'The other day you wanted a treasure map.'

'This is a treasure map?' Olive's voice held childish wonder as she peered more closely. 'But what is the treasure?'

They both looked at the diary.

'Do you think we should read it?' Olive was hopeful. 'Just the first entry.'

'We might put this map inside a large envelope for safe-keeping until we can get hold of the lady we bought it from. Let's see what she has to say.'

She'd want it back. Besides, Harriet was far too busy to go on a treasure hunt, even if her heart had sped up a bit at the thought and her years of reading adventure novels as a child came flooding back with an irrational desire to follow the clues.

FOUR

Every year I get a diary for Christmas and I love writing in it the first time... except today. Today I feel a bit down and keep wondering why does everything have to change? We've all been friends forever but now we're getting older, our differences are more obvious. One day it won't be our little group because R has big plans for her future and won't stay here in Rivers End her whole life. But B might because like me, she loves living here and we can't imagine moving away. Give me friends, the beach, and a pony and I'm happy.

Bess, Ruby and I huddle around a fold-out road map which is open on the sand. I borrowed it from Dad but had to promise to put it back in the car tonight. We're inside the shallow cave beside the stone steps on Rivers End beach. The remains of a picnic are more or less back inside a basket and we all have our cans of Tarax. It's our weekly routine. Spend some hours together using up a bit of our pocket money on things like soft drinks or a sausage roll. The world is ours to explore, but Rivers

End is becoming too small for our plans. Well, not mine. But Ruby's, who at fifteen is a year older than Bess and me. We all used to live in the same street and have been best friends ever since.

'If we started early enough, we can catch the bus here.' Ruby points to a spot near the bridge. 'I know which one goes to Warrnambool and we could spend the day there and try on dresses and have lunch in a real restaurant.'

'That sounds expensive,' Bess says. 'I don't get as much pocket money as you two.'

'Then ask your parents for more. Or do more jobs around the house.'

'It isn't that easy, Ruby. My dad was laid off for ages and only just started working again. You two should go though and you can tell me all about it.' Drawing her legs up against her chest, Bess takes a long sip from her can. There are tears in her eyes and she blinks at them to go away.

Ruby shrugs.

Recently, her tolerance for our lack of pocket money and willingness to follow her every suggestion seems to be tested more often than not. Her family isn't exactly wealthy, not like the Ryan family who lived at Palmerston House and employ half the town, but they are more than comfortable since her father got a big promotion to help run the timber mill. Now they live in a bigger house and he has a nicer car.

'We could pool our money and share.' I lean over and hug Bess. 'Don't be sad. I have some extra shillings saved from my birthday so we can all go on a day trip.'

With an annoyed sigh, Ruby folds the map. 'Well, when then?'

Bess doesn't say a word.

'I'm sorry if I upset you,' Ruby says. 'I'm just so bored and want to do something this summer instead of hanging around the town or helping at home.'

'We could go riding when there's a cooler day.' My family has a small farm and there are a couple of ponies we are allowed to ride. 'If we pick our timing we can go around the cliffs either direction. Or go into the hills.'

'I do love riding,' Bess says.

'But what about Warrnambool? Actually, I'd prefer we find a way to go to Melbourne.'

Bess and I laugh, which makes Ruby scowl.

'Sorry, Rubes. But we can't do that. The bus takes half a day and we'd only have to get straight onto another bus to come home,' I say.

'No, Nettie. I mean for a proper visit. Stay there overnight at the very least.'

Overnight? We're fourteen.

We gape at Ruby and she frowns even more.

'Why don't you two want to do more than just the same old stuff? We are almost adults and before you know it, our lives will pass us by. There's nothing fun to do here. And not many nice boys, either. The only vaguely interesting event ahead is my sister's birthday.'

'Mum would never agree to me going to the city for a whole night,' I say. 'But if you are that bored, why don't we come up with a special birthday present for Violet and plan some fun stuff for her?'

Everyone loves Violet, with her endless chatter and curiosity and smile which always brightens a room. She's like a little sister to Bess and me and we have fun teaching her stuff, like playing card games.

'I know Mum and Daddy have already bought her some really nice presents,' Ruby says. 'They are doing over her bedroom to be a bit more grown-up with a new desk and her own armchair in her room. But I still don't know what to give her.'

After tossing my empty can into the paper bag we've kept

for rubbish, I open my satchel and pull out my sketchbook and brand-new diary. 'We should write down some ideas.'

Bess leans forward, her earlier woes forgotten. 'What did we all love getting when we turned eleven?'

We each come up with different ideas, from books to toys for older kids, but none of them feels special enough.

'Let's do this another way.' I draw a line and start afresh. 'What does Violet love to do? What makes her happy?'

'She wants to be just like me,' Ruby declares solemnly. 'Sophisticated, beautiful, and special.' Somehow keeping her face straight, she gazes at us but we begin to giggle and she joins in.

'You are very, very special, Rubes,' Bess says.

Ruby makes a show of tossing her silky, golden hair over her shoulders. 'I certainly am.'

We all feel a bit happier after that silliness.

I'm writing again. 'So let's see. We've established that the poor child has to contend with her sister, so how do we help her forget that for at least one day?'

'By giving her a break from Ruby?' Bess offers with a grin at Ruby. 'Violet is so clever. She talks to me about the shipwrecks along the coast all the time. Where they are, how some of them move a bit with the bigger tides. Even one which completely disappeared... was it the Mahogany Ship? I think she'll grow up to be an explorer.'

'Or a pirate,' Ruby says. 'That's the latest thing, reading books about pirates and their treasure.'

Silence falls for a moment, then, as one, we speak.

'Treasure hunt!'

We wander along the beach with our feet in the surf. It's so warm today and we want to climb to the top of the far cliff and sit beneath our favourite tree to keep working on the plan.

There's a piece of driftwood in the shallows and grabbing it, I begin making giant 'X' shapes in the firm, wet sand.

'Is the treasure here?'

I run a few yards further and make another.

'Or here?'

'Do you think we should bury the treasure?' Bess asks.

'Don't be silly,' Ruby says. 'Someone might dig it up first. Or the ocean might wash it away.'

'I didn't mean this close to the edge. But what about in the cave? Or in the tunnel beside the river?'

By the time we've climbed the narrow track to the top of the other cliff, we've come up with and discarded dozens of ideas. We flop onto the grass beneath the drooping sheoak –which is one of the few trees able to withstand the winds from the Southern Ocean – and each drink from our water canteens.

Even though Ruby doesn't like the idea, I circle back to it. 'I was thinking about the cave—'

'No! Really. We can't go and buy something precious and then leave it in a damp cave where anybody might find it or the conditions might ruin it.' Ruby crosses her arms. 'And we haven't even decided what to get her so this is probably all a dumb idea.'

Opening the sketchbook to a fresh page, I begin to draw. After a minute, the other two lean closer to watch as my pencil creates a map. I like drawing all kinds of things but I'm not very good at animals or people.

'Gosh, you've got so good at this, Nettie,' Bess says. 'The beach. The town. There's the river going all the way to the hills on one side. And the other hills. Is this for Violet?'

'Just a draft. Once we work out the details then I will do a new sketch until it is as perfect as possible. And then I can trace it and we can burn the edges to make it look really old. If we all agree that Violet should have the best birthday ever, then we should leave clues in different places for her to find.'

I sit back and look first at Bess then Ruby.

'Like, notes?' Ruby asks.

'Each in its own handmade envelope with a cryptic message. We'd give her the first one and if we are clever enough, she'll be able to discover each clue and lead her to the treasure.'

Ruby nods, smiling. 'We have a few weeks to plan. Shall we meet in the morning at my house and we can try and work out the gift? Mum and Violet are going shopping so come over about ten and then we'll have the house to ourselves.'

Bess claps her hands like a little child. 'This is a wonderful idea. We get to do something fun *and* give Violet a wonderful adventure.'

I can't wait to get started. V is such a sweetie and it'll be so much fun making this a perfect day for her.

FIVE

NOW

It was barely six in the morning and little stirred on the streets of Rivers End.

A man walking his dog whistled out of tune as he strode past the bookstore, not noticing Harriet busy at work. Her head lifted for a moment and then returned to the job at hand. She only had the light on above the counter while she emptied the float into the till drawer.

The very first float.

In three hours, she and Olive would open the doors to the good people of the town. Thanks to a lot of help from local tradespeople, they'd transformed the interior in a bit under six weeks, which for her and Olive included quite a few late evenings. The official opening was in about a month and involved competitions, local author readings, giveaways, and a day of free food. By then, any issues she found could be sorted out, not that she expected any. The biggest challenge was being a trader instead of a librarian.

The till closed, she took the money bag back to the safe and locked it in, then turned on the coffee machine to begin heating.

Who knew when she'd get a chance to have a coffee once things got underway... unless no customers came.

She'd had many sleepless nights going through a range of scenarios, from nobody stepping inside the bookstore to a rush on the first day which depleted the stock until the next delivery. Either wasn't ideal, although the latter would at least bring some much-needed money into the bookstore's bank account. Somewhere in between the extremes was perfect but she was nothing if not a realist.

The town had never had a bookstore, so readers already had established buying patterns, either going to one of the neighbouring towns, buying online, getting second-hand copies from the op-shops, or reading e-books.

It was also possible there would be an early flurry of interest which didn't then translate into sufficient regular sales to run a business. But Harriet was a big believer in doing market research and before making the final decision to move here had spent hours poring over reports from sources such as census data, local council demographics, and an anonymous Facebook poll which Olive had set up. They'd paid for it to be an advertisement and sent responders to a landing page with several questions.

How many books do you read each month?

Where do you find your books:
1. Bookstores
2. Online retailers
3. Libraries
4. Other (please feel free to add specific details)

Would you shop at a local-to-you bookstore?

There were a couple of other options but it was the results

of the first ones which had heartened Harriet. By targeting people in an area of Rivers End plus a number of kilometres, and who were readers, they had a good response. An encouraging one. Three common answers showed up in a question about what would encourage you to become a regular customer: price, range, and atmosphere.

Her coffee made, Harriet wandered around the darkened shop.

Price was one of those things she'd keep a close eye on. For now she was going with the distributor's recommended retail prices but was offering discounts if customers became a VIP member.

She felt good about the range, but only time would tell and she was prepared to listen to customers about the selection she carried. There were the usual beloved perennial authors, latest releases and bestsellers, a lot of Australian authors, and a good selection of locally written books. No matter the taste of the reader, there would be something here to offer them and if she had missed anything would order in.

And as for atmosphere?

The shop was beautiful, with timber bookcases, reading nooks, the children's area, and a small book-related gift stand. There was plenty of room for prams and wheelchairs to navigate the aisles and quirky signage on timber in the shape of open books. Harriet had deliberately not used the entire space while she worked toward running a book club or having guest speakers.

At this point, a large bookcase blocked off the spare area.

'I can't believe we did this.'

The difference in a few weeks was immense.

This is my dream coming true.

Her own bookstore. She'd always hoped it would happen but hope wasn't a good plan and her energy had always been poured into Jason's needs, both work and personal, and their beautiful daughter, as well as working outside the home. Her income had helped them but even as Jason's pay packet soared, hers barely moved. She'd just enrolled in a part-time course in business management when his illness ground their lives to a stop.

She shook her head. This wasn't the time to be rehashing the past.

There was a floor to sweep and final touches to complete.

And then the doors could open.

At eight forty-five there was a group of people outside the bookstore.

'There's at least ten people out there, Mum!' Olive's eyes shone as she straightened the pile of catalogues on the counter. 'Shall we open now?'

'Well... I guess we could. Everything is ready. Go on.'

'Me?'

Harriet smiled. It was impossible not to be proud of the young woman who had been her right hand through all of this. Olive looked smart and approachable in the soft, wide-legged pants and silky blouse she favoured.

'Yes, you.'

When Olive turned the sign from 'closed' to 'open', there was a ripple effect on the pavement. People lined up, some chatting to one another.

'Here goes everything!' Olive whispered and she turned the lock. Pushing the first door open, she secured it and grinned at the people. 'Good morning! Please, come on in.'

Standing back a bit, Harriet blinked rapidly at the friendly greetings from people as they wandered in. She wasn't about to cry in front of all these lovely new customers.

The three older ladies who had waved from outside the

window on several occasions as she and Olive worked came in together, straight to Harriet.

'Hello, dear. We want to welcome you and your daughter to our town and tell you how much we've been waiting for this day.' The speaker was a slender woman in her late seventies. Her silvery hair was in a bun on top of her head and she leaned on a walking stick. 'I'm Annette, and this is Bess and Marge.'

Bess had very short, bright red hair and a huge smile, while Marge's sterner features were framed by a salt-and-pepper bob. The three were clearly dear friends and Harriet had always seen them together.

Except, they were normally accompanied by an adorable Cavalier King Charles spaniel.

'No little dog today?' Harriet asked Marge, who was always the one holding the dog's lead.

'James Regal is visiting my ex-husband today. Part of our custody arrangements.'

Harriet beckoned Olive over.

'Olive is happy to show you all around, unless you'd prefer to wander?'

'Perhaps you could take us to your mystery fiction books? Then we can explore from there,' Annette said. 'Do you have a basket?'

'We certainly do.' Olive dashed off and collected three small wicker baskets from near the counter. 'Would you like one each, or shall I carry and let you all fill them?' Her smile was pure innocence but she managed a wink at Harriet when the ladies weren't looking.

That's my girl.

As Olive led the ladies away, Harriet busied herself checking in on customers, encouraging them to look around and to ask for help if needed. After a few minutes there were people waiting at the counter and she hurried back to serve. The very first sale for the bookstore was three children's books and two memoirs as gifts and the woman was delighted when Harriet offered to gift-wrap them.

The next few hours flew by in a blur of running between customers and the counter, taking a few orders, and fielding phone calls – mainly from people wanting to know the opening hours. Olive periodically appeared with her arms or a basket full of books and would grin and leave Harriet to finish the sale. She was so good with every customer, from the three older ladies to toddlers and everyone in between.

When there was a lull, with a handful of browsers all occupied, Harriet rushed to the bathroom and then refilled her water bottle in the small kitchen. Her stomach was growling but there was no time to eat.

'Mum? Oh, there you are. Good, stay in there and take a break.'

'I'm on my way back, honey. You are doing great but how about you stop and have some lunch?'

'All the customers have been served and there's actually not a soul in the store!'

The phone began to ring and they both laughed.

'I'll go.' Olive rushed off.

As much as she wanted to sit for a few minutes, Harriet was more concerned about her daughter. They'd been on the go for hours and Olive having a break and some food was more important. Sitting could wait.

Olive was talking to someone on the phone and heading to one of the aisles and it sounded as if she was looking for a particular book.

Harriet rested her arms on the counter top for a minute to catch her breath. Next she'd tidy and restock the shelves. Over at the café, a woman emerged from the door and crossed the road carrying a tray. It was Sylvia, the owner. She made almost everything herself from scratch with the help of an apprentice, a couple of casual assistants and, over the holidays, her younger daughter, Jessica. Sylvia had been so welcoming from the beginning without ever being intrusive and Harriet liked her immensely. And admired her.

Sylvia came into the bookstore and when she saw Harriet, offered the small smile which was about the most emotion she ever gave away.

'Thought you might be run off your feet so we made you both some lunch, coffee, and a few treats to keep you going.' She walked behind the counter and placed the tray – filled to the brim with boxes and cups – onto a spare spot. 'The trick is to keep half an eye on the customer and half an eye on the street. If the customer is occupied then it's safe to take a bite. If the street is quiet, maybe two bites.'

Good advice. I never even thought about how to eat.

'You are so kind, Sylvia. How much do I owe you?'

'Not a thing.' Sylvia came back to the front of the counter. 'Business has increased today with people coming in with their bags of books wanting coffee and pastries. Enjoy.'

With that she was gone before Harriet could insist on paying.

How on earth had she and Olive managed to find such support and generosity so quickly? Even after years living in her Melbourne home she'd barely known her neighbours, and she wasn't close to many people aside from her family, but Rivers End had rolled out a welcome mat the size of the ocean.

'Is that for us?' Olive returned with the phone and a book. 'Did you order it?'

'I'm afraid I didn't even think about food today. Sylvia did this and she won't let me pay.'

'Well, we can always give her some nice books to say thank you.'

Olive wrote on a post-it note and touched it to the top of the book, which then went onto a shelf behind the counter. 'A customer is coming in this afternoon to buy that one. And I mentioned the other two in the same series. Should I get those as well?'

'Can't hurt and if they don't want all three then at least they will know what they look like for another time.'

'I'll get them and you, my dear mother, can sit and eat.'

For once, Harriet was happy to sink onto a chair and do what Olive said.

By late afternoon, Harriet and Olive began to restock shelves and tidy the shop. Olive had taken the tray back to the café and managed to find out from Sylvia's daughter that books about food and gardens were the best gift choices. Tomorrow Harriet would find something suitable and take it over the road as a thank-you.

'I'm going to the stockroom for a minute, honey.'

'Everything is totally under control out here.'

Harriet had no doubt it was.

The stockroom was small and filled with shelves as well as a stepladder and little table. Boxes with a range of mixed items were on the bottom two shelves but excess books were in clear plastic tubs split alphabetically by author surnames. Harriet found the half-dozen titles she was after then pulled out the box which she thought had more catalogues. Instead, it had the collection of books she'd bought the day when the seller wasn't home. And on top was the diary.

Adding it to the pile, she flicked off the light and returned to the counter.

'I'll just phone Mrs Prentice.' Harriet nodded at the diary. 'I'll try her again to see what she wants me to do with it.'

Harriet dialled the number she'd already called twice without managing to reach the woman. She didn't want to throw it away but keeping it felt wrong when it was probably a mistaken inclusion in the box of books.

It was a landline number and went to a voicemail.

'Hello, Mrs Prentice. This is Harriet Main from Rivers End Bookstore. Would you mind phoning me back on either of the following numbers so that we can arrange to return the diary or otherwise? Thank you.' She left the shop number and her mobile number and rang off.

Olive held the diary, gently stroking the cover as if expecting magic to happen.

'Maybe we'll keep it at home for now,' Harriet said. 'I hadn't meant to bring it here and the envelope with its map is in the safe at home.'

'The map might be all there is to it,' Olive said.

'True.'

'We won't know unless we read some of it.'

'Which we shouldn't be doing.'

Olive gave her one of those looks, as if Harriet was spoiling her fun. Then she handed the diary over and Harriet slipped it into the pocket of her briefcase under the counter.

Some people wandered in with a cheery hello and the phone began to ring.

'I'll look after them.' Olive zipped around the counter and greeted the customers.

Harriet answered the phone.

'This is Jan Prentice and I wish you would stop phoning me!'

Taken aback, Harriet sat. 'I'm sorry... I just don't know what to do about the diary.'

'I didn't even notice it was in that box because all I've been doing for weeks is getting rid of the mess in my father's home now he's died.' She took a sharp breath. 'Throw the thing away, for all I care. Or go right ahead and read it. That horrible diary is ancient history and can't hurt anyone ever again and that is the only blessing about it.'

'I don't understand—'

47

'Look, you sound like a nice person but I'm about to leave this godforsaken town for the last time and when I do, I don't intend to ever think about Rivers End and all its tragedies ever again.'

The connection was cut.

Harriet reached down to touch the edge of the diary in the briefcase. Whatever in that little book had caused such anger and distress for Jan Prentice? And what on earth was Harriet going to do with it?

SIX

'We have to read it, Mum. I'm dying of curiosity and now I know it caused all kinds of tragedies I'm doubly interested.'

'I didn't realise you were such a macabre person. Do you mind grabbing forks?'

'Since when can't you use chopsticks?'

'Since I tried to eat and type at the same time.'

Harriet's laptop was open on the kitchen table and Olive had just arrived back from picking up their takeaway. Neither of them was up to cooking and an early night was on the cards.

'Here you are. What are you looking for?' Olive dropped a fork into the bowl Harriet had made for herself from the take-away containers and began to scoop noodles into her own.

'Anyway, the diary didn't cause tragedies... she said Rivers End had them. And I'm not looking for anything but replying to a few emails. I made a note on our shared calendar about the grand opening. We need to sort out food for the day.'

'The café?'

'Sadly no. Sylvia has new kitchen fittings being installed the same week and won't be baking until that is completed. But there's other options in town so let's look at that in the next day

49

or so.' Harriet closed the laptop and pushed it to one side. 'This smells so good.'

They ate in silence, both starving after the long and active day in the shop. The meal finished, Olive rinsed out the take-away containers and took them out to the recycling bin while Harriet stacked the dishwasher. She filled the kettle and made tea for herself and hot chocolate for Olive.

'Shall we sit outside? It's really nice.'

Olive took her drink and led the way to the front verandah where they had a small round table and two chairs. The air was warm without any bite and sitting here in the dark as people wandered by on the street and cars drove past, was pleasant.

'Are you happy with today, Mum?'

'I am. Actually, I'm a bit shocked at how many customers we had and how many books sold and while I don't expect things to continue at that level, we've made a good start. I haven't looked but I know I signed a lot of people to the VIP program.'

'Me too. Everyone loved the idea of getting discounts and being invited to special after-hours events once we have them up and running. Even the BAMs joined.'

Almost spitting out the mouthful of tea she'd just sipped, Harriet covered her mouth with a hand, swallowed, and tried to speak. It came out croaky so she tried again. 'Olive, you aren't nicknaming our customers? Please tell me no.'

Olive loved assigning her own tags to people and places based on whatever helped her remember them. It was a harmless habit from when, as a young child, she'd struggled with people's names but perhaps it was time to stop.

'George Campbell at the jewellery shop is Father Time and Sylvia is Cookie Queen and so on. Bess, Annette, and Marge equals BAM. Although, I probably need to add James Regal in there somewhere, being Marge's wee dog.'

'No. You don't need to do that and perhaps now that you

are a grown woman and part of a soon-to-be thriving business you shouldn't. What if you accidentally use one of your names instead of a real one?'

'Never happen.' Olive grinned and somehow managed to draw her legs up and sit cross-legged on the chair. 'Let's talk about the diary.'

Harriet laughed and had some more tea. Her daughter had inherited her own curiosity about the past along with the adventurous spirit her father had when he was young – and recently rekindled. It was a potent mix and sooner or later, Olive would want to spread her wings.

A lump formed in Harriet's throat. Olive had tried to spread her wings with her law degree. Moving onto campus was her first real time away from home but how could she have known that trusting the wrong person would do such damage?

'Okay, what about the diary?' Harriet forced a smile.

'If Mrs Prentice doesn't want it and even said we could read it... well, we should.'

'It is intriguing. A diary from the early nineteen sixties. But you know it most likely belonged to a child or young teen and is only filled with daydreams and wishes.'

'I like daydreams and wishes. But what if the contents of the diary are connected to the map? I mean, why else was it folded inside it?' Olive yawned. 'So it's settled?'

'Fine, we'll read it but if we work out who owns it, or once owned it, then we'll return it. But I think sleep is the first priority, honey.'

Olive uncrossed her legs, stood, and stretched with another yawn. 'Sorry. Caught up with me. Are you coming in?'

'I might sit here for a bit longer. Finish my tea.'

After giving Harriet a kiss on the cheek, Olive paused at the door. 'Mummy? You did great today and I'm so proud of you. Get some sleep, okay?'

'Back at you, superstar. Nightie night.'

Harriet leaned back in her seat with a sigh. She couldn't imagine anyone better than Olive to open the bookstore with – not even Jason. He was too impatient and too finicky.

Or had been.

He was a different man now from the one she'd married. Jason had been committed to his future – their future and family – and worked hard on his career. Now and then, usually on a holiday, she'd see glimpses of a carefree spirit who yearned for more of the adventure he'd tasted before settling down. But it was always fleeting and then he'd be busy with work and as the pressures there built up again he'd want things his way at home. After his illness, if he'd only have asked her to meet him halfway on his journey of self-discovery, she'd have been there for him.

The road was quiet, with only the occasional car passing on its way to one of the other small towns along the coast. Only a couple of hundred metres away, on the other side of the cliff over the road, the ocean whooshed and sighed in its endless rendezvous with the beach. The air was salty, not as much as the handful of times she'd stood on the beach, but enough to resurrect old feelings of longing for a boat of her own. A fair wind and an open sea.

One day.

The diary had to wait until Sunday.

Deciding the best days and hours to be open was a work in progress and Harriet would adjust them once she had more data from customers on their shopping habits. For now it was Tuesday to Saturday, nine to five, with a four p.m. finish on Saturdays. She'd been tempted to open six days a week but with just the two of them working was afraid it was too much, and there probably wasn't the need to do so in a town the size of Rivers End.

By the time they closed up on Saturday, both were ready for a break. The entire week had been busier than Harriet could have dreamed and at last she was seeing some financial return for the hard work and expenses to date. They'd gone out for dinner that night and been greeted by so many people that Harriet's head spun from trying to remember names and what books each new customer had bought. Olive teased her later that giving everyone a nickname might help. Harriet went to sleep content.

After a morning of attending to household jobs and a much-needed grocery shop, Olive retrieved the diary and map from the safe and joined Harriet at the dining-room table.

'Are you ready, Mum? This might lead us on the adventure of a lifetime.'

'Or like so many diaries, only have writing for the first month.'

'Don't be a downer,' Olive said. 'I think the contents of this little book will change lives.'

Harriet raised her eyebrows and Olive laughed. That on its own was worth doing this for. This was more like the young woman she knew.

They pored over the map again after removing it from the envelope.

'Whoever drew it had talent.' Harriet pointed to one corner. 'Can you read that?'

Olive squinted at a line of tiny words. 'A something something. Hang on.' She opened the camera on her phone and took a shot, then zoomed in on the image. 'A Treasure for a Treasure. Treasure is with capital "T" both times.'

'Hm. For a spouse or partner?'

'Ooh... newlyweds honeymooning in Rivers End. He buys a beautiful bracelet from Father Time—'

'Olive!'

'From Mr Campbell. Or *she* buys a watch or hand-crafted handcuffs for her new husband.'

'Handcuffs? Whatever books have you been reading?'

With a giggle, Olive gestured to her wrists. 'The things which go into the sleeves of some men's shirts. Dad has some.'

Harriet burst into laughter and Olive looked downcast.

'Sorry. Cufflinks.'

'Yes, those. Anyway, one of them wanted to make a simple gift into a treasure hunt so found a clever place to hide the jewellery and then created a map.'

Harriet picked up the diary. 'I love your scenario but this looks more like one owned by a young teen. Nice enough to have been a Christmas gift, possibly, but not elegant enough for an adult. And even if the map was drawn by a man, I doubt the diary belonged to one.'

'You do realise that sounds sexist, Mum.'

'Well, it isn't. Look at the cover, honey.' Harriet turned it in her hands. 'Although a bit faded now it would have been bright pink and before you say anything, think in context. The year is 1961 and the country is Australia. Feel free to do your own research but my understanding of the fifties and sixties is that pink was not a real choice for boys.'

'Sexist gender profiling. Not you, Mum, but society.'

'Agree. And we still have a long way to go, but imagine living in an era where there were such clear demarcations between male and female and goodness help any poor soul who wasn't clearly one or the other.'

Olive's eyes were cynical. 'We all need more conversations but unless people have an open heart, what is the point?'

As soon as Harriet opened the diary, Olive leaned closer to read with her.

'Isn't it odd that there's no name or address on the first page? Just this line... I guess it is a dedication?'

Every year I get a diary for Christmas and I love writing in it the first time... except today.

'That's kind of sad,' Olive said.

The first entry was dated 3 January.

Today I feel a bit down and keep wondering why does everything have to change? We've all been friends forever but now we're getting older, our differences are more obvious. One day it won't be our little group because R has big plans for her future and won't stay here in Rivers End her whole life. But B might because like me, she loves living here and we can't imagine moving away. Give me friends, the beach, and a pony and I'm happy.

Olive reached for a notepad and pen. 'I wonder who 'R' is.'

'And how many friends are in this group. Whoever the diary belonged to was happy with her life and her future. Do you think she was a teen?'

'Well, she talks about "R" having big plans which I doubt a child would... or at least, not any which would alarm her friends because kids talk about stuff that they have no idea about. I know I did.'

Harriet gazed at her daughter. 'Do you remember what you wanted to do when you were eight or nine?'

'Ballerina. And a scientist.'

'Both worthy aspirations.'

'I don't have the focus for science. Not once I hit high school and delved into it more. And you've seen me dance.' Olive grinned but there was a flicker of sadness which crossed her face. 'Ballerinas have grace and I don't even have a sense of rhythm.' She bit her lip.

'You are a beautiful dancer and you need to begin believing

in yourself – the real Olive – again, not someone else's version of you.'

About to say something, Olive just nodded.

'You also wanted to be a teacher and a poet and move to the high country to protect the brumbies.'

Olive's mouth dropped open and her eyes widened.

'Did you forget?'

'No, but how do you remember?'

'My darling daughter, I treasure the memories of your childhood.'

'Before it all went downhill as a teenager?' Olive asked.

'Not even close.'

'Brock!'

His name sent a jolt of electricity through Harriet. He'd crossed her mind a few times since that magical visit to his property but this reaction was unexpected and completely unwarranted.

Olive explained herself. 'I just thought that we could ask him to cater for the grand opening.'

'How did you think of him?'

'Horses. He said his are all rescues and we just spoke about my love of brumbies. Or are you at an age where memory loss is imminent?'

'Cheeky girl.'

As she made a note on the paper, Olive spoke aloud. 'Ask Brock for his availability and cost to provide enough delicious pastries and possibly some kid-friendly goodies for grand opening.'

'You're serious.'

'Why not? We already know from first-hand experience that he's a brilliant baker and capable of producing large quantities. And we could go a step further and let him leave a short survey for anyone who wants to provide feedback for him which might help with the development of the menu he is doing.'

She made good points. Harriet was all for building relationships in the town and networking with other traders, which was why she'd wanted to work with Sylvia.

'Alright. Are you able to work on a plan for the day with an estimate of numbers and just how much we want to provide? And then create a document with the information and we will talk to Brock as well as a couple of other local places.'

'He's the best option, Mum.'

You really did connect with him.

'I think we owe it to ourselves, to the bookstore, to have several options to consider. And I'm happy you've thought about this because I sometimes get a bit overwhelmed by how much there is to do.'

Before she knew it, Olive had wrapped her arms around her. 'You are doing great, Mum. And I'm very happy to look after as much of the planning for the grand opening as you need me to.'

She understood exactly what the owner of the diary meant about wanting things to stay the same. For as long as Olive wanted to be here she was welcome. More than that, she was a life raft in a stormy sea.

SEVEN

9 January 1961

*Planning V's birthday treasure hunt isn't as easy as expected.
It's been almost a week and we all seem to be busy at the
wrong times. R is acting weird a lot. Sometimes I wonder if she
thinks B and I are too young for her now. But today we are
getting together and hopefully everybody comes with good
ideas.*

I'm getting impatient after waiting almost a half hour under the
sheoak near the edge of the cliff. Today is unseasonably cool
and the wind makes the waves below grey and choppy. Out at
sea a small yacht tosses and rocks in the water which looks
dangerous and uncomfortable for whoever is aboard. As dark
clouds scuttle toward land I decide I have had enough of
freezing here and go in search of Ruby and Bess. Clearly
neither of them cares for punctuality.

The meadow is easy to cross with its soft grass and wild-
flowers and then I reach the winding track down to Rivers End.
A horse and rider approach at a canter and I move to one side to

let them pass, but instead, the girl in the saddle slows her charge and stops close by with a broad smile.

'I thought you must have gone away for summer, Nettie!'

'My parents are both so busy working and anyway, I love it here in summer. Where are you going, Martha?'

Martha Ryan is a year older than me and lives at Palmerston House. Despite being the youngest child of the wealthiest family in the region, a family who helped found the town and still employ a majority of the residents, Martha is sweet and friendly and unaffected. Sometimes Bess and I meet up with her to go for a ride or a swim.

'Willow Bay. I think it will be quiet enough there to have a swim with this one if it warms up a bit and then lunch under the trees. The sky is a bit dark though so it might be a quick trip.' Martha pats the neck of her horse, whose head lifts up and down. 'Mother and Dorothy and I are going to Melbourne next week but I'd rather stay here with Father. But when I get back, shall we go for a ride again?'

'I'd like that. Have a nice ride today.'

Martha's horse is keen to go so she waves and they are off, the powerful hindquarters of the chestnut mare powering up the hill as if the incline is nothing. How I'd love to be alongside Martha and spend a carefree day in the saddle and on the beach.

'Nettie! Nettie, here we are!'

Bess calls out – Ruby trailing behind her – from the bottom of the track so I jog down to meet them.

'Was that Martha?' Ruby asks.

'Yes. She's riding to Willow Bay.'

Ruby does a pretend shiver. 'Too cold to be near the water. Anyway, I want to show you both something for Violet. Back in town.'

'I waited for ages. Where were you both?'

Bess slips her arm through mine as we start walking. 'Mum

needed me to run an errand and then I met Ruby on the way up.'

Ruby doesn't say anything but her face is unusually pink.

'So what about you?' I press.

'What about me? I was busy. Sorry. Saw someone at the last minute... a friend.'

'We're your friends.'

'No, Bess, you are *two* of my friends. I have others.'

'Was it a boy... friend?' Bess giggles.

When Ruby's colour turns to beet red, my mouth drops open. 'It was!'

'But Ruby, you're too young for a boyfriend.' Bess sounds shocked.

'Oh for goodness' sake!' Ruby stomps faster and we speed up to keep pace. 'I'm fifteen, almost fifteen and a half, and he isn't my boyfriend. There's nothing you need to know and he wouldn't want me to talk about him anyway. Just drop it.'

Bess and I look at each other but drop the subject because it is better to wait until we're alone to properly dissect this information.

Once we reach the town, Ruby leads the way to Rivers End Fabric and Remnants.

I hesitate near the door.

'It's okay, she's not working today,' Ruby says. 'That's why I thought we should go in now.' She pushes the door open and holds it.

Sometimes Ruby is incredibly thoughtful and the 'she' referred to is Frannie, a classmate of hers who can be a bit unkind to me and particularly to Bess. Frannie's mother owns the shop so there is always the chance of running into Frannie.

The small shop is packed full of rolls of fabric, a wall of quilting and sewing accessories and patterns, and a selection of sheets, blankets, towels and curtains are displayed along another wall. It's a funny shop in some respects as there's also a small offering of shoes with fancy shoeboxes, half a dozen sewing machines for sale, and a glass cabinet with collectables. Ruby heads straight through the shop to the cabinet.

With a grin, she points to the middle shelf.

It is a compass.

We gather round, each trying to see the detail on the object.

Set into rich and dark-red polished timber, the compass looks old with some foreign words in the gold rim which secures the piece into the wood. It is quite beautiful.

'For Violet?' Bess asks. 'She would love this.'

'But where on earth has this come from?' The other 'collectables' in the cabinet are nothing like the compass. Several miniature paintings. A porcelain doll. A rather horrible silver gravy boat. None of them are anything like this piece of history. 'And look at the price. Five pounds.'

'Oh dear. That is expensive.' Bess frowns.

'I have a five pound note on me,' Ruby says. 'So if you girls agree with me that this is the best idea ever for a present for Violet and will make it up to me by putting a lot of effort into the treasure hunt, then I can buy it.'

Something about the compass bothers me and I can't explain why or how. I just feel a bit... unsettled by it. Almost as if it is sad and lost.

'How do you have a five pound note?' Bess asks. 'That is so much money.'

Ruby folds her arms. Her face is getting red again like it does talking about that boy. She wouldn't have got it from him? Surely not. 'It doesn't matter where I got it. Are we buying it?'

Again we are in a circle in the cave. The compass rests on the fabric bag it came in. We've each taken turns holding it and trying to work out details but so far we know hardly anything.

I've copied the words into the sketchpad and drawn the front and the back of the object.

'I'll look up the words at home. They do look like Spanish or something similar and I have a dictionary.'

'It doesn't really matter, Nettie.' Ruby returns the compass to its bag. 'Violet will probably make up a story about it. What *we* need to work on is the treasure hunt, so what ideas do you both have?'

Bess pulls a piece of paper from a pocket and unfolds it. 'I wrote down some landmarks if you'd like to hear?'

'Go on.'

'The railway station,' Bess said. 'There's lot of places there.'

'Ooh, that's good.' Ruby and I nod.

'The grocery store.'

That gets a blank stare from us both.

'There's a noticeboard inside and we could ask to put up a note.'

Ruby smiles. 'Not so silly an idea.'

With a bit more confidence, Bess reads off the rest of her list. Some of the suggestions are too far away or too hard to do but she's almost glowing with our praise.

'Do you have any suggestions?' I ask Ruby. After all, this is for her sister.

'I think it should start at my house, say with the letterbox. The first clue might appear to be posted and addressed to Violet. Then I'd think the grocery store, or somewhere similar, might be fun because it isn't too far. But I'm stuck after that.'

'What about this? The letterbox leads to the cryptic clue which then sends Violet to the stables at my place. I'm thinking that she could borrow one of the ponies and that lets us plant clues further afield.' I can just see us following her on foot across paddocks.

'She shouldn't be riding alone though. Mum wouldn't like that.' Ruby frowned.

'We can go with her because she won't be fast – or one of us can ride with her. And we can take a camera and take a picture when she finds each clue. Then later we'll make a book for her with all the clues and the photos and stuff.' I check my watch. 'I have to go home. Mum wants to shop this afternoon and I said I'd come.'

'We'll keep planning and writing down ideas.' Bess grins. 'I can't wait!'

Despite having to be home soon, first I walk along the beach for a bit and go to stand on the end of the jetty. I like the sea for paddling and swimming close to the shore but not the idea of going out on a boat so much. The same yacht from earlier makes its way around the far cliff and is probably going to Willow Bay where there are half a dozen or so boats moored most of the time.

Since we've been in the cave the weather has brightened. The sea is still more grey than blue but the wind has dropped, letting the sun warm my shoulders.

About to turn to go home, a distant ship catches my eye. It doesn't look like a cargo ship but one from days gone by with tall masts and billowing sails and a hundred sailors. It wasn't too many years ago a ship like that might come to grief on the rocks and reefs along this coastline. A captain might have had a compass made of timber with a gold rim and words I don't understand but still not seen disaster until it was too late.

As I watch the tall ship on the horizon I wonder if the compass came from a shipwreck. I know a little bit about scavenging rights from a school assignment and would think something so nice as the compass would have belonged to an important ship. So why did it end up being sold in a fabric shop for five pounds?

EIGHT

NOW

'Do you understand any of the words?' Olive rewrote the line of writing from the diary on her notepad. 'I'll do a search a bit later.'

Harriet nodded. 'Only a couple which are tree and strong, or strength... or close. It's Portuguese. If it was on a compass then it might be quite old.'

'And the friends bought it from a fabric shop in town?'

'Pretty sure there isn't one here now but most businesses wouldn't last more than sixty years. Although the jewellery store has, so we could always ask George Campbell.'

'Or the BAMs. Sorry.' Olive grinned at the disapproval on Harriet's face. 'I'll try to avoid the term. Plus Sylvia's lived here her whole life, and I know she's not that old in comparison but she might remember it.'

'It is odd though that a fabric shop would sell something such as an old compass. Well, we know that this was the gift planned for Violet and that there were some ideas for the treasure hunt. What does it say beneath the words from the compass?'

Olive picked up the diary. '*Wherever did the compass come*

from? Was it a shipwreck? I wonder if we should find out because it may belong to the family of some poor soul lost at sea.'

What a caring young person to think beyond the here and now. To consider the ethics of ownership rather than simply accept such a special item might have a history.

'And there it ends... at least for this entry. Should we do another, Mum?'

'She mentioned Willow Bay. Would you fancy a drive?'

Without hesitation Olive was on her feet. 'I'll put these back into the safe. Actually, now that we know Mrs Prentice doesn't want the diary, do we need to lock it up?'

'I'd feel happier if we did.'

It was only an old diary belonging to a teenager from the past. What could possibly be important enough to keep it locked up? Harriet couldn't find a logical reason, but her instincts urged her to err on the safe side. Though why anyone breaking in would take it over computers and jewellery and other obviously precious items made little sense.

'I'll make us a picnic. Get into your old lady swimwear and we can go into the water,' Olive called from the kitchen.

Harriet stuck her head in. Olive had an Esky on the table and the fridge open.

'Old lady swimwear?'

'Big flowers, little skirt thing. Oh, we'll need towels, please.'

Unsure if she was offended or amused, Harriet found herself smiling as she collected beach towels and stowed them in a big bag. Old lady swimwear indeed. Not everyone had the body of a twenty-year-old who ran miles a day. But after donning her swimsuit, which did have big flowers and a skirt, she glanced in the mirror. A long glance from the front, side, and back.

You could almost go back to a bikini.

The past few years, particularly the last, had played havoc with her health and fitness. Once a keen cyclist – a passion shared with Jason – she'd not been on a bike since the day he'd been told he had a life-threatening brain tumour and possibly only months to live. Despite the change in her exercise levels she'd lost weight, which went against the experience of most women her age she knew. Worry. Stress. Divorce.

'Ready yet?'

'Almost.'

'I'll pack the car.'

After slipping into shorts, top, and sandals, Harriet grabbed a sunhat and followed.

Willow Bay wasn't what Harriet expected. Instead of the small, deserted beach she'd envisioned, it was a hive of activity. Several four-wheel drive vehicles waited to use a ramp to back their boats and jet-skis into the water. At least a couple of dozen families and couples were on the sand having picnics or sunbaking, with several having joined up to have a party of sorts, complete with music.

'Oh dear.'

Harriet and Olive looked at each other and burst into laughter.

They moved out of the way as one of the vehicles drove back up the sand with an empty trailer.

'Let's go over here, Mum.'

Olive carried the picnic basket and the towel bag and had an air of happiness about her Harriet hadn't seen in a while. They tramped through the heavy sand closest to the bushland which lined the beach until they were almost at the end. It was quieter here with no cars or people and the music was faint.

They stopped near some rocks and laid out the towels to sit on, then slathered themselves with sunscreen.

With warm sun on her body and the salty air on her lips, Harriet relaxed. They were in a small bay with cliffs cradling a natural harbour. There was a fairly small gap leading to the open sea, making for a protected area. Yachts of different sizes bobbed slowly where they were anchored while others, under sail, came and went through the cliffs.

'This is nice, honey.'

'Not too noisy?'

'Not up here. For some reason I imagined Willow Bay would have a handful of moored boats and a few horses.'

Olive laughed at that.

'I know. The diary got to me,' Harriet said.

They unpacked the picnic.

'I can't believe you pulled this together so fast. It looks delicious.'

'I was hungry and the beach is my heart-home so I had to move fast while you were keen. Bread rolls, a super-quick salad, some cheese, pickles. Oh, and there's some leftover apple pie from the other night.'

Olive piled a plate for herself after passing one to Harriet. 'I remembered to fill our travel bottles with water as well.'

'You said the beach is your heart-home. What a lovely way to describe it.' Harriet went straight for the cheese.

'Isn't it funny, though? Where we lived was miles from the beach and it was only on our holidays I spent any time on one, but here, with the sea breezes and warm water and clean sand... I just love it so much.' Olive bit into the roll she'd been filling with salad and cheese. Her face was content and her eyes bright.

The move is better for you than I expected.

'I have to admit, Olive, I had a million doubts about uprooting us both but on a day like this, what's not to love?'

'I'm glad we moved. The idea of being in the same city with... him... it was making me feel ill.'

'You thought you might run into him again?'

There was no response.

67

'Honey?'

'It doesn't matter.'

Olive took another bite and looked away.

It was frustrating that Olive still kept so much of her hurt and thoughts closed off from Harriet. She'd refused to see a therapist and it worried Harriet that without someone to talk to, Olive might lose some important part of herself.

But I can't push her too hard.

For a while they ate in silence, both of them gazing out at the deep blue water and activity in the bay. The vehicles had all gone and kids splashed about in the shallows. Further out, away from the moored boats, several swimmers did laps along what was not a long stretch of beach, certainly not like the kilometre or so expanse of Rivers End beach.

'I had a picture in my mind after we read that part from the diary,' Harriet said. 'The young woman on her chestnut mare all alone on the beach with a handful of old-fashioned yachts moored and nothing but the sound of the sea and the birds.'

Olive pointed. 'Like that yacht?'

The boat in question was small compared to most of the others but was beautiful. Built from timber with a sleek, classic design, it might have been here for half a century or more, despite the good condition it was in. On the side was the name: *Jasmine Sea.*

'Exactly like that one.'

'You do love the past.' Olive grinned as she began packing away what little was left of the picnic. 'Your perfect world is one without technology. Filled with old buildings. Swimwear from the seventies.'

'I'll have you know that this is a modern design. But, perhaps if I'm going to spend more time on beaches I should update my wardrobe.'

'Best news all day. I'll help.'

'But you are right, honey. I've always had an interest in

history and Rivers End as a town appeals to me a lot. Not too much in the way of the modern conveniences people seem to want but a charm of its own. Thanks for the food.'

'All good. I might wait a bit to have a swim.' Olive lay on her back with a contented sigh. 'Wake me before I burn.' She pulled her sunhat over her face.

Harriet gazed at Olive, tempted to join her in an uncharacteristic afternoon nap. She knew she'd struggle to sleep tonight if she did, so found her phone and took some photos of the beach, the boats, the beautiful surrounds. Even one of Olive's hat. She caught herself writing a message to Jason to send the photos. A lifetime of habit, sharing moments he'd missed.

But he doesn't want to share my life any more.

She deleted the message and put the phone away, her fingers shaking a little. It was time to create new habits, ones which were for her and Olive. As much as she knew in her soul that she'd always love Jason, a line had to be drawn and never crossed. None of this was what she'd asked for. Not leaving the life she'd lived for her entire adult years and the house she adored. A divorce thrust upon her. Even the bookstore was *her* dream to fulfil rather than its appearance in her life as if... well, as if it was a consolation prize.

Lose your husband and secure world. Gain a bookstore.

Olive turned onto her side.

If her daughter had embraced Rivers End, or at least its beach and ocean as her 'heart-home', then it could be Harriet's starting point. The town, the friendly welcome from so many of its residents, and yes, even the bookstore with all its hard work and challenges, all were conspiring to inch their way into her heart. The heart she'd written off as too broken to feel anything unless it revolved around her daughter.

Was it time to let Rivers End become her heart-home?

. . .

Long after Olive had gone to bed, Harriet worked on her laptop from the comfort of the sofa in the living room. Her muscles ached a bit after a swim at Willow Bay but it felt so good to have been in the water. Floating and diving beneath the surface and a lot of breaststroke back and forth across a hundred metres or so of water in sight of their bags.

Before making the decision to move to Rivers End – rather than ask Jason to sell the building, which had been her first reaction – Harriet had spent weeks reading about the region. The research into the potential of a bookstore came later, once she'd assured herself the change of lifestyle was worth considering further. Born and raised in New Zealand – where her parents enjoyed their retirement and her brother had a large family – Harriet had moved to Melbourne to attend university and fell in love – not only with Jason, but with Victoria. They'd travelled over the years, but never to the western reaches of the state. The more she'd pored over images of the town and region, the more confused she'd been why Jason had purchased a building there of all places.

'I was born there, Harry,' he'd said with a touch of impatience, as though she was supposed to have known this already. 'Left as a baby, but we visited my auntie a few times, and I liked the feel of the place.'

'An aunt?' This was the first she'd heard of one.

'I think she died decades ago. Long before we met.'

His family history had always been sketchy and Harriet only met his parents once – at the wedding – before they tragically died in a small plane crash on a trip through India. Like Jason, they'd been adventurous travellers. He'd never spoken of any other living relatives.

Even if his aunt had died, did she have children? It would be nice for Olive to know more about her family tree, if nothing else.

Jason hadn't mentioned his aunt's name so Harriet began by

searching his. She found that he'd been born at Green Bay Hospital, the closest large town to here. This was something she should have known but he'd taken his birth certificate when he left their home and it had never occurred to her during their marriage to ask where the town was.

She found the birth notice for him and copied it to a file she'd created. Tonight was only about gathering data and then she'd see if Olive wanted to help. The only thing which was at odds with his comment about being born in Rivers End was an address in Green Bay. Perhaps he'd left too young to have memories and was going off the visits to his aunt, some twenty minutes further west.

Her next search was on his father, and then his mother but neither got a result when coupled with Rivers End. Without a name or year of birth for Jason's aunt, the effort was a bit pointless and Harriet found herself typing something completely off topic into the search bar.

Brock Salisbury.

His face appeared on one side of the screen with a bio and for a moment as Harriet stared at him, her heart sped up a little. The image was a shot from a kitchen where he stood, both palms on the counter on either side of a plate of food. He wore a chef's hat and whites and his expression was almost serious. Almost. She'd already seen that glimmer of humour in his eyes once – first hand.

Beneath the image, his bio was cut off partway and she ignored the urge to click on it and read about him. It wasn't as though she was interested in him in any way other than as a potential part of her bookstore's grand opening.

The rest of the screen had a lot of results and she scrolled down.

Articles about him.

Articles he'd written.

His career profile on LinkedIn.

Different restaurants he'd worked at.

Stop it, Harriet. Time to get some sleep.

She forced herself to close the laptop. If she began to read those different results she'd be awake for hours longer. Brock might be worth talking to about the catering and she'd give Olive the go-ahead to ask him. That was all. And that was enough.

NINE

'I'm sorry to trouble you again, but the girls and I are having coffee over the road so I thought I'd pop in and see if that book has arrived?' Annette's wide smile crinkled up the lines around her eyes even more than usual. 'Since I finished the first two in the series I'm eager to read the new one.'

In the two weeks since opening the bookstore, Annette, Bess, and Marge had become regular customers and Harriet knew exactly what book she was talking about. 'We're expecting a delivery anytime today and I just finished loading the invoice so can assure you it's only hours away. At the most.'

'Oh, that is wonderful news.'

'And you are never any trouble. Olive and I love seeing you and the other ladies. You've made us feel so welcome here.'

'It goes both ways!' Annette waved her hand in the general direction of the rows of bookstands. 'You've made a beautiful and comfortable place for shoppers and both you and your darling daughter are so friendly and helpful. This bookstore is an asset to Rivers End and I hope you stay here for a very long time.'

Annette began to hobble away, leaning a bit more on her

walking stick than Harriet had noticed before. She caught up with her at the door.

'What if I drop the book around to you after work? That way you don't need to make a special trip back for it.'

'Well that is kind. My silly leg is playing up today... old injury which has come back to haunt me.' Annette's face dropped. 'A lot comes back to a person as you age.'

Unsure how to reply, Harriet took out the pen and notepad she always had in a pocket. 'Let me have your address and I'll be there before six. And if for any reason it doesn't arrive in, I'll call you.'

A moment later she had the address and directions and watched Annette carefully cross the road. Marge and Bess waved to Harriet and she smiled and waved in return.

Olive appeared from around the corner of the bookstore carrying a carton of huge strawberries. 'Are you out here trying to get customers?'

'Funny. Where did you find those?'

They went inside and Olive offered Harriet one of the decadent and aromatic fruit. 'I walked up one of the side roads and there was a little shelter out the front of a house and an honesty jar. Walked past then got a whiff of them and went straight back.'

Harriet was too busy savouring the strawberry to answer but she followed Olive to the kitchen.

'Do you want to have lunch, Mum? Go for a walk if you like.'

'That was delicious. I will take a break but I'll sit out here and read the catalogue which arrived earlier. There's a few interesting new releases coming up and I'm trying to get my head around the volume to order.'

Olive put the strawberries on the table. 'Help yourself but please leave some for me. Anything you need me to do?'

'Can you make space on the front table for two new titles?

They'll be in today and so will Annette's book. I'm going to take it to her house after work.'

'Home deliveries! I like it.'

After refilling the water bottle Olive usually kept close, she headed out to the shop. Harriet took one more strawberry while she collected her lunch from the fridge. Now that they were settling into a daily routine, both of them brought lunch from home most days, saving money and making it easier to keep close to the shop.

Harriet had almost finished her salad when there was a tap on the frame of the door, and mid-mouthful, her eyes shot up, straight into the steady gaze of Brock Salisbury. Her mind went somewhere ridiculous... had he known she'd searched his name the other night?

Well aware that heat was rising from her neck upwards, she quickly swallowed and grabbed her water bottle to take a long sip, hoping he wouldn't notice her response.

'Apologies for the interruption. Olive said I should speak with you.'

His voice was as deep as she remembered.

'Please, come in and take a seat. Would you like a coffee?'

He glanced at the coffee machine. 'I would. Short black, please.'

Harriet tossed her lunch container into the sink and busied herself making two coffees. The machine was noisy enough to make conversation difficult and she appreciated the couple of minutes to collect her composure.

'One short black. I had to buy a decent machine because coffee is life.' She sat again.

'It is. Thanks.'

The kitchen was smaller with Brock in it and being so close to him, the fine lines around his eyes were noticeable for the first time. There was a hint of silver running through the hair she'd remembered as jet black. It suited him.

The small smile on his lips made her stomach flip-flop and Harriet picked up her coffee and took a sip. She hadn't meant to be caught dissecting him.

'Olive spoke to me recently about catering the grand opening of the bookstore. She prepared some information for me and I want to say—'

'Oh, it really is fine. I can only imagine how busy you are and a man of... a chef of your stature would find our little event...' Harriet ran out of words.

'I'd love to cater for you.'

'You would?'

He smiled, all the way to his eyes. And she smiled in return, holding his gaze until she had to glance away.

'Well, thank you.'

'Thank me only if your guests enjoy the food. Olive suggested I have a feedback form on the table which would help me with my continuing quest for the menus I'm creating. Unless you feel it would be an encroachment.'

'Please do that.'

'In that case, I will provide all the food you need for the price of ingredients.'

'I'm quite willing to pay you whatever your commercial rates are. Your time is valuable. What will you need from me?' Harriet glanced around. 'The kitchen is at your disposal of course, but isn't well equipped.'

'Apart from the coffee machine.'

'True.'

'Before we formalise the arrangement, I would like to construct a plan. My leaning is toward a tasting table-style menu. Savoury and sweet finger food which are bite-sized and mix and match well. I can provide recycled paper plates and wooden forks and spoons and all I will need is one, maybe two trestle tables.'

Harriet blinked. 'You have thought so much through.'

'Some of my fondest memories are around catering for local events when I was only a trainee chef. Mum would arrange for me to take on as much as possible to give me the opportunity to challenge myself, and there were some early disasters.' He chuckled. 'Imagine this. Mid-winter. A dinner for the local school board and invited VIPs to help raise much-needed funds to expand the sportsground. I'm all of nineteen years old and in my first year as an apprentice working a day a week at a Warrnambool restaurant while I studied.'

Brock leaned back in his seat.

'I was in the school kitchen all day prepping and cooking – it was school holidays so I had the place to myself. The menu was good. Pumpkin soup with bread rolls. Choice of fish or chicken with roast vegetables. And my crowning glory. Soufflé.'

He was such an engaging storyteller that Harriet imagined herself in a kitchen with pots bubbling away and aromas making her mouth water. 'It sounds delicious.'

'It was.' Brock paused for effect and moved forward in his chair, putting his elbows on the table and locking his fingers together. 'Until the power went out.'

Harriet gasped.

Brock's expression was mournful as he nodded.

'The chocolate soufflés had just gone into the oven. They were to be served warm with ice cream and a tuile I'd agonised over.'

'What did you do?'

'The gas was still working on the stove tops so I was able to serve hot soup. The bread rolls were already cooked. First course was fine, although it was by candlelight while a storm raged outside. I managed to salvage the mains by reheating the vegetables in hot frying pans and the same with the proteins, albeit with caution. I slathered everything with two sauces I whipped up at the last moment.'

That poor young apprentice.

Almost afraid to ask, Harriet had to know.

'And dessert?'

He lifted his shoulders in an exaggerated sigh. 'I invented a new dish. Chocolate pudding puddles, with the emphasis on puddles. Even my beautiful ice cream couldn't save it and it was all I could do not to slink away from the dinner and become a sailor on the high seas.'

Her lips were quivering. She couldn't help it. Laughter burst out and Brock joined in.

'What on earth is going on in here?' Olive appeared in the doorway, hands on her hips and mock outrage on her face. 'I have a hundred customers yet you are both cackling away. Some help please?'

The minute she was gone, they both laughed again. Only much quieter.

'You would have made a wonderful sailor,' Harriet said as she stood.

'I would?'

'Even pirates need feeding. Perhaps not soufflé though.'

'So Brock is going to cater?' Olive climbed into the passenger seat.

The shop had closed and they'd gone home to collect the car because where Annette lived was a bit further than Harriet felt up to walking. The day had become busy with deliveries and more lovely customers and Harriet longed for a bath and a glass of something relaxing.

'Yes. He's going to put together a menu and also a list of what he needs access to and then you and I will go over it.' Harriet started the car. 'I liked his idea of having an hour after we close just for the VIP members and some special guests.'

'Me too. We can invite all the local shop owners and staff. The press. And the mayor... is there one? Anyway, shall I start making up a flyer? Then once we get Brock's info we can finalise it.'

Harriet smiled at her. 'You love this, don't you?'

'Retail? Organising stuff? Party time? All of the above,' Olive said. 'First time in ages I've felt... useful.'

'Good grief. You have always been useful, honey! And think about it. You only finished school two years ago and have done time at university since. It isn't as if you've just been lounging around the house.'

'Done time at university... makes it sound like prison. I wish I had just lounged around the house though, because I'd never have met Tyler, which became its own kind of prison. Drive through the intersection and keep going straight.'

Did you just talk about that little creep? Good girl.

'Then take the third on the left.'

It was as though Olive hadn't even mentioned the name that she'd kept to herself for months.

'Did you notice Annette was struggling a bit today? She said she has an old injury which was hurting,' Harriet said.

'Oh, the poor thing. And she'd walked all the way to the bookstore.'

'Unless one of them drove her. Or she did.'

'Have you ever seen any of them with a car? One more block, Mum.'

'All three of them are always on foot. They're the best of friends, from everything I've seen. Almost every day they're at the café for coffee. How nice to have such close ties.'

Harriet turned into the road.

'I think it's the third on the right. Yep,' Olive said.

Pulling up on the opposite side of the road, Harriet glanced around. 'We can walk over.'

The road was wide, with no footpaths on the broad grass verges and only a handful of houses with large gardens. They climbed out and Olive collected the book – which she'd tied with a bright ribbon and popped, with a bookmark, into one of the bookstore's smaller fabric bags – and they crossed.

'Look, Mum. There's the new assisted living centre. Well, the construction site for it.' Olive pointed past the houses toward a series of half-finished buildings with a few portable offices which were surrounded by high mesh fences.

'So it is.'

'And Brock is going to be in charge of the kitchen. Isn't that exciting?'

Harriet smiled at Olive as they reached the other side of the road. 'You really do like him.'

'He's the real deal. You know. Genuine. Mind you, Mother, a bit less hanging around in the kitchen with him and a bit more helping me sell books wouldn't go astray.'

There was no chance to respond as Annette appeared at a gate. 'Oh, this is so kind of you both!'

'Hello, Annette. What a pretty garden you have.'

There were roses and hedges and weeping trees behind a picket fence.

'You need to praise our Bess. This is her lovely home where the three of us – four if you count the furry friend – live and she's put a lifetime of work into making it a wonderful haven from the world. I do enjoy pottering around out here though and Bess indulges my need to prune and plant. Please, will you come in?'

Annette turned and hobbled along a path to the front door. There was one step up to the door and she took a moment to balance herself while Harriet held the door for her.

With a welcoming yip, James Regal bounced around in the hallway, tail wagging. Once they were all inside and the door closed, Olive handed the bag to Harriet and sank onto the floor to pet him and he climbed in her lap. Annette led Harriet around them and through a doorway into a living room.

'Look who I found!' she announced.

Bess and Marge were in armchairs, both reading books which Harriet recognised as ones she'd sold them. It gave her a warm glow, knowing her little business was making people happy.

'Hello, Harriet.' Bess got to her feet, closing and putting her book on a coffee table. 'Welcome to our home. Would you care for a glass of something refreshing?'

'We have wine, spirits, even beer,' Marge added.

'Oh, that is lovely of you to offer, but we drove over so I won't drink, plus I have a pile of work at home. Another time?' Harriet smiled at the ladies. She lifted the bag. 'Here's your new book, Annette, and I'm glad you didn't wait around as it was late arriving in.'

Annette took the bag and peeked in. 'Ooh. Look how pretty it is, with a ribbon. Was that Olive?'

'She's good at making things look nice.'

Olive and James Regal appeared. 'Hello, everyone!'

'Hello, dear. Thank you for the book. The ribbon and bag makes me feel special.'

'You are special,' Marge muttered.

When Olive's eyes widened, Bess and Annette laughed.

'How long have you been friends?' Harriet asked.

'Before Marge says "too long", it is close to a lifetime. At least for Bess and me. Marge, we met in our twenties, wasn't it?' Bess glanced at Marge.

'At your sister's wedding, where my ex, who was at that time my beau, was a groomsman.' Marge nodded. 'Hit it off immediately, and our friendship outlasted my marriage.' She turned her attention to Olive, with a serious gaze. 'Female friends matter, young lady. Men come and go, but the women in your life will stick by you through anything.'

'Almost anything,' Bess said sadly.

All of the ladies shared a long look and whatever passed between them had meaning. The sense of history permeated the room and then, when James Regal flopped against Marge's leg, the atmosphere lightened.

Whatever was that about?

Harriet caught Olive's eye. 'We might head home. Are you still going for a run while there's light left?'

'Probably. Enjoy the book, Annette. And you,' she reached out to scratch the top of the dog's head, 'are welcome to visit the bookstore any time at all.'

'He can come in?' Marge's expression brightened.

'No reason why not. We don't sell food. Maybe not to the grand opening though, because we'll have the most delicious finger food imaginable.' Olive grinned and straightened. 'You really do have to come along and as valued VIP members, you'll receive a special invitation to the members' evening.'

'Isn't it wonderful?' Annette's smile lit the room. 'My son is such a talent and nobody will go home without falling in love with his cooking.'

Wait. What?

'Your... son?' Harriet asked.

'Brock.' Annette stepped closer. 'Did he not tell you?'

'Um, er... it actually just never came up. When we first met it was to purchase books, and he told us how much his mother was looking forward to the bookstore opening but didn't mention your name.'

'Hmph. He never thinks to elaborate. Always his head is filled with recipes and flavour combinations and horses.'

Olive nodded. 'Well, he is pretty good as a cook. And with the horses.'

'He's a good boy and I'm very happy he's home again.'

At the front door, Annette suddenly hugged Olive and then Harriet. 'We love the bookstore and know that you both will become a big part of our town.' She waved until they were back in the car, then closed the door.

'Brock is her son,' Olive said. 'How funny that we're only finding that out now.'

Harriet started the car. 'Those three ladies are so nice but did you get the feeling... no, my imagination.'

'When Marge said that women will stick with you through anything and Bess kind of looked sad and said "almost anything". What do you think she meant?'

'I guess everyone has past hurts and betrayals and sorrows.'

'They are all too sweet to deserve that.'

And you are too sweet to see anything except the good in people. Even bad people.

But something real had passed between the women. Something which bound them together.

TEN

14 January 1961

I think I've read half a dozen books about the shipwrecks along our coast this week. Mum loves talking about local history so I've asked her about what would happen with any artefacts. She believes if they are from an important ship then they'd go to a museum. R is so happy with the compass that I don't want to upset her by asking too many questions. But I'm so curious.

I've been cautious with who I've talked to in case the compass is taken away by an adult. Taking a bus to Green Bay one afternoon, I spent hours in the library poring over reference books about the region and its shipwreck history but there'd been no specific mention of a missing compass or, for that matter, anything not already salvaged and catalogued.

But one story stuck with me – the Mahogany Ship.

This story is so fascinating because an actual shipwreck washed up onto dunes and then disappeared a long time ago. Completely disappeared. Some say it was a Portuguese vessel exploring around Australia long before the English did. Others think whoever saw the wreck was drunk. I've deciphered two words or at least I think I have because Spanish is kind of like Portuguese and I had a Spanish dictionary and that fits with the legend. The words are 'tree' and 'strong'.

I even asked George Campbell if he had heard of any missing items of value from any shipwrecks. He only just took over the jewellery shop from his father and he seems very serious at times. All I'd said was that it was a compass with foreign writing inscribed and nothing more. He suggested I bring it in to let him evaluate it.

I didn't go back.

For some reason I'm the only one of us worrying about the origins of the compass. Bess just thinks it is interesting and Ruby got annoyed when I wanted to ask Frannie's mother where it had come from. So for now I'm keeping my thoughts private.

Today we are arguing about silly things, yet again, because Ruby is in a mood and wants to boss us around.

'I can't see the point in doing a test run,' Ruby says. She arrived at the cave armed with pen and paper and has spent the past half hour making lists of jobs for us each to handle. 'If we write out all the clues and read them to someone then follow them around… that is getting tedious.'

'And what if Violet gets lost?' Bess asks. 'We should check for accuracy.'

'I'm accurate.'

'Then prove it. Look, I think Bess is right. We've written up all these wonderful clues but we've done it here in the cave and up under the tree. Shouldn't we get a better idea of how long the whole thing will take and whether we have enough, or too many stops?'

Bess offers a grateful smile and Ruby looks at us both and then shrugs as if giving up.

'Fine then. I'll pretend to be Violet and Bess can read me the clue and you can write down any changes.'

As I scramble to my feet I toss the sketchbook, notepad, and canteen into my satchel and use a cajoling tone of voice. 'Come on, *Violet*, we're going on a treasure hunt.'

'Aw... Nettie, wait up. And can we get ice cream?' Ruby does a good enough impression of her younger sister to have us all giggling as we leave the cave.

It all started well at Ruby's house where we'd stopped near the letterbox while Bess read out the first clue.

'You'd usually push a trolley
But that would be a folly
Look there on one side
A new clue you will find.'

We'd each agreed it was an easy one which clearly led to the information board at the grocery store. A good way to start.

But as we begin walking, Violet appears from the house curious about what is happening. Bess quickly hides the book of clues and we pretend we are doing a school holiday assignment about letterboxes. I don't remember who came up with it but Violet is immediately suspicious and wants to come along.

As we have decided to time the whole process, we have to start over once Violet is persuaded – well, bribed with promises of a trip to the milkbar later – to go back inside.

We don't go into the grocery store to read the next clue.

'I'm dark and cool and near a pool
There's steps close by and ocean tides
Upon a wall you'll find it
Another clue of what to do.'

'Do you think the word "pool" confuses it?' We cross the road in the direction of the river.

'It rhymes. Anyway, the other bits give it away,' Ruby says. 'I'm more worried about where to put the next clue.'

'Violet doesn't like the cave,' Bess mentions. 'What if it is too scary for her to go inside?'

'Rubbish. She'll be fine.'

Ruby never listens. She used to but not these days and I blame her boyfriend. Or her 'not boyfriend' who doesn't like being talked about. Anyone would think he is hiding something. He'd better not be because Ruby is honest and will tell everyone if he's up to no good.

At the bridge we follow the river as it flows through the natural break in the cliff. I hurry along the path at the side of the water. I've never been entirely comfortable cutting through to the beach this way because something about the way the tunnel echoes, and imagining the weight of stone overhead, is kind of scary.

But we're in the sunshine in a minute and we throw off our shoes and trudge through the soft sand until the river becomes a lagoon and there we cross, splashing each other and squealing as we get drenched.

'Whoops... my bag is wet.' Bess inspects the oversized bag she wears over her shoulder. She climbs onto the sand on the other bank and peers inside. 'Not in here though.'

Ruby, who stands knee-deep in water, has her thinking face on.

I nudge Bess with my elbow and we both grin until Ruby notices.

'What?' She steps out and brushes droplets of water off her arms. 'Bess's bag is made of canvas, right? So I was thinking that we get a piece of that kind of material and wrap it around the pouch with the compass. Even tie it with leather laces or something to look authentic.'

'Good idea. And it will protect the compass just in case it

gets dropped or wet.' I start off toward the cave. 'That's a clever idea.'

'It is! I'm glad I noticed my bag.' Bess follows.

Ruby is pleased with herself. 'And I can go into the fabric shop and find the perfect piece. I might do that on the way home.'

Once inside the cave, I open my sketchbook to a rough outline of a map – this one with only the landmarks where the clues would be. It is an evolving process and with every piece of the puzzle I have a bit more of an idea of how the finished map will look.

'We are still going to frame the map for Violet?' I really hope so.

'Yes, of course. She can have it as a keepsake after she finds the compass.' Ruby stands in the middle of the small space, hands on her hips, gazing around. 'Exactly where will we leave this clue?'

Scattered around are several rocks big enough to sit on and most likely dragged in here by people over the years. Between the three of us we pull and push one rock against a wall.

'Stand on it, Bess,' Ruby commands.

'Why me?' Bess pants a bit from the exertion.

'Because you are the shortest of us and I want to work out if Violet can reach that little crevice or not.' Ruby points. There's a crack wide enough for an envelope to be slid part way in.

When Bess climbs up she easily reaches so Ruby nods. 'Okay, then we'll change "upon" to "up... on a wall".'

Jumping down, Bess digs her notebook from the bag and makes a note.

We stop for a few minutes to drink some water and sit. Outside, the day is a lot warmer than expected and there's still a long way to go to finish the route.

'Do you think we've made the hunt too long?' Bess asks.

'Are you complaining about a little walk?'

'No, Ruby, I'm not. But Violet is heaps younger and we're going from one end of town to the other and back.'

'So you are complaining but on my sister's behalf. Well, if it is so hard—'

'Stop squabbling.' I've heard enough. 'Violet is fit and healthy and runs everywhere, but it is kind of you to worry, Bess. Enough resting. Time to test the next clue.'

After glowering at Ruby, who pretends not to notice, Bess turns to the appropriate page.

'*Our town is known for tall plants grown*
From Rivers End they must be sent
Where steam is loud and people crowd
A new clue waits on a field's gate'

This clue is much harder and might potentially mislead Violet. She is only ten. Or eleven on the day of the treasure hunt.

'I think she'll work it out.' Ruby doesn't seem to have a lot of confidence. 'I mean, if she works out the tall plants being trees and the steam thing being a train?'

'Let's go and see, because if we really want to leave a clue on the gates then one of us will need to go ahead to do so. Can you imagine the stationmaster finding an envelope on his gate and throwing it away?' I joke.

Rather than the laugh I'd hoped for, the other two are a bit glum.

'Come on. We've done well so far and we're smart.'

'Sure are.' Bess jumps up. 'Look at Ruby's good idea about the waterproof fabric.'

We leave the cave and begin the climb up the stone steps. Halfway up, I pause and gaze back along the beach.

The ocean is deep blue and calm. A handful of people swim in the shallows past the old jetty. And at the far end, high on the other cliff, the sheoak we use all the time is just visible. Everything is perfect.

So why am I worrying so much? V will have a terrific birthday so it isn't that. I do have R on my mind a bit because something isn't right about this boy she's seeing but she won't come clean with me. I'm probably over-thinking things because new stuff always bothers me a bit. I'm sure that is all it is.

ELEVEN

NOW

There was less than a week until the grand opening of the bookstore and the dining room had become planning central. A two-sided whiteboard on wheels was almost filled with notes, lists, and sketches of the shop, while the dining-room table was organised chaos with paperwork, small boxes, and plastic containers.

Harriet finished writing a line beneath the heading 'Attending authors', replaced the lid of the marker and moved on to the pile of invitations on the table.

The front door opened and closed followed by the sound of shoes dropping onto the floor. When Olive stuck her head around the door she was glowing from the sun and glistening with sweat.

'You okay, honey?'

'Tired. The run was good though and sorry to leave you halfway through all of that. As much as I'm excited about the event, I'll be pleased when it's over.'

'You've outdone yourself, Olive, and I appreciate every single thing you've done. I doubt this would be happening at all if not for you.'

'I might jump into the shower, then shall I get dinner ready?'

'Is it that time already?' Harriet checked her watch. 'Why don't we go and have dinner in town? I wouldn't mind a walk and chance to get away from this as well.'

'Perfect. And we can take the diary and keep working on it.' Olive grinned as she hurried up the hallway. 'I'm starving.'

'I should finish these first.'

Olive returned. 'The invitations? What needs doing?'

'I was going to fold them and put them in an envelope and write out the recipient... you think that's overkill?' Harriet picked up one of the brightly printed sheets. There was an image of the front and of the interior of the bookstore with details of the VIP evening and some other information.

'Why don't you bring the invitations with you, no envelopes, and after dinner we can walk around and slip them under doors.'

Harriet was on her feet in seconds. 'And that is why I pay you the big bucks.'

The noise which came from her daughter might have been agreement.

Unlikely.

After sliding the invitations into a large envelope, Harriet turned off the light and paused to look back in. Making this event come to life was a joint effort but Olive was tireless with ideas and implementing them. If she was tired then that was a sign she was being pushed too hard and as soon as the opening was behind them, Harriet would insist Olive take a few days off. She could manage alone for a bit and her daughter could do something nice for herself for once. It was long overdue.

The wine bar was more than the name implied. There was a baby grand piano being softly and ably played by a young man who wore black pants and a colourful waistcoat. An eclectic mix of seating options made for an inviting space where one could relax in a tub chair beside a low table, or sit at a table for two or another for many more. Although the room had no overhead lighting turned on, strategically placed standing lamps and recessed lanterns along the walls cast a moody glow.

Almost every table was occupied and happy chatter competed with the piano. Harriet and Olive had a spot near the window, able to see most of the wine bar as well as the street, including the bistro diagonally over the road.

'This is gorgeous!' Olive's eyes widened as she gazed around the room. They paused on the piano and a small smile touched her lips.

The wine bar or the young man?

Harriet kept the thought to herself. It was doubtful Olive was ready to date again. She had never shown much interest in having a boyfriend through high school, saying she wanted to find a relationship as good as her parents and didn't care how long it took because one day she'd have a family every bit as wonderful.

She'd stopped talking about it the day Jason announced he intended to leave.

And then she'd met Tyler at university. She was first year and he was in his last.

Harriet drew in a sharp breath.

Had they ruined Olive's life? First by the separation and then by Harriet being so distracted by her own sadness that she'd paid little heed to Olive's increasing plight with a wolf in sheep's clothing?

'I thought I might have a glass of wine, Mum. How about you?'

How about a whole bottle just for me? With a chaser of another?

Olive still smiled but now her eyes were on her mother, her head tilted in question.

'Actually, yes. Wine sounds lovely so what about we get a bottle to share?'

'Shall I go and order it?'

She didn't wait, slipping out of her seat and weaving her way around tables.

Sinking back in her chair, Harriet entwined the fingers of both hands and squeezed, focusing the sudden anxious response onto the feeling of tightness then releasing the pressure. She hated Jason for changing the rules overnight. For hurting Olive and making her wary of romance. But it wasn't just him. What was the saying? It takes two to tango? Two sides to every story?

That is two sayings and neither of them is right because you had no choice in it.

What Olive needed was a strong mother. A good influence who was able to rise above life's twists and turns and do so with grace. Even if deep down inside she wanted to tear Jason's photographs to pieces and scatter them over a... well, not the sea because she'd hate to pollute it with scraps of paper. Perhaps a bonfire?

Over the background noise, Olive's laughter was enough to make Harriet smile. The pianist was leaning against the beautiful timber bar, talking to her, and she was smiling and saying something, her hands animated.

Being hard on herself for the loss of her marriage was ridiculous.

Tonight was to be enjoyed.

Olive was going to be okay.

A moment later Olive returned, her cheeks reddened and her eyes bright. 'The wine will be over in a minute. I asked them to recommend something special for us and they said there's a lovely local winery and they thought the Riesling was perfect. I hope that's okay?'

'If they think it is perfect then so do I. And I think you are perfect.'

'I know I wasn't gone all that long but did you sneak out and have a drink already?' Olive leaned forward. 'Nobody is perfect, Mum. Not you. Definitely not Dad, who has a lot of life lessons to learn.' She suddenly smiled. 'Now I think about it I probably am pretty close to perfect.'

'Do you think we should follow the clues ourselves?' Harriet picked up her glass of pale gold wine. 'As if we were Violet?'

After the wine had arrived with a plate of delectable tapas to share, talk had turned to the diary.

'Oh, yes! How much fun to follow their footsteps!'

'Well, what about tomorrow we push hard to finalise everything we can for the grand opening, then take the afternoon to take the map and the diary and see where it leads us. Having Mondays off is meant to be for us to have some downtime.'

'I think we are pretty close anyway,' Olive said. 'Our local ads are going to run right up until the day. All of the attending authors have confirmed and they know how the day will run and their timeslots. We still need to put together the goodies to go into each of the bags we hand out but everything is there and ready.'

'The extra books are on their way. I've arranged for a couple of people to help us move the front stands the night before so there's nothing to do in the morning. Oh, we still need to make up some hampers to give away and signage for those.' Harriet was pleased with the progress they'd made. 'What am I forgetting?'

'Over there,' Olive said, gesturing with her head to across the road.

Annette, Bess, and Marge stood outside the bistro looking along the footpath as Brock strode toward them, flanked by a young woman about Olive's age. As they met, there were hugs and kisses all round and Annette held on to the young woman for a while, her smile huge even from the distance.

'Who's that, I wonder?' Harriet asked.

'I think it is Kasey.'

'Kasey?'

'Brock's daughter. The other day when he'd been in the bookstore he said he was driving to Melbourne to pick her up from the airport.'

'Is there anything you don't know?'

So somewhere there's a Mrs Salisbury.

Brock held the bistro door open until the others were inside then followed.

'Lots. But when it comes to our new town and business, then I feel it is my duty to know who is who, what is what, and where is where.' Olive giggled. 'Think of it like an airplane where you have to know the exits.'

Harriet held her hand over the top of Olive's wine glass. 'I think you've had quite enough.'

'All of two sips so far.'

'In that case, I'm uncertain whether to keep a travel bag packed at all times, or rename you Agatha. Or Nancy or Jessica.'

Retrieving her glass, Olive nodded. 'Good thinking. Agatha Jessica Main.'

'Nope.'

'What do you mean, nope?'

'Jessica Agatha because that way I'll remember your name.'

Try as she might, Harriet had no hope of keeping the laughter in as Olive caught up.

'JAM? You'd call your own child JAM?'

'We could change your surname to Main-Sherlock.'

'Mother!'

TWELVE

Harriet and Olive were stumped at the very first clue.

'If we don't know the name of the person who owned the diary, how can we have a proper starting point?' Olive complained.

'We should just skim through it all and see if we can find any addresses or people we can identify somehow,' Harriet said.

'Absolutely not, Mum. Where would be the fun in that? Okay, we have the first clue so it shouldn't matter where this is supposed to begin... not unless it comes up in something later.'

They stood on the corner of the main road near the bookstore. Olive had the diary open at the first of the clues for the birthday girl, V. Harriet carried a notepad and pen and both wore hats, small backpacks with water and other bits and pieces.

'Mum, this might be an issue anyway because so much will have changed in all those years. Some places might not even exist now.'

'Then we use our ability to think critically. Go on, read it.'

'*You'd usually push a trolley. But that would be a folly. Look there on one side. A new clue you will find.*'

'Thoughts.'

Olive closed the diary. 'Supermarket? Did they even have them back then?'

'Oh my sweet child.'

With a chuckle, Olive started along the footpath. 'Come on then. Don't you remember I did an assignment on mid twenti-eth-century life in Australia? I can even tell you what soft drinks were around and banks, and why a town like this closed its rail transport.'

Good girl.

Harriet caught up. 'Back then in a small town a super-market was more like the local grocery store. I think this one has had a bit of renovation over the past couple of years to extend to the next shop over as Rivers End gets busier.'

Inside the supermarket, they didn't go through the turnstile but looked to either side. To their left the wall was brightly painted with images of fresh produce. To the right was a huge black and white aerial photograph of the town behind a row of trolleys.

'A map of Rivers End? That gives us a lot to decipher.' Harriet moved closer. 'Such a great photograph.'

'*Look there on one side. A new clue you will find,*' Olive said. 'So is the clue in the fresh produce painting or the photograph?'

'Or neither. Look at the image, of the hill just out of town. That's Rivers End Heights.'

'Oh. Which is new.'

'New and horrible.'

The voice behind them was familiar and they turned, both smiling.

'Hello, Marge.'

She was wearing her stern face. 'An estate like that should never have been permitted in this area. Have you seen those massive homes squashed into small gardens? And half of the owners only come here every so often but leave their blasted boats all over the place.'

Marge wasn't the first person to comment to Harriet about the estate which was only a few years old and for some of the old-timers was an eyesore which detracted from the charm of Rivers End.

'And that's been there only a few years?' Olive asked. 'We were wondering if there'd ever been anything on the wall before the photograph?'

'Well isn't that an odd question. But yes, there used to be a community board. There's still one but over there.' She pointed to the inside of the front wall where a large corkboard displayed dozens of notices, including one for the grand opening of the bookstore. 'I've been shopping here since it was a little grocery store and the board was always where the photo is now.'

'Like I said earlier, Mum. Things will have changed in all those decades.'

'Whatever are you up to?' Marge spied the diary. 'Goodness me, I haven't seen one of those old things since I was a girl. All the rage for the younger teens.'

Harriet's mind raced back to the initials they'd come across so far. R and B and V. No M. Unless she'd owned the diary?

'Was yours just like this?' Olive held it up so the front faced Marge but she kept it firmly in her fingers. 'Same colour?'

'I didn't have one. My mother was highly religious and believed the only writing a girl should do was at school or for church studies. Some of my friends and schoolmates did but I wouldn't be able to tell you who.' Her expression softened. 'Is it silly for an old lady to suddenly want her own secret diary?'

Without waiting for an answer, Marge turned her back and powered through the turnstile, leaving it shuddering from the impact as she disappeared into an aisle.

'Poor Marge.' Olive stared after her.

'You do know we sell diaries. What if we find one which is

pretty and a bit girlie and when she comes to the grand opening we'll make sure it is in her goodies bag.'

Olive flung her arms around Harriet, almost driving them both backwards. Once they'd steadied themselves and Olive had released her mother, they stepped outside. Olive pulled her phone out and tapped away. 'Just making a note about the diary for Marge. You are the most generous person I know.'

'Just a little thing, and how could I not do something when she seemed so downcast? Poor woman.' Harriet smiled. 'But what we do know is that Marge remembers a lot about life here, even though I recall her saying she grew up in Driftwood Cove, so perhaps we can ask her more questions if we get stuck.'

'And we also know whatever clue was once here is long gone.' Phone away, Olive opened the diary and read. '*I'm dark and cool and near a pool. There's steps close by and ocean tides. Up on a wall you'll find it all. Another clue of what to do.*' She looked at Harriet, eyebrows raised. 'Any ideas?'

For a few minutes both of them did internet searches for mentions of pools in the area. Swimming pools – none. Not public anyway. Waterholes – a few, but quite a way out of town and if V at the age of just eleven was on foot then that made no sense.

And then a thought stuck Harriet.

'What if it means the lagoon on the beach?'

Olive frowned. 'That is kind of a pool and close to ocean tides. Hah! Come on, Mum. I know exactly where this is.'

Harriet might have missed the narrow entrance to the cave had she not been looking for it. The base of the cliff was craggy with rocks jutting out, casting shadows on the limestone. But Olive knew exactly where to go and disappeared inside without a word. Although Harriet preferred the sunlight to the dim space, she followed.

Olive's phone flashlight offered enough brightness to see the cave was no bigger than the dining room at home.

'It goes up a long way,' Olive said, directing the light over their heads.

'You've been in here before?'

'Once or twice when I've wanted to sit out of the sun or escape a downpour. It would make a good spot for kids to hang out.'

Footprints covered the sandy ground and a few empty beer bottles littered one side.

'Doesn't the diary mention the clues being inside home-made envelopes?' Harriet asked, now using her own flashlight app to examine the walls. 'We could assume the clue in the supermarket was pinned to the community board but where on earth would it be hidden in here?'

'And within reach of V who is only just eleven. The walls are pretty smooth. What if they left the envelope on one of the rocks?'

'Or stood on one?' Harriet stepped onto the smallest of a dozen or so. 'If I'm not mistaken, there's a crack here.'

Olive climbed beside her, adding more light. 'There is. I think an envelope would slide in there just fine and the height is probably okay for a kid. Can you imagine how much fun V would have had doing this?' She stepped down, grinning widely.

'Would you like me to set up a treasure hunt for your next birthday?' Harriet joined her.

'Absolutely. But as you can see, I'm pretty good at this so you'll need work hard to outsmart me.'

'Easily done. Might not be able to outrun you though.'

Opening the diary again, Olive was grinning and it warmed Harriet's heart to see her happy like this. They'd always been close but those couple of years of darkness changed how much

Olive was willing to share of her thoughts and feelings – even the more positive ones. This was better.

'Next clue, Mum. *Our town is known for tall plants grown. From Rivers End they must be sent. Where steam is loud and people crowd. A new clue waits on a field's gate.*'

She closed the diary and slipped it into her backpack, pulling out a water bottle and drinking. Harriet followed suit, thinking about the clues.

'We need to think back to the sixties,' Olive said. 'The town today isn't really known for anything but there was a thriving timber industry until the train line closed. And it was mostly trains which took the timber away.'

'When did the trains stop? Was this part of your school assignment?'

'It was and happened in most places when the gauge – the width – of the lines were changed. It wasn't for the first time and the government wasn't about to pay for every little town to keep their trains. The ones who couldn't contribute just gave up and many lost their local industries.' Olive was tapping on her phone as she spoke. 'Okay, so Rivers End closed its railway station in the late nineteen sixties.'

'The old station isn't too far from here if we take the steps.'

Once they left the cave they headed to stone steps which were carved into the limestone cliff, leading up the car park and graveyard above. As Harriet adjusted her backpack at the bottom, something caught her eye.

Deeply etched into the limestone was a love heart.

'How sweet.' Olive traced it with her finger. 'I wonder who the initials belong to. T loves M.'

'Look at how deep the engraving is. Someone wanted this to last forever.'

Young, idealistic love. Because nothing lasts forever.

Harriet noticed herself playing with her wedding ring, turning it around and around. Tears welled in her eyes and she quickly started up the steps, blinking to clear her vision. They were angry tears and it made her even crosser that she could respond so readily to something as simple as two initials and a love heart. Made by strangers to her, no less. Yet she longed to know their story. Had their love lasted or been swept away by time and circumstance? If Jason hadn't been faced with his own mortality then he'd still be her husband. Wouldn't he?

If she revisited the last few years, before he was ill, there were signs of him drifting away. Moments when she'd find him researching a mountain climb or trek across a continent, and never for two. Until the day she'd signed the divorce papers she'd pretended their marriage was perfect and unbreakable and blamed his change of personality on his brush with death.

She reached the top, puffing heavily, her muscles screaming.

This wasn't the time to think about Jason.

'Geez, Mum. No need to turn it into a race.' Olive was panting but not nearly the way Harriet was. 'I had no idea you could go up steps so fast. Next you'll be coming running with me. Shall we see who gets to the station first?'

The road to the station wasn't far from the graveyard and ran inland. For a couple of hundred metres they walked along a narrow dirt road flanked by tall gum trees and bushes. It was peaceful and had few signs of recent human activity, other than an old four-wheel drive which slowly passed them going in the same direction. It bumped over some railway tracks before turning into a driveway further along.

What had once been a busy railway station was now a couple of dilapidated buildings along a crumbling stone plat-form and a single track overgrown with grass and weeds.

'Kind of beautiful in a gloomy way.' Harriet gazed around. 'I can almost hear the steam trains and smell the timber.'

'Ghosts.' Olive shuddered.

'We can go if you're uncomfortable, honey.'

'Oh, no need. There are just times I feel... things.'

'Me too.' Harriet put her arm around Olive's shoulders. 'Let's work this one out and then maybe go for a swim.'

'Really? Cool.'

'So do we agree this is where the clue sent us? Trees are tall plants and the timber trade was the town's main employer back then. Steam and crowds would be the trains and workers. But a field gate?'

'Maybe those, Mum?'

On either side of the tracks as they crossed the road were raised boom gates.

'They look as if they've not been operated in decades. See the handle? They'd be moved manually and I can't imagine a group of youngsters being allowed to access them to attach an envelope.' Harriet wandered onto the platform with Olive right behind. 'Watch your footing on the edge.'

There was no sign of another gate and they headed back to the road.

'Is that a gate there?' Olive changed direction and spoke over her shoulder. 'See near the shed and fence?'

Alongside the railway line a faint path led to another old building, but this one storm-damaged and very small. The railway track ended at a row of concrete blocks and old sleepers were piled to one side. A long wooden and metal gate – in some disrepair – was pushed open just past the blocks, leading to open fields.

'We found it!' Olive jumped up and down. 'A field's gate.'

'I think we did! I can just see the girls sneaking along here so as not to be stopped from accessing the gate. And then did they have to sneak back or do you think they would have gone through the gate?'

Olive reached for the diary but it flew out of her hand and hit the ground.

Both of them stared at it.

Although still closed with the little clasp intact, a photograph had partly fallen out. It was a polaroid in black and white. Olive picked up the diary and then Harriet carefully slid the photo out.

'I had no idea, Mum.'

'Same. But we'd agreed to read it one entry at a time so how could we know? This must have been toward the back.'

Harriet held it so they both could see.

It was taken from outside the entrance to the cave on the beach. Three girls smiled at the camera. Two were teens and the third was smaller and younger and held up an envelope.

'V?'

'I'd say so, Olive. Well, now I'm wondering if a photo was taken at each clue site.'

'The lady who sold this to us? She said the diary didn't matter or something.'

A sense of foreboding seeped into Harriet. 'More than that. She talked of tragedy and heartbreak or words to that effect. The photograph has to belong to someone and if there are more... well, we might have more than a harmless treasure hunt on our hands.'

THIRTEEN

18 January 1961

Something is up with R. I can't ignore it anymore because she's acting strange – stranger than usual. Even V told me her big sister keeps getting in trouble for forgetting her chores. We just don't have a lot of time to waste now.

We worked on the treasure hunt for another few days and made a few small changes. Instead of the original ten clues we now have seven because it was taking so long to complete. After one final walk around the map we know to allow two hours for Violet to find the compass and then we will have a lovely picnic ready under the tree afterwards.

Ruby missed a few of our meet-ups and when she did attend, she was either unusually quiet or more bossy than ever. It is annoying. One minute she's her usual self but then she'll look at her watch and say she's going. Bess and I figured she was busy sneaking around to meet her new boyfriend but it wasn't fair of her to keep leaving the two of us to plan so much for Violet. As much as we adore her, she isn't our sister, but Ruby's.

Today is the perfect example.

Bess and I both had chores to do at home all morning and when we finally were able to meet under the sheoak, there was no sign of Ruby.

'What if she doesn't come today?' Bess hasn't sat yet but instead gazes down the track for Ruby. 'There's still so much to get ready.'

'We can cover most of it but you need to sit and help. Do you want to fold the clues? You are much more precise than me.'

Bess sinks onto the grass and empties her bag, taking out the notebook and using that to fold on. For a few minutes she is occupied and together we do a last check of each clue and then get them into the correct envelope. I'm writing which number clue and draw a little creature on each one. A bunny, a horse, a cat and so on.

'The envelopes are so good, Bess. Violet will love them.'

'Do you really think so? I liked making them. And the paper is pretty.'

Ruby had bought some fancy sheets of thick paper which are pale pink with a faint pattern of flowers. Violet would probably have preferred horses or a different colour but Ruby liked it.

We finally have all the clues in the envelopes and still Ruby is absent.

'Maybe she had to help at home?' Bess suggests, putting her stuff back in her bag.

'Or is with that boy again.'

'Do you know who it is?'

'No, not even a whisper of his name so I guess she's making sure it stays a secret. But she could tell *us*.'

Although I think she's too young for a boyfriend, I am curious. Since Bess and I first teased her about seeing a boy, we've both watched Ruby like a hawk but haven't seen her even glancing at any of the boys we know from school. She'd better not be dating an older boy. I mean, she's only fifteen and we all know enough about older boys to avoid being alone with them in case they want more than a kiss.

'Here she is!'

Ruby waves as if she isn't the one holding everything up. When she gets closer, she's smiling and I don't remember seeing her look so happy in ages.

'I've got the material!' She holds up a carry bag.

'Is that where you've been? At the fabric shop?' Bess asks.

'No, silly.' Ruby sits and opens the bag. 'Sorry I'm late. What else needs doing?'

'Not much. Bess and I have done the clues and envelopes.'

She gives us both a big smile. 'You are the best friends ever! Violet is going to love her birthday and I couldn't have done it without you two.'

As true as that is, I say nothing and Bess is too happy with the praise to remind Ruby how much work she managed to avoid.

'So I bought this piece of oilskin and think its perfect.' Ruby unfolds a dark brown square which is softish on one side and sleek on the other. She puts it sleek-side down on the grass and reaches into the bag again, this time extracting a long piece of thin leather and the pouch holding the compass.

'May we see the compass again?' Bess leans forward.

Ruby hands her the pouch.

'We need to hide this really well at the last point,' she says. 'And because we'll be with her almost all the time I think we should do that in the morning, before the hunt begins. Can we go and have a look for the perfect hiding spot?'

'Now?' Bess asks. 'I don't feel like walking all the way up the big hill and back because I've got a swimming event on in Green Bay later.'

I hold out my hand and Bess passes the compass. 'How many races are you in?'

'Two. Oh, and the relay. So three.'

The compass is as interesting as I remembered but again, the feeling rises that this belongs to somebody else. But Ruby takes it back and in a moment she is wrapping it in the oilskin. She has already bitten my head off once for asking about getting it evaluated and all I can hope is once Violet has it, their parents might investigate a bit.

Bess helps Ruby tie the strips of leather around the oilskin until it is secure and protects the precious gift.

'Are you coming with me?' Ruby gets to her feet and gives me another smile. She's in a good mood today. More like herself. And much nicer to be around than last time I saw her when she'd snapped at me for mentioning the boy.

I'd rather not go with her because I'm uneasy about too much. Her boyfriend. The real story behind the compass. But if I don't go I won't know where the compass is hidden, should Ruby forget. Or not bother to show up for the treasure hunt.

'Sure. Do you want the envelopes?'

'You take them. I'll carry the compass.' She starts down the hill then calls over her shoulder. 'Hope you win your races, Bess!'

'Thanks!'

Bess and I follow Ruby. It feels I'm always following Ruby. But then she runs back and gets between us and she slips her arms through ours and we chatter and giggle about stupid stuff until we get to the road.

Ruby and I find two possible places to hide the compass and because we can't decide, we flip a coin. Ruby's choice wins.

'You don't think it might be a bit hard for Violet to reach?'

'Why do you worry about every little detail? As long as she

thinks the clue through and doesn't mind sticking her arm in there, she'll find it.'

I guess we can always prompt her if she struggles. Most people wouldn't want to dig around in a tree trunk but Violet will. I've seen her wriggle under a house in the narrowest of spaces to rescue a lost kitten and come out covered in dirt and cobwebs without caring.

'Are we leaving it in there?' I ask. 'It would save one of us coming back.'

'I'll bring it early, before she's even up, and be back for her birthday breakfast so she'll never even know I left and then once she's had her other presents we can start the treasure hunt.' Ruby's eyes are shining with excitement. 'This has been fun to do with you and Bess. I'll never forget it.'

She suddenly hugs me.

'You really are my best friend, Nettie, and nothing will change it.'

I'm a bit surprised but it feels nice to be close again, and as long as Violet enjoys the day then all the work will have been worth it.

We walk back to town and I suggest a milkshake, but Ruby has to go home and help. With only one day until Violet's birthday, there's a lot to get ready. Violet's having a sleep-over party at her house with her friends tomorrow night and her parents have a lot of people coming over for a barbecue.

I order a chocolate-vanilla milkshake and while I wait I look over the road. Frannie hurries along the footpath and goes into Rivers End Fabric and Remnants. What has always puzzled me is that she's Martha's best friend but they are so different. Martha is kind and friendly and laughs a lot whereas Frannie rarely has a nice word to say and looks grumpy most of the time. Because I like Martha, I put up with Frannie when we are all together, except for if she is mean to Bess. I always tell Frannie to be nice and cheer up Bess.

Taking my milkshake outside, I perch on one of the windowsills of the milkbar rather than take up one of the tables. And as has happened so often, the compass fills my thoughts. There has to be a reason why it ended up for sale at the fabric shop but nothing I come up with makes sense. I really need to find out because I have even had some dreams about it.

The door of the fabric shop swings open and Frannie runs out. She gets as far as the corner and stops and I notice she's crying. My heart hurts for her. Whatever could have upset her so? I suck the last of the milkshake through the straw and return the glass but when I come back out, Frannie is nowhere to be seen.

I could go looking for her. She'd probably hate for anyone to know she's upset. I would. Instead, I cross the road and go into the fabric shop.

Frannie's mother has her back turned and is talking to the other lady who works there.

'She always wants money but does so little to earn it. You know that I've asked Frannie to work here more during the school holidays but as it is she resents her few hours of regular work. I tell you it is the fault of those Ryans. If Frannie wasn't always at Palmerston House she wouldn't have these high and mighty ideas.'

So, Frannie is crying over money. I don't feel so sympathetic anymore. But her mother is being unfair about Martha's family.

I look at the glass cabinet. There's a fancy gold fob watch sitting open. The face of the watch is cracked and the hands don't move. There's no photograph on the opposite piece. My father has one a bit like it and he keeps a photo of me and my mother.

'Are you interested in it or just looking?'

The other lady who works here... I don't know her name, comes over. Frannie's mother goes behind the counter, picks up her handbag, and leaves.

'Don't these usually have a photo in them?' I point at the watch.

'Yes. This had one but it had been in the water and was too faded and damaged so we disposed of it.'

'My friend purchased the compass which was here.'

The woman sighs and glances at the door. Maybe she wishes she was going home but they don't close for another couple of hours.

'I really like the compass. My dad always wanted one of these watches,' I fib.

She brightens. 'If the new owner takes it to the jewellery shop I am certain Mr Campbell could fix it. We think the watch is very old and quite precious.'

'Like the compass?'

'They both came from the same seller so I imagine they were part of an estate which was sold or else were inherited by the seller. Quite valuable pieces.'

I don't say what I'm thinking but if they are so valuable why were they being sold here and for so little money? Five pounds is a lot but not for a collector.

'Who was the seller?'

She looks affronted.

'My father told me it is important to know the history of precious items.'

'That is confidential. Are you going to purchase the watch?'

My face becomes all sad and disappointed. I am surprised I can act so well as I never enjoyed school plays. 'I'd better not if the history is... unknown.'

With another glance at the door, she snaps at me. 'It isn't unknown, but it is not for you to ask. If your mother or father wants the details then they need to come in but I can assure you that they are not stolen. If that is what you are insinuating.'

With a heavy sigh, I nod. 'Thank you. I will let them know.'

And I don't wait around another moment because the woman's face is red.

Outside, I almost laugh aloud. I didn't mean to offend the lady but she wasn't helpful. But then I frown. There is a story behind the watch and the compass and it would be awful if they were stolen and Violet gets in trouble for having one of them.

I'm not ready to give up searching for the truth.

My mind keeps trying to connect the facts. R found out about the compass somehow and then had the exact amount of money – a lot of money – in her purse when we went to look at it. And the fabric shop aren't being helpful either. But what has my mind racing is seeing the fob watch. There is more to this than anyone is saying.

FOURTEEN

NOW

The line along the footpath on the first day the bookstore opened was nothing compared to the one today. Olive had gone outside and handed out grand opening flyers to everyone and assured them it was only minutes until the day's trade began.

'There's like a hundred people, Mum!' She locked the door behind her then smiled at the closest people. 'Some of them are carrying bags. Big ones. And there are lots of kids who are super excited.'

Harriet was rushing around to do a final check of everything. They had ten minutes until nine o'clock and she made good use of it.

The morning was geared toward young families with a couple of local children's authors doing story time and talking about their books. There was a table set up for kids of all ages to use to write their own story and it was well stocked with paper, pencils of different colours, snacks and drinks. Each story could be swapped for a free book from a lovely big pile donated by Harriet with the help of a couple of publishers. The stories would be placed in the window for a week to share with everyone.

Around midday, the table would be converted to a food station and different authors would come in for a couple of hours each. There were lots of giveaways planned as well as a major prize drawn from all purchases – a store gift voucher.

Everything looked amazing and the store was ready for its biggest day yet.

Children's laughter filled the bookstore as Olive read passages of one of her favourite childhood books in funny voices.

'And that, kiddies, is all.'

There were cries of 'more' and 'no' but in a matter of minutes smiling parents and children – clutching kid-sized goodie bags – were waving at Olive as they left. Harriet finished a sale and went in search of her daughter.

Olive had flopped onto a chair at the end of the table. Somehow she'd managed to collect all the stories and get the children to return their pencils to a plastic tub. Even the empty paper plates and cups were piled neatly. With a tired smile, Olive got to her feet and reached for the stories. 'Children are hard work, Mum.'

'You had them eating out of your hand,' Harriet said. 'I'll get a bag for the rubbish if you want to put the stories somewhere safe for now.'

They were able to clear the table before anyone else came in and both managed to get a coffee to take back to the counter.

'Are those orders?' Olive ran a finger down ten or so entries on the book they used to keep track of customer queries. 'I know I sold two of that book this morning but thought we had more?'

'We did. Five more. And guess what? Two ladies were here from up at Forrest... it is a little town in the mountains. They are part of a book club and want to do regular orders of ten to fifteen paperbacks for their book of the month. Each month.'

'Outstanding. I wonder if we will sell out of more books. Anything still in the storeroom?'

'Not much. Feel free to check a bit later if you are between customers. Or we can try to restock after we close the first time.' Harriet took a quick sip of coffee. 'Here are the next two authors. I'll go and show them where to set up.'

'And Brock. You look after him and I'll take the authors.'

Brock must have parked around the corner because he went past the windows pushing a box-shaped multi-level oven on wheels. The front door was open and he carefully navigated around a couple of displays before stopping near the counter with a broad smile.

'Special delivery, ma'am.'

It was all Harriet could do not to giggle like a child but she kept her composure and smiled in return. 'I wasn't aware I'd ordered a new oven. It looks very... professional.'

'Only the best for you. May I park this in the kitchen?'

'You remember the way?'

He grinned and resumed his efforts.

Harriet got busy with customers and then spoke to the signing authors for a moment or two and when she went past the table it was in the process of being set up for food by the young woman she'd seen with Brock the other night.

'Hello, I'm Harriet.' She offered her hand.

'Oh, hi. My name's Kasey, I'm Brock's daughter.'

Kasey had the same eyes as her father, dark brown with a touch of humour lurking in their depths. There was something so friendly and warm about them.

That must be why I'm drawn to Brock.

Satisfied with her self-analysis, Harriet hurried off to serve another group of customers. As busy as the day was, it was deeply fulfilling to see her dream being embraced by so many in the community. She had made notes all day as people mentioned their likes and dislikes and she'd overheard snippets of conversations about book clubs, libraries, and online book-stores. At the very least, the grand opening was helping her formulate long-term plans.

She carried a box of books out to an elderly customer's car. Even one of the second-hand books was in there and she'd had some great responses about the little section. While she waited for keys to be found and the boot unlocked, Pam, who owned the inn, ducked into the store with a small wave in her direction.

Hopefully Olive was managing.

Once she was free she rushed back inside, her head down, and ran straight into a rock-hard chest.

Firm hands steadied her and she raised her head.

Brock.

Of course.

The heat from his body was intoxicating. He smelled of caramel and apples and spices.

'I'm so sorry. Wasn't looking,' she managed.

'I was.'

Pure electricity sparked through her body.

He still had his hands on her arms. Not too tightly. Or loosely.

'So you deliberately ran into me?'

There was an intensity in his gaze. The humour wasn't there for once as they roamed her face. Pushing aside a ridiculous urge to reach up and touch his lips with hers to see if they tasted of caramel and apples and spices, Harriet took a tiny step back and he released her. She had to resist a need to rub her arms where the warmth from his fingers still lingered.

Please tell me you don't have a Mrs Salisbury.

'Dad? Sorry, I need the car keys.'

'I was on my way there,' he said. 'The oven is plugged in and the sides are pretty hot if you go into the kitchen.'

'Okay, thanks,' Harriet said. 'I'll tell Olive.'

'Come on, Dad. Still have to bring the rest of the food in.'

'Well, let's go then.'

The humour was back in his eyes and the moment between them, whatever it was, had passed.

By five o'clock the store was empty of customers and the last of the authors were leaving. Brock and Kasey began to remove the remaining paper plates and cups and empty platters. Olive helped, she and Kasey chatting like old friends. That done, Brock disappeared to the kitchen and after a few minutes the most delectable aromas wafted out.

Harriet couldn't help herself and followed the smells.

Brock had magicked a portable stove from somewhere and had both elements going with pots on each. He stirred one and then the other. Lined up on the counter were dozens of pastry shells waiting on trays for filling. The oven he'd brought was still on.

She leaned against the doorway, unnoticed by the man whose focus was purely on the pots. There was no denying her attraction to him. It wasn't something she'd act on because a new relationship wasn't on the cards in the foreseeable future. If ever. And it was presumptuous to think he was interested in her. He had a daughter and most likely a wife.

'Do you like lemons?'

How do you know I'm here?

'It was the tang of them which drew me here. Are those little lemon tarts?'

He switched off the heat to one pot and reached for a spoon, glancing her way. 'From my own lemon trees. Well, Mum originally planted them decades ago but I guess they are mine these days.'

Lifting the pot, he deftly spooned thick curd into pastry shell after pastry shell.

'These will be served warm with whipped cream on the

side. That's the last of the sweet pastries. The savoury pastries are ready to go out. Oh yes, I also have cheese tarts cooling.'

'Is there anything I can do to help?'

The question sounded silly and Brock didn't immediately reply, finishing his task before setting the pot down. He began stirring the contents of the second pot but his eyes were on her.

'Harriet, you have already outdone yourself with this event. Do you have any idea of how many people you've made happy today?'

Harriet didn't know how to respond. Her heart had done a flip-flop when he said her name and the rest of what he said was fuzzy. Something about happy.

I am happy. Look at what I've created from nothing.

'Are you closing the doors now?'

'Very soon. I should go and... um, I'll help Olive restock the shelves.'

He began spooning more lemon mix into pastry shells and didn't seem to have heard her. Brock had so much to do in such a short time. Harriet smiled at his back and went in search of Olive.

'Look at the B— whoops, look at the ladies, Mum,' Olive whispered, her eyes on Bess and Annette.

They were seated in tub chairs, each with a glass of wine and a plate of food. Bess was trying to get Marge's attention but the other woman was browsing the second-hand books and seemed unaware of her friend's arm waving.

'Do you think I should disturb Marge?' Olive asked.

'No. She looks content there and that reminds me, I've popped her goodie bag behind the counter so we mustn't forget to give it to her. Oh, she's coming over.'

Marge went straight past Bess, who was still waving, and

held up a book as she got closer. 'Do you have any idea who this once belonged to?'

It was the poetry book from Brock's place.

Harriet frowned while she tried to recall why it was special. Marge opened it and the handwritten dedication was an instant reminder.

'I've been meaning to research who Henry and Eleanor were. 1852 is a long time ago.'

'Let me fill you in. Henry Temple was the recipient and Eleanor, poor woman, was his wife.'

'As in Temple River? And Temple Road?' Olive's eyes brimmed with curiosity. 'The man who built Palmerston House?'

'The very same. Wherever did you find this?'

Annette was staring in their direction.

'Let's have a chat over here, Marge.'

Harriet led the way.

'You finally found us, Marge! I've been waving for ages,' Bess said.

'I know.'

'Well then. I had saved you a lemon tart but if that's your attitude I shall eat it.'

Marge seemed unimpressed and held up the book. 'Anyone here know anything about this?'

After peering at it, Annette shrugged. 'Brock sold it for me.'

'*Your* Brock? Did he mean to?'

'Of course he did, Marge. And before you start, I know it is valuable and probably should go to a museum or library, but I just couldn't find the bandwidth to follow through with that.'

Olive giggled and everyone looked at her.

'Sorry. I just never heard someone old... I mean older than me, use the term bandwidth.'

'I learned it from my granddaughter.' Annette gazed steadily at Olive.

'I think there are some customers going toward the counter, honey,' Harriet prompted and Olive tore away.

'It is an odd term,' Bess said.

Harriet was mortified. 'Annette, I had no idea. I'm so sorry and will return it to you.'

'But then I'd have to bring back some of the books I bought from you because I imagine I have used up what you paid for it. You are welcome to donate it to the appropriate body though.' As if the matter was decided, Annette bit into a tart.

Marge handed the book to Harriet. 'There's a lot of interesting local history with the Temples.'

'Gossip, you mean,' Bess piped up. She had finished her glass of wine and Harriet was fairly certain it was her second. Or third.

'Remember to collect a goodies bag each in case I forget. Marge, yours is behind the counter. I might go and put this book somewhere safe, if you'll excuse me?'

Harriet took it to the safe and locked it in. Something about Annette's response didn't sit well. She'd known the book was valuable but had sold it for far less than its worth.

I'd love to talk to her away from the others.

The rest of the hour raced by and Harriet was certain she wouldn't remember half of the people who introduced themselves. And so many more books were sold. Olive had shown Kasey how to use the till and they'd both kept busy ringing up sales and handing out bags. As people began to trail out, Kasey went to help Brock and Olive farewelled folk as they left.

'I have to tell you what a gorgeous shop you've created.' The young woman on the other side of the counter had a beautiful face and kind eyes. 'The town needed a bookstore but you must have known that.' She laughed and gestured at the shelves, many with big gaps where books had once been. 'I'm going to bring my great-aunt in when she returns from her latest jaunt overseas.'

'Please do. I'm happy to extend the grand opening special pricing to her.' Harriet found one of the flyers and wrote across it – *discount approved by Harriet for* – and she glanced up, 'May I have her name to add?'

'Martha.'

'*Martha.*' Harriet finished writing and handed it across. 'There's no rush to redeem it.'

'You are so generous. And I have something for you in return.'

The woman took an envelope from her handbag. 'Two free beauty treatments, one for you and one for your gorgeous daughter. I have the beauty spa down the road, Harriet.'

'Olive has been trying to get me to book in for a while. Thank you so much... oh, I don't know your name?'

'Christie. It's been so nice to meet you and please do book into the spa.'

When almost everyone had gone, Harriet found herself at the food table. Brock was missing and Kasey was helping Olive collect plates and glasses from tables and shelves. The food had been a delight and so many people had commented about it. Harriet's stomach rumbled and she rubbed it. She'd eat once the bookstore was back to normal and ready for tomorrow's trade.

'I made this for you. There's one for Olive in the kitchen.'

Brock had appeared from nowhere but a second before he'd spoken, Harriet knew he was there. It was both a bit scary and a lot exciting to have this weird connection. He put a plate down in front of her.

'How?'

He chuckled. 'Me chef. Me know stuff.'

Harriet laughed as well and without meaning to, she reached out a hand to his arm.

His own hand covered hers. 'But quite apart from my super-powers, I guessed you'd be hungry.'

They looked at the plate. Nested in rocket and baby spinach

with balsamic dressing were several of the cheese tarts. Alongside was a piece of grilled sourdough with herbs, fresh tomatoes, and glistening with oil.

'I am so hungry, Brock.'

'Olive just locked the front door. The guests have gone. Eat.'

She mouthed, 'thank you', picked up the plate which had a knife and fork neatly wrapped in a napkin, and took it behind the counter. After sinking onto a stool, Harriet bit into the sourdough and closed her eyes in bliss.

'Don't go to sleep yet, Mum.' Olive's voice was amused.

She pulled up the other stool and joined Harriet with her own plate of food. In between mouthfuls, Olive chatted about customers, the food, Kasey, the food, how on earth they'd restock the shop... and then food. She still managed to finish before Harriet and began showing her photos on her phone.

'I'll put a lot of these onto our Facebook page later. I did ask people if they minded and nobody did but I won't show the faces of any of the children. I took heaps more than I thought... Look at this one of how busy we were!'

Brock ducked out to move his car closer, now that the street outside was quiet. He and Kasey had moved most of their equipment closer to the front door, including the oven and portable stove. Olive took off again to help Kasey who appeared to be her new best friend, and Harriet carried both plates to the kitchen.

It was spotless. Not a sign that a chef had been hard at work in here and created delectable finger food for a lot of people. Well, only one sign, which was a note on the counter.

In the refrigerator are the remains of the day... please eat within twenty-four hours or freeze.

In the freezer you will find packets of sweet and savoury. These will last up to three months... if you can wait that long.

Harriet couldn't stop smiling. She held the note against her chest. Her stomach was happy. The grand opening was more than she could have imagined. And a certain man was getting under her skin in the nicest of ways.

I'm happy. At this moment, I truly am happy.

FIFTEEN

'Are you sure you don't want to come with me, Mum?' Olive stood at the open front door. 'I'm sure everyone will be disappointed.'

'You and Kasey enjoy your day, honey. There's a few things I want to do here and I might go shopping as well. Anything you want me to get?'

'Yes please, some more of the yoghurt I like and some cherries.'

'Yoghurt and cherries it is. Have a lovely time and don't let that pony bite you.'

With a laugh and a wave, Olive stepped outside and closed the door.

Harriet went into the living room and watched her daughter climb into Brock's car, which Kasey had driven down. Their friendship was an unexpected bonus of getting to know Brock, and seeing Olive with a friend around her own age again was wonderful. In a moment they'd driven away and a bit of Harriet left with them. A day wandering around Brock's mountain property and getting to know him more was close to irresistible.

And that scared her.

He'd been on her mind too much since the grand opening and she had to find a way to manage her expectations. For one thing, he had an adult daughter. He didn't act as if he was happily married but perhaps he liked to play the field. Harriet didn't believe that. But either way, as interested in her as she thought he was, Harriet was still reeling from the break-up of her marriage and unsure if she could trust her feelings. Saying no to the invitation extended via Kasey gave her a chance to be alone and think.

'And talk myself out of anything.'

Rather than talk aloud to herself, Harriet moved to the dining room and spent the next hour packing up what was left from the grand opening. She and Olive had been tired for a couple of days afterwards and it had been so busy in the book-store. Now it was Sunday, she finally had time to attend to turning the room back to its real purpose. The final thing she did was clean the whiteboard. Instead of returning it to the shed though, she wrote on it.

The Diary

The Map

A Treasure Hunt

The Poetry Book

The final line was at odds with the others... or was it?

Henry Temple was one of the founders of the town and in the safe at work, Harriet had a book which once belonged to him. How had it made its way to Annette? And why had she sold it for far less than its potential worth? That was enough to justify its inclusion on the whiteboard because although doubtful it had any bearing on the events in the diary, it was an anomaly. Like the compass.

There was so much Harriet had to learn about Rivers End. The people, its rich history, no doubt full of scandals and plenty of gossip... just as Bess had said. Harriet stepped away from the whiteboard with a sigh. After living here for such a short time she couldn't expect to know everything or even skim the surface.

It would have been nice if Jason had brought her and Olive here before buying the building. Such arrogance to assume this was the best place for a bookstore, let alone that Rivers End was a town they'd want to live in.

She went to the kitchen for a glass of water. Thinking about her ex-husband wasn't a good idea. But she and Olive wouldn't be living here if not for him and his decisions. Harriet sank onto a chair.

'The day after I was diagnosed I began searching for a suitable place for you.'

They'd been in the hospital waiting room. He was about to be admitted for surgery and the prognosis was poor. The tumour in his brain had grown rapidly in the short time between diagnosis and the operation. It was only weeks after they'd first heard the news which had sent their family into shock and Jason's health was visibly deteriorating.

'What do you mean? What kind of place?'

'For your bookstore, Harry.' He'd taken her hand and kissed it. *'Your never-failing support got me to where I am in my career. This is the least I can do in return.'*

It hadn't made sense. For a moment or two, Harriet had seriously considered that the medication and illness was playing with his mind.

'There's a sweet little seaside town called Rivers End. You'll love it. Olive will love it. And I managed to buy one of the best

retail spaces on the main street so that you, my book-loving wife, can open the bookstore of your dreams.'

'But I don't want that. I want you. Jason, I want you to be well and for us to go back to our happy life.'

Something had shadowed his features. At the time Harriet put it down to his fear of dying but later, when he'd filed for divorce, she'd wondered – over and over – if it was her use of the term 'happy life'.

The conversation had been interrupted by hospital staff and Jason had his surgery and came through it better than even the surgeon expected. Within a fortnight he was home and recuperating with expectations of a full recovery.

And a new mindset.

Harriet's heart pounded and she wiped tears from her cheeks.

They'd never returned to being the family of the past. Jason had new dreams and needs. He'd only ever said sorry one time and that was to Olive. Perhaps Harriet could have fought harder. Persuaded him to seek couples' therapy. Begged him to stay. But he'd made up his mind so what was the point? She'd given in. Stepped back. Signed paperwork. Watched her home go on the market and her husband become happier and more carefree by the day while she barely held it together. He thought she was okay with it. Even told her once he was surprised how cold she was about the situation.

Cold? I was heartbroken.

Poor Olive had been shattered and she was the one who railed against her father's decisions, which were incomprehensible to her. She'd got through her last year of school with excellent results and that was a measure of her determination. But university was a different matter and she'd failed her first exams and promptly dropped out. It was as out of character as the gradual change in Olive from an outgoing and bubbly young woman to one who wanted to stay in her bedroom all the time.

And I still thought it was all about her father.

While Harriet had been there through Olive's grief and anger, Jason hadn't noticed. His focus was on removing himself from his partnership at work and putting his share of the finances into long-term travel plans. One day Olive asked if she could go with him and he'd laughed. He'd actually laughed. As tears had poured down her face he'd given her a hug and said something about needing to explore the world and find out who he really was. He loved her and always would but wanted to be alone.

She'd pulled away and in a steely tone of voice Harriet had never heard from Olive, told Jason he was selfish and childish and that until he changed back into her father, she would treat him accordingly.

It was only occasionally – such as the night when Harriet had asked Jason to call – that Olive showed how young she was and how much this had affected her. For the most part, even recovering from the emotional damage inflicted by Tyler, she was the poised and funny young woman Harriet was so very proud of.

They'd got through the worst of it together and now was the time for Olive to grow again, with new friendships and skills and dreams.

And so should you.

Harriet couldn't spend the rest of her life trapped in the past. The bookstore was the best thing she'd ever done apart from raising Olive. At the very least she could build some friendships because that way, when Olive eventually went out on her own, Harriet could get a cat or two and have the perfect life. Books, friends, and cats.

She removed her wedding ring. Inside was an engraving. *Our unbreakable bond of love.* There was a heaviness in her chest. The bond was still there, no matter how angry she felt. Harriet slipped the ring back on.

. . .

Friendships were still on her mind when she drove to the supermarket. She'd normally walk but wanted to do a decent shop and without Olive to help carry bags, she decided it was fine to be lazy every so often. Seeing Bess and Marge – with James Regal – settled in at the café for a coffee, reminded her she wanted to talk to Annette alone. Bess saw her and waved, so Harriet wandered down to the ladies. They were seated under a large umbrella outside the café, and James Regal jumped up and whined in greeting.

'We were just talking about you!' Bess called. 'Nothing bad.'

'Seriously, Bess, that's the first thing you say?' Marge shook her head. 'Come and join us, Harriet, unless you have somewhere else to be.'

'I'm going to do some grocery shopping but thought I'd come and say hello first.' Harriet pulled up a chair. James Regal wiggled under the table and she scratched the top of his silky head. 'No Annette today?'

'She's visiting with Brock and Kasey. For that matter, why are you here and not there?' Bess tilted her head. 'I thought you and Olive were both there today.'

Why would you think that?

Bess didn't wait for an answer. 'Kasey hasn't been home in months so Annette takes every opportunity to be with her. Such a lovely young woman. As is Olive, you must be proud of her.'

'I am. And thank you. I had some things to take care of today and I really don't think Olive needs her mother looking over her shoulder while she visits her friend.'

'*Friends*, dear.' Marge wore oversized sunglasses which made it difficult to gauge her mood. Even more than usual. 'You'll never find a sweeter human than Brock and he is a decent man.'

'Did you enjoy the food at the grand opening?'

Both of the other women nodded.

'And as long-time residents of the region, how do you think the evening went?'

Bess leaned forward, her eyes bright. 'I've lived in Rivers End my whole life and can safely say that in the last couple of years we have been blessed with the most wonderful new places. Your bookstore, of course. The beauty salon. The new wine bar... mind you, we haven't been in yet.'

'I have.'

'You have?' Marge removed her sunglasses. 'Every time we walk by in the evening it is packed.'

'For a good reason. Terrific service, lovely food, and there's a piano as well.'

'Played by young Billy. Such a talent and not bad on the eye,' Bess said.

Marge reached over and smacked Bess's arm. 'He isn't even twenty-five. You are more than seventy-five.' She turned to Harriet. 'Please do not sell her any more romance books.'

That made Harriet laugh and the other two women joined in.

They might be quite a bit older but to Harriet they were the kind of people she enjoyed spending time with. Age had never mattered to her when it came to who a person was and having worked in a school library, she'd met children wise and level-headed beyond their years and had many interesting conversations. The world was in good hands with youngsters like that.

'Speaking of books,' Marge said, 'I haven't thanked you for the gift of the diary. So thoughtful of you to remember our conversation and come up with such a kind gift.'

'It was our pleasure. I had one when I was about twelve but I rarely wrote in it and I know when I gave Olive one she was the same. But some girls really do use them to record their thoughts and feelings and special events.'

Bess sat back in her chair, her face unusually sombre and

her eyes gazing down the street. Harriet couldn't see anyone in that direction, which led past the jewellery store to a part of town she'd not explored. In the distance, the hills rose with only a few houses scattered around.

'We all enjoyed the contents of our bags from the other night, although I think my diary might have surprised Annette.'

'Surprised?'

'She seemed a bit emotional. Thought I saw a strange glistening in her eyes and she's not one to cry. I didn't ask her, but I hope she was happy for me.'

'Or it upset her.' Bess hadn't moved.

'But Bess, why would me having a diary upset Annette? Or do you mean she might have wanted another one of her own?'

With a sudden smile, Bess nodded at Marge. 'Yes. Yes, that must be it.'

'I have plenty at the bookstore so please let her know she is welcome to choose one.'

'Oh, I don't think she wants one.'

I'm not following this conversation very well.

Perhaps Marge was equally confused for she patted Bess's arm with a soft, 'Are you quite alright, dearest?'

'I am, thank you. But we shouldn't talk about Annette behind her back, should we?'

'What would you like to talk about?'

Bess looked at Harriet. 'We've been curious about why you chose Rivers End for your bookstore. Was it because we didn't have one?'

The sudden change of topic must have surprised Marge for she raised both eyebrows.

'Not directly, although had there been one already here, I imagine another town would have been selected.'

If anyone might be able to help her then these two and Annette were high on her list.

'My ex-husband actually made that decision. He knew I'd always dreamed of opening a bookstore and a couple of years ago he purchased the building without me knowing a thing about it.'

'That sounds very generous,' Bess said.

'It was unexpected.' Harriet smiled, unsure of how much to say. 'He was dealing with an illness and felt it was important in case he—'

'Oh goodness, he didn't pass away?'

'No, Bess. Fully recovered and travelling the world. Anyway, he gifted the building to me. Fully paid for. It was the last thing I expected or wanted and I had every intention of selling it, but then Olive and I came for a visit and fell in love with the area.'

'We are very glad you did,' Marge said. 'But why Rivers End? Aren't you from Melbourne?'

'We are. It turned out that my ex had an aunt in the area and I only recently found out he was born in Green Bay.'

Bess and Marge both leaned forward.

'But I have no idea of the name of his aunt, only that he said she lived in Rivers End and he visited her as a young boy. He thinks she passed away a long time ago, which is a bit sad since Olive won't meet her.'

'If you can find out her name, then we will help find out who she was,' Marge said.

'Or is. How lovely if she's still living and you find you have family here.'

'When I next hear from Jason I'll ask again if he remembers,' Harriet said.

They chatted for a little longer but only about the weather and the chance of a storm the next day.

Harriet excused herself in order to do the shopping. But all the while the questions hammered away. Why didn't Annette like talking about her school years? Why would Annette be upset seeing her friend with a new diary? What did Bess know that she wasn't sharing?

It was unlikely that Annette was one of the people involved in the treasure hunt.

Wasn't it?

SIXTEEN

Harriet wrote a message for Olive on the whiteboard in big letters and pulled it to the doorway so she couldn't miss it going past the dining room.

She had no idea whether Olive would stay at Brock's for dinner and didn't want to disturb her day by messaging to ask. The fridge, freezer, and pantry were full again thanks to a full trolley shop and there were multiple options for a dinner for one or two. For now, Harriet yearned for some sand beneath her feet.

This was her first visit to the beach without Olive and she chose a different way from their usual wander along Temple Road to the bridge then following the river through the cliffs. Perhaps it was the diary and treasure map which inspired her to turn the opposite way and walk toward Palmerston House. The stately old home was only a block or so further along the same road and she'd admired it from outside a few times. Today she kept going but couldn't help gazing at it as she passed.

Built of limestone and timber, the huge home had two floors, wrap-around verandahs, and an air of history. The grounds were beautiful, with old deciduous trees and hedges complemented by hundreds of flowers and flowering bushes. A long driveway circled around a multi-level fountain.

There was a similarity between this and Brock's property, so perhaps that was built around the same time.

The road began to rise as it approached Rivers End Heights in the direction of Willow Bay and Driftwood Cove but Harriet took the only road on the left. If she was correct, this led to the cliff top where the girls from 1961 often sat beneath the sheoak.

After a few twists and turns – and a steep incline that had Harriet puffing – the road levelled out enough to create a vehicle turning space, which was just as well as it abruptly ended at the edge of the cliff. Only a low series of logs and posts stood between the road and a sudden drop.

The view was glorious. Harriet took a few minutes to catch her breath, eyes hungrily drinking in the expanse of green-blue sea and a dramatic coastline back toward Melbourne. It felt so far away... not so much the distance but the life she'd had there. As busy as she'd been with work and family commitments, it was nothing compared to owning and running a shop. She and Jason often entertained but more for business than with their friends, who were mostly from their respective workplaces anyway. Once a month she'd go out with some of the women from work – dinner, theatre, even the occasional fun visit to the casino – but she wasn't missing that. And it came as a bit of a sad surprise to realise she didn't miss anyone she'd known in Melbourne.

The beach was a long way down and it was only when Harriet stepped over the logs that she noticed a track leading along the cliff face, which was rugged rather than sheer. Was this the same track the girls used all those years ago?

Harriet glanced around and immediately spotted the sheoak. *A* sheoak. Not the most attractive of trees, the species was widely scattered in different terrains around the country, hardy and determined to survive even against the sometimes buffeting winds coming off the ocean. It had grown at an angle to accommodate the conditions and its long spiny leaves covered branches which had seen better days.

It was on the other side of a post and rail fence and beyond the tree was a house about fifty or more metres away. Whoever lived here had a wonderful view and privacy and she wasn't about to trespass.

Taking her time, she descended, watching her footing where the stones were loose and staying close to the rock side of the track as it zigzagged down. It wasn't a difficult walk but needed concentration and when the ground levelled out she stopped again and had a drink of water from her backpack.

She stood upon rocks which extended around the cliff, some boulder-like and others filled with pockets of water. With the incoming tide they'd be under water, making the track inaccessible. Getting caught there during high tide wouldn't be fun. Another day she'd see how far the rocks went but for now the beach was calling.

Although Harriet didn't go for a swim, she walked the length of the beach along the wet sand, stopping periodically to savour the warm whoosh of sea water over her feet or to pick up a shell to inspect before returning it. With only a couple of hours until sunset the colour of the sky and sea were shifting and thin clouds very high above barely seemed to move. There was something in the air. A change coming.

Just as Bess and Marge predicted.

At the far end of the beach she touched the engraving in the rock face.

T loves M.

This time there was no accompanying swell of unwanted emotion. She felt as though she was moving past Jason. But she was curious about the person who must have spent hours with a chisel and hammer declaring their love. Taking her phone out, she snapped a couple of photographs, then turned and took a few of the beach. Surfers were taking advantage of the incoming tide and many other people were doing as she had – wandering through the shallows.

Her stomach reminded her she'd not eaten since breakfast other than an ice-cream cone she'd bought on a whim after shopping. Harriet crossed through the heavier dry sand toward the usual path home, wading through the lagoon and laughing as a gorgeous golden retriever bounced in beside her for a pat and sprayed water all over her.

He might have stayed there for more scratches behind his ears but someone whistled and he tore off, bounding across the sand to meet up with a man carrying a surfboard.

We need a dog.

Olive had wanted one her whole life and once they found their own house there wouldn't be a single reason not to fulfil that dream. Harriet was still smiling at the idea when she reached Temple Road and crossed over.

Brock's SUV was drawing away from outside the cottage, and thinking it was Kasey behind the wheel, Harriet waved.

The car pulled over and the passenger window wound down.

'Are you a goddess emerged from the sea and seeking a home on the land?'

It was Brock.

Harriet leaned on the door. 'I have a home.'

He was smiling and his eyes were as warm as the summer sun. 'I just dropped Olive there. She is exhausted. Kasey took her riding and then she helped me work out which ingredient was missing from a pasta dish I was puzzling over. She and Mum did some gardening. And she brushed all the horses. Perhaps I should pay her?'

'You sound like you are handing her back to me after a day having custody.'

It had sounded better in her head than out loud.

Brock leaned closer, his face serious. 'The thing is, goddess of the sea, if she was my daughter and you were my wife, the word custody would never be spoken. Love is for life.'

Her heart completely stopped.

He wasn't touching Harriet but her body was on fire and it took all of her willpower not to reach her arms through the window to cup his face and draw him closer.

Love is for life.

'Do you know who made the engraving near the beach cave?' She blurted it out.

It was as good a response as any.

Brock blinked, raised an eyebrow, and nodded.

Harriet waited. She hadn't moved an inch.

The seconds passed... or a lifetime.

'Would you have dinner with me, Harriet? Perhaps next weekend?'

'Is this invitation connected to my question?'

His smile returned. 'You see through me. But okay, yes, I will tell you what I know over dinner.'

Just say yes, Harriet.

'I would like that. Dinner.'

He settled back into his seat. 'There's joy in your eyes today. The ocean does that to me as well. Goodnight, Harriet.'

''Night.'

She stepped back and he drove away.

'I even managed to make friends with the bay horse. You know, the one who nips?'

Olive hadn't stopped talking since Harriet arrived home,

apart from the few minutes of having a shower to wash off the salt and sea.

Now, Harriet sat at the kitchen table with a glass of wine poured by her daughter who was attempting to replicate the dish she'd worked on with Brock. Half of the fridge seemed to be on the kitchen table.

'And you went riding?'

'How do you know?'

'I talked to Brock. He was leaving when I was almost home and we... caught up. He said you'd had a busy day.'

Stopping long enough to take a sip from her own glass, Olive nodded. 'Gardening, horses, cooking, hanging out with Kasey. I'm tired but in a happy way. Does that make sense?'

'It does. What was the best part?'

'Hmm. I actually can't remember how he did this. Do you mind if I just do a simple sauce?'

'Not at all. Are you sure I can't help?'

Olive gave her a look. 'I was told today that mothers matter. Annette had gone for a little nap and Brock said how much she had done for him over the years. All the support when he went through bad stuff and putting herself last. And it made me realise that you do the same.'

What bad stuff? What did Brock go through?

'Honey, have you met Brock's wife?'

'Oh, she's been gone for a long time.'

'Gone? Did she leave him?' Harriet asked.

'She died when Kasey was a little girl.'

He's single... but how heartbreaking for a young man. A young father.

'So sad for him and Kasey and I guess that's why Brock said about mothers mattering. I'm going to cook at least a few nights each week and make sure you go and have a massage and do things which make you happy. Okay?' Olive said.

Harriet got up and held her arms open. 'There is not a moment when you don't make me happy.'

Olive came in for a cuddle.

'The thing is, Olive, we are a great team. But seeing you happy today makes me happy. Making new friends and trying new experiences. That's what life is all about.'

'Same goes for you.' Olive grinned as she stepped back. 'You looked like some kind of sea queen when you got home. Hair sprinkled with water, skin glowing, and eyes alight. I think living in Rivers End is great for us both.'

Dinner preparation took a bit longer than expected but Olive was determined to do everything, other than the tossed salad which she allowed Harriet to make. They ate on the verandah with a candle as the only light, apart from two citronella flames burning in little tins on the railing to help keep mosquitos at bay.

'Can you feel the storm approaching?' Harriet asked. 'Bess and Marge assured me there will be one tomorrow.'

'I don't mind the humidity. And speaking of the BAMs – sorry – I have something to share from Annette.' Olive put a forkful of pasta into her mouth.

Harriet had recounted her time with Marge and Bess. She'd kept some of her thoughts to herself, though. Those about Annette being one of the diary girls. And so far she'd said nothing about dinner with Brock.

'She was showing me some other books which are in that lovely library room and told me that her husband had been given the poetry book by a patient. He was a doctor and when he retired was given a lot of presents by his patients and colleagues. Now, Annette knew that patient and didn't like him very much so wasn't interested in keeping the book after her husband passed away.'

'I don't suppose she mentioned a name?' Harriet asked.

'No. But she did say he came from a family of thieves and she hadn't felt she could donate it to a library without there being some retaliation. And then Brock came in and she changed the subject.'

Harriet put down her fork. 'She was frightened of retaliation? Olive, this is serious. It sounds as if that person still has influence or family locally. But do you think she meant they'd be upset she didn't keep it? Or that it being publicly available might draw unwanted attention to them?'

'Don't know, Mum. She didn't seem scared. More annoyed than anything.'

'But she let me buy it. Wouldn't any retaliation then be redirected to the bookstore?'

Olive's eyes widened. 'Do you think we're in danger?'

'Oh goodness, no, sorry. I was thinking financially. The original owner might object to it being sold after it was gifted elsewhere and seek compensation or else request it be returned to them,' Harriet said.

'But by giving it to Annette's husband they'd made a contract, and unless there was some arrangement about it staying in the Salisbury family then the giver has no recourse.'

With a short laugh, Harriet picked up her fork again. 'See, those months in law school weren't wasted. And you are right, of course, but I think we might do something about the book. If there is any kind of cloud over it, best that it resides somewhere official.'

After dinner was eaten and the washing up done, Olive, although yawning, was keen to read more from the diary.

'We must be close to the birthday,' she said. 'And now we have the photo to look at too. I wonder if there are more.'

'Well, we could skim over the diary entries and see if we

find any more?' Harriet held the closed diary and squeezed it a bit. 'I'm sure there's more in there than just the pages.'

Olive reached across and took the diary. 'Absolutely not, Mother. This was their adventure and I think we should be following along, not jumping ahead.' She grinned. 'But you can guess what happens next if you like.'

Harriet laid out the map and placed the photograph beside it.

There was something haunting about the image of three girls who now would be elderly, if they were even alive. Was Annette one of them? None of the girls looked like her, but age changed people.

'The next entry is the morning of V's birthday. Do you think she followed all the clues?'

'We haven't even followed them all so I hope we get the chance before the story ends.'

What if there were no more clues and this entry was the last? Harriet didn't want that. She'd become heavily invested in the lives of these youngsters from more than half a century ago. She *had* to know if their carefully made plans worked out perfectly... because the occasional unease from the narrator had rubbed off on Harriet, particularly about the mysterious young man R was seeing behind everyone's backs. After Olive's experience, it might be nothing more than seeing a parallel between two boyfriends who were controlling.

In the distance a long, low rumble of thunder sounded, followed by a flash of lightning.

SEVENTEEN

20 January, 1961

All those weeks planning and its finally here. We're all so excited about today and when I wake early, I think about running up to check R hid the compass properly. But I trust her.

Today is Violet's birthday and everything is going wrong. It's bad enough that the air is already unpleasantly humid. And Ruby turned up late for the birthday breakfast which upset Violet and in turn, their mother. By the time Bess and I arrived Ruby had apologised and promised Violet that the rest of the day would be perfect, but it was obvious stern words had been spoken. Ruby couldn't wait to get out of the house.

Bess only waited until we were all by the front gate. 'What did you do?'

'Nothing. I just lost track of time.'

'But you remembered to hide the compass?' That is my only concern. I think Ruby brought her mother's wrath on herself and she needs to stop letting people down so much.

'Of course I did! That's why I was late, because it took a bit longer to get there than I remembered.'

I don't believe her. Why would it take longer to get to the hiding place when we only went there yesterday?

Ruby looks back at the house. 'Violet is still a bit cross with me but she said she'll be out once she changes her shoes and gets a hat. I've already put the first clue in the letterbox.'

'And the second clue is on the board inside the grocery store,' Bess said. 'What about the third clue?'

'One of us can run ahead and plant it once we go into the grocery store. Can you do it, Nettie?'

I was expecting that. I'm the fastest and less likely than Ruby to mess it up. Bess is best to stay close to Violet and encourage her if she gets stuck. I nod and pat the satchel I've slung over my shoulder. Inside are all the other clues and I imagine I'll be doing a lot of running today.

'Bess! Nettie! Today is my birthday!'

A blur of excitement throws herself at me and then Bess. She really is the sort of sister everyone should have. Cute with her two braids, a cheeky smile, and she's smart and kind. Most of the time.

'Ruby forgot it was.' Violet has her hands on her hips and glares at her sister.

'I did not. And if you'd stop being cross long enough to check the mailbox, you might understand why I was running late to breakfast.'

Her big blue eyes dart to the mailbox. 'But it's too early for the postman.'

'Not on your birthday it isn't. Go on, look inside,' Ruby says.

Violet opens the back of the mailbox and peers in. 'Oh, there is something.' She pulls out the pretty envelope and brings it back to us. 'It has my name on.'

'Open it.'

She's a bit uncertain and looks at each of us. We are all smiling and waiting. This is so exciting. We are about to start the treasure hunt!

'Is this a present?'

'We all got together to do something special for you, Violet. Open the envelope and see.' Bess looks like she's about to burst with excitement.

Violet carefully opens the flap and pulls out the card with the first clue. As she reads it her forehead wrinkles up in an adorable way. 'This is strange. *You'd usually push a trolley. But that would be a folly. Look there on one side. A new clue you will find.*' She glances up. 'Clue? So this is a clue and there's another one at the grocery store?'

Knew she was clever.

'Happy birthday, little sister.' Ruby gives Violet a big hug. 'This is one of the reasons I was late this morning because I had to leave the treasure in its special place.'

'Are we doing a treasure hunt?' Violet begins to jump up and down. 'Like a pirate? This is the best day ever and I have to tell Mummy.'

With that she runs back to the house. Her mother is on the front steps waiting, glaring at Ruby even when she hugs Violet. The image will stay in my mind forever.

The minute we are close to the grocery store, I drop back and cross the road and once Violet, Ruby, and Bess go inside, I start running. After a few minutes I wish I'd left the camera with Bess to carry and my water canteen because it is already warming up and the extra weight is a bit tiring as I sprint across the beach. But I get there and dive inside the cave.

It is much cooler and I scramble onto the rock while I fumble around in the satchel for the envelope. My eyes haven't adjusted to the dark and I jump off the rock to check in the entry that I have the correct clue.

The second the envelope is in the narrow crack I race back out and around the side of the cliff so Violet won't see me. I lean against the cliff wall, panting. In the distance, Violet calls something out. Perhaps 'there' or similar. Once I catch my breath, I take out the camera and get it ready for the photograph. We'd completely forgotten about taking one at the grocery store but at least we had one from outside Ruby's house.

The voices get closer until it is easy to hear.

'Let's stop for a minute, Violet. Tell me the clue again,' Bess says.

'Okay. *I'm dark and cool and near a pool. There's steps close by and ocean tides. Up on a wall you'll find it all. Another clue of what to do.* So it has to be in the cave.'

'Better see then,' Ruby says.

'Are you both coming in? It's kinda dark.'

'I will!' Bess is cheery. 'The others will follow.'

'Where *is* Nettie, anyway?'

Her voice sounds muffled now so I figure it is safe to leave my hiding spot. Ruby is just disappearing into the cave.

Inside, Violet holds on to Bess's hand and gazes at the walls with wide eyes. She really isn't comfortable being in here and Ruby should have listened when Bess raised the possibility back when we were writing the clues. I don't like small spaces but the cave doesn't bother me because the entry is big enough. Violet is fine with small spaces but hates the dark.

Sometimes Ruby lacks compassion and lately she's worse than ever. If that is the result of having a boyfriend then I'm glad I don't want one.

'Is it there?' Violet points to the envelope peeking out from the crack. Releasing Bess's hand, she climbs onto the rock and grabs it. 'Got you! Let's go outside in the sun to read it.'

Violet wastes no time opening this envelope. 'Another clue.

Our town is known for tall plants grown. From Rivers End they must be sent. Where steam is loud and people crowd. A new clue waits on a field's gate.'

Figuring I might as well get going while Violet works it out, I check the camera is on. 'What if we get a photo? Bess and Ruby go either side of Violet. And hold up the envelope. And smile.'

I aim in their direction and push the button and the camera whirs and clicks and everyone gathers around as the photograph slowly emerges. I hand it to Ruby to hold. 'The image takes a minute. You should all watch for it appearing.'

'Good idea. Violet, let's watch.' Ruby faces them all the other way and glances over her shoulder with a grin and mouths, 'Go'.

Go indeed.

This part is the hardest so far, with the steps followed by a race across the graveyard to the main road. I know I have to get to the other side and be at least partway down the road to the railway station before the others reach the top of the steps to avoid giving away the next clue. It feels like I won't make it but then I'm in the shade of the big gum trees which line the road and I slow to a walk.

At this time of the day there are a lot of people around. Train and timber-mill workers unloading huge logs and packing them onto special cars which a steam train will come and collect. Anyone who grew up in Rivers End knows to take care around here because accidents have happened before and people have been hurt. Maybe this wasn't the best idea.

I keep close to the trees so that I'm not walking on the road and have to wait a couple of times when trucks trundle by, stirring up clouds of dust. At least the siding is clear to walk along and in a few moments I have the new clue secured on the gate.

There's not really any good place to hide so I go into the field and sit beneath a tree where I can watch for the others.

. . .

'I think this one was a bit too dangerous,' Bess whispers. 'We're not meant to walk near the trucks and logs and stuff.'

I've just taken the latest photograph and Violet is sitting beneath the tree holding it and watching it like a hawk. The rest of us are a little distance away so we can talk.

Ruby looks downcast. 'I hope my parents don't find out because I don't need to be in more trouble. For some reason I forgot how busy it gets during the week and we've only walked the course on weekends.'

I pat her shoulder and she gives me a small smile.

'So far Violet hasn't worked out the next clue so we might need to get her to think about it, but then explain we have to start it from a different spot.' I point down the field a bit. 'We can climb through the fence and cross back to the main road and avoid the railway station completely.'

'And what about we all go for an ice cream once we are closer to town? I think we all need a little break.' Bess wipes perspiration from her forehead.

'I'd like an ice cream!'

We haven't noticed Violet come over. She holds out the photograph.

'I like this one but we need one with Nettie as well.'

'Next one. Promise,' I say. Being the person planting the envelopes is getting exhausting.

'And I know where to look next.'

'You do?' Ruby asks.

Violet nods and smiles. 'This is so much fun and I love you all so much for doing this.'

My heart fills with love in return. I don't have any siblings and Violet is the closest thing to a little sister. I'd do anything for her.

I'm so pleased we decided to take photographs of today. I don't have any photos with all of us in, not even school photos because R is in the higher grade. So far I've taken all the pictures but if we come across anyone we know I'm going to ask them to do some with our camera of the four of us.

EIGHTEEN

NOW

Harriet gazed out of the bookstore window, the one overlooking the corner. Rain steadily fell and the gutters on the road were overfull. Cars drove slowly, leaving a wake of water behind them, and the few people who braved the weather all scurried along with umbrellas.

Grey. Wet. And too quiet.

Across the road, the café had covered their outdoor seating and there was only the occasional customer running in and then leaving again hunched over coffees or cake boxes in an attempt to keep them dry.

This was the first day without a steady stream of customers and who could blame them? If she wasn't at work, Harriet would be curled up on an armchair with a book.

A police car went by, turning the corner.

'I probably need to talk to the police about the poetry book,' she said aloud, and then glanced over her shoulder in case a customer had snuck in.

But she was alone. Olive was at home today. They'd figured there wouldn't be too many people shopping thanks to the forecast so Olive was planning on doing some cooking and updating the bookstore's social media. It was odd being here without her daughter but good practice for the future. Olive was happier than in ages and she'd want to be more independent once she decided on a path to follow.

Standing here wasn't getting any work done. Harriet collected a box of books from the storeroom and restocked the one shelf she hadn't done today.

The police car was back but this time it pulled up outside and parked.

By the time Harriet took her now-empty box behind the counter, a police officer was heading in, not bothering to wipe his wet feet on the mat. Raindrops dripped off his jacket.

She offered a smile.

He nodded in return and stood for a moment while his eyes roamed the shop.

At a guess he was in his mid to late thirties. He didn't look fit, carrying a fair amount of weight around his stomach. His face was round and his cheeks and nose were red in stark contrast to white-blond hair.

'So this is what all the talk is about,' he said. 'Heard there was quite an event the other evening.'

'We had a successful grand opening day followed by a VIP hour.'

He plodded to the other side of the counter. 'Didn't get my invitation.'

Harriet's smile grew wider. 'I slipped one beneath the police station door myself. We would have brought it in but it must have been outside hours. I'm Harriet.'

'Yes. Harriet Main, owner. Your daughter is Olive. Not here to say hello?'

And that isn't at all creepy.

'Not today. I didn't catch your name.'

'Senior Constable Mick Hammond. Born and bred in Rivers End.'

'Nice to meet you. Is there a book in particular you are looking for today?' Harriet asked. 'Something for yourself or a family member?'

He made a scoffing sound in his throat. 'There isn't a relative of mine alive who deserves a gift from me.'

'For you then?'

'Nah. Reading's a waste of good time. But all the same it's nice for the town to have the bookstore. Good for kids, I guess. And the old people with nothing better to do.'

Then why are you in my shop?

'Heard you'd been buying up old books to resell. Often thought about doing something similar. Not with books of course but other stuff. Do you think I'd need a whole shop to sell it in though?' He leaned his arms on the counter. 'Probably not. These days everyone uses online selling. Wouldn't be hard.'

Harriet had no idea how to respond, so simply nodded.

'Anyway, back to work. Better make sure people are keeping to the speed limit in this weather.'

He was halfway to the door when he stopped and turned to look at her with a different expression. One which sent an unpleasant shiver up her spine.

'Yeah, and I like to keep crime down. Thefts and stuff. I hope you've been careful where you bought those second-hand books, Harriet. Wouldn't want to have to arrest you for receiving stolen goods, eh?'

Her chest was tight.

Mick burst into laughter. 'Aha, you look so serious. Have a nice day.' He pushed the door open with more force than needed and stomped out to the patrol car.

Harriet sank onto a stool. Her heart was thudding and she had to fight the urge to lock the door and close for the day. Was he talking about the poetry book? How would he even know she had it, unless somebody had seen it on the shelf before she'd put it into the safe. Or was it a different book altogether? A stolen book?

After getting a glass of water and telling herself to calm down and be rational, Harriet collected a book trolley and went to the second-hand section.

One by one she checked each book, putting on the trolley any that looked suspicious.

Listen to yourself. Suspicious books?

It had never occurred to her to ask sellers for proof of ownership. These were just preloved items in search of new readers. Olive had made good records of each one and it wouldn't be difficult to cross-reference which books came from a particular seller. But after she'd checked each book – flicking through the first and last pages to look for any indications of ownership other than the seller – there were only a handful of titles on the trolley.

She wheeled it back to the counter and transferred them, pushing them out of sight from anyone who might come in. Olive had added all the information to the computer and it only took a few clicks to find the file containing all the data.

Picking up the top book she found its listing. This was a thirty-year-old picture book on local flora and fauna. It was a limited edition and numbered and the only reason she was checking it was because of the photograph on the front. It was a sheoak and looked a lot like the one at the top of the cliff. But internally there was nothing to indicate it belonged to anyone other than the seller. She sighed and put it to one side.

The next three books also passed closer inspection, leaving one.

The bible she'd bought from Annette.

In hindsight it didn't belong on the shelf and Harriet chided herself for being careless with several of the more precious books. What she needed was to source a small lockable glass cabinet for them. And talk to a valuer about this bible and the poetry book.

Inside the back cover was a line of words.

Gifted to the first son of each generation.

Was Brock the eldest of his generation? Olive would probably know. Either way, this bible wasn't going anywhere until she'd sorted out a few things.

'The safe is beginning to look like one for books instead of money,' Harriet said. 'And what smells so good?'

Olive grinned as she opened the oven a crack to peer in. 'Baked mushroom risotto. It does smell nice. And once I add fresh lemon juice it will be even better. And I made coleslaw to go with it.'

If this was part of Olive's plan to help out more, then Harriet was all for it. Then again, since meeting Brock, Olive's interest in cooking had come alive so perhaps it might be her real calling.

'Go and change, Mum. And dry your hair because you're dripping onto the floor.'

'Oops, sorry. Just call me Mick.'

About to dry the floor with paper towel, Olive gave her the weirdest look.

'I'll explain later.'

Earlier, Harriet had decided to keep the police officer's visit to herself, not wanting to alarm Olive, but she'd changed her mind. It was better she knew. In fresh clothes and with dry hair, Harriet returned to the kitchen just as Olive served two bowls of steaming risotto.

'Did you have lunch, Mum?'

'I did. There are still some of Brock's cheese tarts in the freezer at the shop so I had a couple.'

Olive patted her stomach. 'I am now running twice as far each time because since we met Brock, all I seem to do is eat or think about food; but only the good types.'

'Good types? Salads?'

'Should be but no. Baked goods. Pasta.' She gestured at her bowl. 'Risotto. Do we have Italian blood somewhere?'

Dinner was delicious, with the rice cooked to perfection.

Once they'd finished, Harriet insisted Olive sit while she cleaned up and told her about the strange visit from Mick Hammond. She left out her feelings and didn't go into detail about some of the conversation.

'I'll open my laptop while you talk,' Olive said. 'Let me see what I can find out about him.'

'Why?'

'Best to know what kind of people run this town. Like, is he a bad sheriff who throws strangers behind bars for looking at him the wrong way?'

Harriet chuckled. 'He's a senior constable and doesn't run the town. Wrong country.'

'Can't be too careful. You said he was born and bred here?'

'His words.' Harriet hung up the tea towel and sat beside Olive.

'Michael "Mick" Hammond. Thirty-four. Born at Green Bay Hospital... isn't that where you told me Dad was born, after you did a bit of a search?'

'It is.'

'He went to school in Rivers End and Green Bay at different times. Graduated from the Victorian Police Academy and was in several Melbourne police stations before moving here to take up the role as senior constable at Rivers End single station. That means one officer, I guess.'

She clicked around and Mick's face appeared. 'Is this him?'

'That's Mick.'

'He doesn't look very police-like.'

I'm not going to voice my uncharitable thoughts.

'His Facebook page is full of... well, now I know he likes watching hot-dog eating competitions. A lot of them. And strangely opposite to awful eating habits, he plays football in winter. No information about wife or kids and so on.'

'How about the Hammond family in general? His parents. Siblings.'

Olive did a search for Hammond Rivers End and got a few hits.

'Everything is pretty old. Birth notices, deaths... but decades ago. Let me jump onto Trove.'

'Why didn't I think of that? I used Trove all the time at work.' The online research database was a collaboration between the National Library and hundreds of information source providers and kept records going back to the eighteen hundreds.

'We can't think of everything, Mum.'

'You do though. Look how much you know about Rivers End already.'

'I still don't know who the diary belonged to or who R, B and V are. Why would anyone use initials? Was it some kind of code or big secret?' Olive peered closer at the screen. 'Ooh, this is interesting. A Desmond Hammond was employed by Henry Temple to work on the construction of Palmerston House and then retained to maintain the equipment at the stables. So it may be that the family has been here since the early days of Rivers End.'

'Thanks for looking all of that up. I'm genuinely interested in the town. After all, it is our home now. But I'm also trying to piece together the events around the treasure hunt and whether anyone who was involved is still living. And still local for that matter,' Harriet said.

'I think about it a lot. Isn't it funny how we've got this common passion about a diary from last century? When I came home from the day with Kasey and Brock and Annette, I saw your note on the whiteboard but also the other stuff you'd written. Do you think the poetry book has some connection to the diary?'

The storm was directly overhead, with thunder booming periodically and rain pounded on the roof. Harriet got up and closed the blinds.

'I hope the bookstore is watertight.'

Olive's eyes widened. 'Oh. I never thought of that. I can run over and check?'

Harriet smiled and squeezed Olive's shoulder on her way back to her seat. 'I'd rather you don't go out in this weather. We're insured. But what I might do is get security cameras installed. Not because I think we're at risk of robbery, but so we can see remotely – as long as there's power of course. And just in case of shoplifters.'

Or anyone else who might wish us harm.

The thought was unsettling and based on little, apart from the peculiar visit from Mick Hammond and the question over the origin of the poetry book.

A clap of thunder overhead startled them both and then the lights flickered and went off. The digital clock on the oven was out as well and the only light now came from the computer screen. With a sigh, Harriet got to her feet.

'Speaking of power going out... I fancy an evening of reading a good book and a glass of Bailey's. Would you like to join me?'

After closing her laptop, Olive picked it up. 'Sounds good

but I might do a bit more research. I'll use my phone. And you need to visit a hairdresser. The one at the beauty spa.'

'I do?' Harriet touched her hair. It was a bit longer than she normally wore it but she didn't mind it on her shoulders.

'Get with the program, Mum. You have a date this weekend.'

Last time I tell you anything.

'I haven't heard from Brock so he may be too busy. We'll see.'

Olive grinned. 'We sure will.'

Reading by candlelight wasn't nearly as romantic and enjoyable as movies made it out to be. Probably something to do with Harriet's eyesight not being as sharp as it once was. After an hour of almost falling asleep with the flickering candlelight, Harriet gave up and had an early night.

She opened her curtains wide to watch the storm from bed.

There was a power, a majesty, and a terror about lightning and thunder swept in from the Southern Ocean. It both scared and delighted her.

Imagine being on the beach.

Harriet had rarely taken chances in her life. Married far too young to explore her own needs and wants, she'd quickly adapted to being the support system for Jason and then Olive. But Olive was different. A child is always different. Jason could have done more and it was only with the benefit of hindsight that Harriet saw their life more clearly.

Her studies came to a halt when *his* became more important.

Why did I lose myself?

She no longer wanted to cry or rail against the unfairness of it all.

Her phone beeped.

It was a message from Brock.

> I heard that Rivers End lost its power. If you need anything let me know. I have multiple generators and can bring one to the bookstore tomorrow if power is still out.

How thoughtful was this man? She typed back.

> Hopefully it will be back in the morning. But thank you.

Since their meeting on the road the other day she'd not heard from him. For that matter, she'd never given him her number... or had she? Thinking back, she'd handed over the card she'd had made up for the bookstore before it opened and that only had her mobile number.

He'd kept it.

She turned in her bed to face the window, taking the phone with her.

Another message.

> Is seven too early on Saturday evening?

Harriet's heart did a little dance.

> Seven is fine. Is there a dress code?

She watched as the dots in the message app rose and fell while Brock typed. Where were they going? She'd eaten at the bistro a few times which was lovely. And the wine bar.

> Dress for a warm evening in the open air. And if you really are a goddess of the sea, prepare to swim.

Whatever he had planned was something special. His use

of words told her so. It had from the beginning. Brock was not an ordinary man. And she was ready to discover the kind of man he was. And the woman she was.

NINETEEN

The bookstore had escaped the storm unscathed. They'd been there early to check the books were safe and dry and with a little extra time free before opening the shop, Olive showed off the social media posts she'd made yesterday.

'At the moment I'm concentrating on Facebook and Instagram because that covers a lot of our demographic. And it saves time because posting to one sends the post to the other. Check out how many comments are on the gallery of photographs from the other night.'

'Oh my goodness, Olive. I didn't realise we had so many followers.'

Harriet had left most of the social media side of marketing to Olive but tried to visit the bookstore's page every few days. It had grown rapidly and was looking bright and interesting with Olive's cheery posts.

'The page is public so there may be people liking and commenting who aren't local or have yet to visit us here, but there are heaps who are customers. Click on the pics from the VIP hour.'

'Doesn't the shop look amazing at night? And all those

customers. Oh, there's Marge but I don't think she liked her photo being taken. Aw. Bess is waving at the camera. Annette is looking the other way. These are great, honey.'

Harriet noticed herself in one and stopped scrolling. The photograph was taken from near the front door by the angle and there were no customers in view. She was smiling and her face gazed up at Brock. Her hand was on his arm and... oh dear, his hand covered hers. 'Maybe we should delete this one.'

She glanced sideways at Olive who was smirking.

'Why delete it?'

'But it isn't terribly professional. There I am laughing with him rather than working and we are... um...'

'Touching? Come on, Mum. The point is that you look so happy and relaxed, which makes for a lovely casual photo. It makes you even more approachable and I can't think of anyone who wouldn't love it.'

She had a point. It was a photo she'd keep for herself, if only to remind her that happy moments matter.

There was a tap on the front door and when Harriet looked up, a lady waved.

'Oh goodness, we're late opening.'

Olive was laughing as she shot around the counter. 'Stop stressing so much.' She unlocked the door and held it open. 'Good morning! Please come in. We've been cleaning up after the storm and time got away from us.'

The little fib made Harriet smile. She glanced at the photo again and rubbed her hand. Brock's touch had been warm.

'Seeing as you are out on a date on Saturday, do you mind if I go out as well?' Olive bit into the pointy end of a homemade pizza slice and made an 'mmm' sound.

About to take her own first bite, Harriet's hand stopped on the way to her mouth.

Did you say you want to go out? Socialising? Oh, that's wonderful.

She kept her voice even. 'I don't think it's a date I'm going on. But as far as you are concerned, you never need to ask me.'

Olive swallowed. 'I know. I just think we only have each other now so should know where the other one is. Within reason. I mean, I don't text you my location when I'm running. What? Why are you hiding a smile?'

'Don't think I'm being one of those helicopter parents, but the first time you said you were going for a run when we'd been here all of two days, I did check the location finder app on my phone.'

'Haha. That's so funny. You watched me go from one end of the beach to the other and back, what, three times?' Olive took another bite.

'There's a thought. I wonder if there's some app which allows me to actually see you, rather than just wherever the phone is pinged. But yes. I admit to checking you were okay, or at least in motion, and I am quite happy for you to check up on me whenever you want.'

'Kids don't bother about where their parents are.' Olive pretended not to look at Harriet. 'Only sometimes.'

Like with Jason. You can't find him on his phone at the moment.

'Shall we go back to the diary tonight?'

'Good idea, Mother. Shall we start putting more clues up on the whiteboard, seeing as it's still in the dining room?'

It didn't take much to convince Harriet to do that, so after dinner she stood in front of the whiteboard with a marker in hand. 'How shall we do this? A list of clues, or a timeframe, or our ideas?'

'Um. I'd go by date and add what happened from what we've gleaned. Just in dot point. I wish we could work out who the girls were. And there's the two others now. M and F.'

On one side of the board, Harriet wrote all the initials they knew of, one under the other.

B
R
V
M
F

'What we can do is add any snippets next to an initial which might help us identify them.' Harriet tapped the marker against her hand while she thought. 'The real key is the owner of the diary. I wish Mrs Prentice was more friendly, or at least not so angry and I could ask her more questions. From her voice I wouldn't think her old enough to have owned it, nor did she sound as though it was hers, but she did call it horrible and was happy it couldn't do any more harm.'

Olive held the diary against her chest.

'Honey?'

'Maybe we shouldn't read it anymore. What if something terrible is written inside? Something not meant for anyone else's eyes?'

She had a point.

Harriet sat, going over the conversation she'd had with Mrs Prentice all those weeks ago. 'I may not have mentioned this part. She said she hadn't realised the diary was with the other books because she'd been sorting out her father's house because he'd passed away. It might be that she was still grieving and the diary brought back sad memories?'

'I guess. And I really want to know if the little sister found the compass from the clues or had to get some help.'

'She sounds pretty resourceful.'

Olive placed the diary on the table. 'I always wanted a sister.'

'I can't help with that.'

'But you and Brock could get married and—'

'Stop right there! Brock and I are not getting married and I am far too old to have more children.'

'I'll look after her.'

'A baby isn't a puppy!'

'So can we get a dog then?'

Harriet finally saw the amusement in Olive's eyes.

'You could have led with that.'

'It was more fun teasing you about Brock.'

'Perhaps I should adopt a little girl and raise her to be kinder to her mother.'

'Would you like a cup of tea?' Olive stood. 'I am kind. See?'

The tea was nice.

Olive had dropped the subject of dogs and babies, thank goodness.

'Shall we read the first entry again? The one from January third?' She opened the diary to the first entry and read aloud. '*Every year I get a diary for Christmas and I love writing in it the first time... except today. Today I feel a bit down and keep wondering why does everything have to change? We've all been friends forever but now we're getting older, our differences are more obvious. One day it won't be our little group because R has big plans for her future and won't stay here in Rivers End her whole life. But B might because like me, she loves living here and we can't imagine moving away. Give me friends, the beach, and a pony and I'm happy.*'

When she finished, she looked up. 'That's right. They'd been a bit at odds because R wanted the others to go to Melbourne with her and money was an issue for them.'

Harriet was back at the whiteboard. 'R has more money

THE BOOKSTORE AT RIVERS END

than the other girls from the sound of it but not as much as the Ryan family.'

'The Ryans owned Palmerston House back then. And most of the timber mills.'

'So the majority of the wealth was theirs. I read somewhere that a sizable chunk of the locals worked for them and imagine there'd be a substantial difference of income between a manager of a mill to a simple worker. The girls were friends despite the hierarchy,' Harriet said. 'I imagine as they got older it was more apparent who had more financially.'

Beside 'R' she wrote 'best off'. Then 'B', 'worst off?'.

'What shall we name our narrator?' Olive asked.

'Unless you have a better idea how about "N" for narrator.'

'Original. But sure.'

After adding 'N', Harriet wrote 'middle income?'. 'It may have no bearing on the treasure hunt but maybe it will lead us to identifying the girls.'

Olive was looking at the photograph again, using a magnifying glass she'd recently bought. Harriet joined her at the table.

'The taller girl? Look at her hair. It is well cut and her shoes look like decent quality. For that matter, both she and the younger girl...' Olive handed the magnifying glass to Harriet. 'And then compare the other girl. We know V is the young girl. I think R looks like her and B is definitely from a poorer family.'

There was a clear difference. B's hair looked like a decent home cut and her shoes were quite worn on the toes.

'You really have a good eye, honey.'

'It's so interesting. Can you imagine living then? Lots of homemade clothes and food and people used their feet more than cars.'

There was a wistful look in Olive's eyes that tugged at Harriet.

'Certainly a simpler time,' Harriet said. 'Less intrusion by the outside world.'

'We should have a vegetable garden.'

'No reason why not... I wouldn't be digging one here but we could get some big pots and grow a few things. That way when we buy a home we'll take them along.'

'Do you think the owners would sell us this place?' Olive gazed around. 'I know it's small but it has such a lovely feel to it.'

A sister, a dog, a vegetable garden, and now a cottage.

'It'll be a little while before I'm ready to seriously look for a place to buy, so we can keep our options open. But honey, you might be at the point of wanting your own place by then. Or return to the city to go back to law school.'

With a horrified expression, Olive shook her head. 'Not a chance!'

'But he's left, hasn't he? Tyler?'

'Unless he failed his final exams he'll be working some-where as a graduate but that isn't the point, Mum. If I go back to university it won't be for law and it won't be in Melbourne. Geelong and Warrnambool both have campuses with courses which interest me, but I don't need a degree if I keep working with you and I love my job.'

Suddenly there were tears in her eyes and her lips quivered.

'Oh, my baby girl.' Harriet reached out her arms and drew her daughter against her. 'I love you working with me and you are fantastic at the bookstore. Quite honestly, honey, I don't think it would even be open yet if it wasn't for you. You are clever and kind and determined and I think it's great you have some other ideas about your future. Just please, please don't settle for anything less than whatever fills your heart with joy.' Harriet released her and reached for a box of tissues.

'I just want to be useful. And help you,' Olive said.

'Well you are. More than you know.'

Pulling out a handful of tissues, Olive dried her face. 'What

Dad did wasn't fair on you and I won't leave you to manage alone.'

About to say not to be silly and it wasn't Olive's job to pick up after Jason, Harriet kept the words in. The impact on Olive was deeper than she'd realised and buried under the young woman's resolve to be upbeat. And probably intensified by being in a controlling relationship.

'I forgot to ask you earlier. You said you're going out on Saturday night? Anywhere special?'

At last Olive managed a smile. 'Kasey and I thought we'd go to the wine bar. She knows Billy... the guy who plays piano. We might all hang out for a bit afterwards.'

Kasey was good for Olive. But who was Billy apart from a young piano player Olive had met a couple of times? Harriet had never spoken with him. But Bess and Marge knew him and so did Kasey. And they'd be together, out as friends.

Harriet had to believe Billy might be good for Olive as well and help her to be young again instead of trying to be old before her time.

I'm so sorry I failed you, honey.

TWENTY

20 January 1961

We made a mistake with the railway station but it isn't a big one. But if we ever do anything like this again, please let it be on a cooler day!

I run down the side of the main road to town, hoping Ruby and Bess have kept Violet occupied long enough to give me a decent head start. Last I'd seen, the three of them were sitting under that tree going over all the clues, pretending to Violet that something might have been missed.

Why have I ended up the only person who is planting clues?

There's three of us and rotating the load would be fairer.

I'm missing half of the fun of this.

At the bottom of the hill I slow at last and look back. I think I can just see the others. It surprises me that Violet solved this clue without help because it was pretty vague. At least she says she knows but what if I go and hide the envelope but everyone goes in a different direction?

Perspiration drips down my back and I long for an icy-cold lemonade. I like Bess's idea of ice creams because if nothing else it will slow things down and let me take a breather.

The bridge is just ahead and as planned with Ruby and Bess, I don't cross it but go down the bank toward the river. Although it is a bit steep, there's a track of sorts where people walk down. I have to duck to fit under the bridge which is designed for a river, not pedestrians. There's a narrow ledge just wide enough for me to avoid falling into the water and I pull out the envelope and look up. None of us has checked for a safe place to leave the clue.

A car goes over the bridge, making it shudder. I hate that. I hate being under anything which might fall on me and I won't put Violet in danger.

I get out as fast as possible. My heart feels weird like it is hammering at my chest and I feel kind of dizzy. There's not a chance I can get back up to the road and I lie on the grass, clutching the envelope. I close my eyes but the spinning gets worse so I stare at the sky – at wispy clouds passing – until the pounding feeling starts to fade.

'Found you! Nettie, that is a strange place for a clue!'

Three faces stare down at me. Violet is smiling. Bess is worried. And Ruby is furious.

'Are you alright?' Bess kneels next to me. 'You look really pale.'

'Too much running in the sun.' I manage to get the words out.

Next thing I know, Bess is pouring water over me and I splutter and sit. Violet slides the envelope from my hand but she doesn't open it. Instead, she looks ready to cry.

'I'm fine, Violet. Just needed a rest. I'm sorry this clue wasn't better hidden.'

'I'd have found it anyway. I'll read the other one again.'

She opens the previous envelope.

'Above and below people can go
From near and far with a boat or car
A founding name with a road the same
Will be the place in a tiny space.'

After replacing the clue she sits beside me. 'I knew it was the bridge because Henry Temple was one of the founders of Rivers End and has a bridge and river and road named after his family. And even a house.'

'Good work, Violet.'

'Can we have an ice cream now?'

Ruby takes her hand. 'Up you get. I think that's a good idea and you can open the new clue afterwards.' She gives me such a cross look that I almost stick my tongue out but what is the point?

My patience is almost gone. Everything lately is about Ruby and what she wants and if it doesn't suit her she stops acting like my best friend. It hurts and makes me want to yell at her and make her understand. But Violet is waiting for me and her face is a bit anxious so I let Bess help me stand and wait a minute to make sure I'm fine again.

While the others have ice creams I sip on the lemonade I'd been yearning for, careful not to gulp it down in case I get that awful headache above my eyes. It is so cold and refreshing and after a few minutes I feel less upset with Ruby. She still keeps giving me sour looks but I'm not going to respond. This is Violet's special day.

'May I read the next clue please?'

Violet has wiped her fingers on a napkin and has a big smile. We all say 'yes' at the same time which makes her giggle and then she opens the envelope.

Ruby made Bess take over with the clues and we gave her a full ten minutes before following. By now Violet had worked out one of us was going ahead each time and she was content to be a bit slower. Perhaps it gave her a bit of a scare, seeing me lying on the grass. It gave me one.

'Have you worked out the direction we're going?' I ask.

'Kind of. I think we are taking the road going to the mountains. Inland. But I am getting a bit tired so I hope we don't actually walk all the way to them.'

'Well no,' Ruby says. 'Not nearly as far. What part of the clue are you stuck on?'

Violet gazes at the words and shakes her head.

'Read them aloud and we might help a bit,' I suggest.

Until now, she hasn't had any assistance but this one is hard. I don't know if I'd work it out.

'Toward the mountains
Near the fountain
There is a hush within the walls
Upon their knees the people fall
There's names and dates
And earthy weight
Tread lightly, dear
And feel no fear.'

Ruby glances at me and she is back to normal. It is like she was asking whether she should help or not. The trouble is that Violet sometimes gets annoyed when she helps and will say she's not a baby.

'Talk it through, Violet,' I jump in. 'Can you think of anywhere with a hushed feeling or sound inside?'

She screws her face up. 'At first I thought it was our church. We have to be quiet and listen but I've never seen anyone fall over there. Oh... does that mean praying on their knees?' Her face lights up and she's on her feet again. 'The church is just off the road to the mountains.'

'Are you sure? What about the other clues?' Ruby asks. 'Do they make sense?'

Of course she wants it to because she wrote this one.

'Not yet although bibles have lots of names and dates. We should go and see.'

Without waiting for us, Violet skips away. I don't know how she can keep her energy so high because I'm tired. Ruby and I follow far enough behind that she won't hear us talking softly.

'If she thinks it's a bible, she'll want to go inside and that wasn't the plan,' I say. 'You know the doors get locked if the reverend isn't there.'

'There was a slight change and I forgot to tell you. Sorry.'

'What? Why would you do that?'

'Because I had the same thought, and the other thing is that Bess keeps going on about how we are sinning if we lean the clue against the stained glass window of the Archangel protecting heaven. I've told her it's just a windowsill and it'll only be there for a minute.' Ruby rolls her eyes. 'I mean nobody will ever know and it was such a clever part of the clue.'

'Then what's the new plan?'

'You'll see. Hey, Violet, slow down a bit.'

Rivers End has two graveyards. The one on the cliff is where people like Henry Temple are buried because he took his own life. Because it is so pretty and near the sea, other people began to choose it over the one at the church. And not everyone is allowed to be buried near the church which I don't really understand but my mother said it shouldn't be about where a body lies which matters but who they were in life. I like that. Some people who go to our church aren't very nice but some of the kindest ones I've met aren't part of the congregation. I like the church because the stained glass windows are beautiful.

When Ruby originally suggested we put one of the envelopes outside against the window, Bess was horrified and I have to admit, I thought it was going too far. But here we are, approaching the church where half the town go every Sunday.

'I think the door is locked, Ruby!' Violet stops at the gate. 'Now what will we do?'

We let her make a few guesses but then Bess waves from the back of the car park which runs alongside the church grounds all the way to the graveyard at the back. Ruby mutters something under her breath as Violet runs along the driveway to Bess.

'So much for plans.' I don't mind having a little dig at Ruby after she changed everything without sharing. 'Of all the clues why would you make Bess come here? She'll be convinced she's going to hell now.'

Ruby huffs and stalks after her sister.

I'm right. Ruby should have done this one. This is another example of her lack of care about other people's feelings. I still love her though. We've been friends forever and I couldn't bear for anything to change that. I just don't understand why she's being so mean.

Bess holds Violet's hand and gives us a look of sheer panic. My heart goes out to her and I rush over. 'Why don't you go back to the road? You can... um, look out for anyone coming.'

She nods and tears off.

It seems as if Ruby has given up. 'I wonder what that is.' She points in the direction of the headstone of T. Lightly, a timber worker from 1867.

'Am I allowed to go there?' Violet is uncertain and her eyes flick from Ruby to me.

'Of course you are. It's just a graveyard. Nobody cares. Not if they don't see you, so be quick.'

There's a small gate which Violet opens and then she sprints across to where Ruby indicated. She grabs the envelope and runs back to us.

She looks almost as upset as Bess and as she scoots through

the gate, Violet glances over her shoulder. But she has the clue and I shake my head at Ruby and close the gate.

How on earth did we mess so much up? Not planning better around the planting of the clues – I have never felt so unwell in my life and I've never felt such fear and upset in my tummy before. B is a mess about going into the graveyard. R doesn't care at all. I just want today to be over and everyone safe because now I feel I need to look over my shoulders in case the reverend saw and we get in trouble.

TWENTY-ONE

NOW

'There. That at least makes you halfway presentable.' Olive stepped back from doing something with Harriet's hair. 'Go look in a mirror now.'

'Is halfway presentable enough? Maybe I should have gone to the spa.'

Harriet headed for the bathroom, which had the best overhead lighting, with Olive on her heels. She flicked on the light and drew in a breath.

Her hair was in soft waves touching her shoulders, apart from a few from the sides which were gathered back and held in a pretty clasp. Olive had also done her makeup and although Harriet has insisted she keep it light, somehow managed to emphasise her eyes and downplay a host of lines.

'Oh, honey...'

'Don't you dare cry and mess up all that work.' Olive grinned and put an arm around Harriet's shoulders. They both looked in the mirror. 'Not too formal. You'll fit in wherever Brock takes you, whether indoors or out. The only thing is...'

'What? What's wrong?'

'If you do go swimming I'd take the clip out first. And it's fiddly to get it right so probably leave it out, unless Brock is as good with a hairbrush as he is in the kitchen with a wooden spoon. And I don't mean in a Fifty Shades way.'

Harriet's mouth dropped open and Olive giggled and left the bathroom.

'Let's find the right outfit now.'

How am I going to look Brock in the eye?

In Harriet's bedroom, Olive had the wardrobe open and was sliding hangers along. 'You need more clothes.'

'Olive, have you read that book?'

'I thought you don't agree with censorship.'

'Only where you're concerned.'

'You really don't need to worry, Mum. How are you going to go on a date wearing any of these?' Olive stepped and put her hands on her hips. 'Brock said you'd be outside and near the water. You can't wear shorts. Oh, hang on a sec.'

'Where are you going?'

Olive had already left. 'Throw your swimsuit on and I'll be... oh no.' A second later, her head popped around the door. 'You *cannot* wear your old lady swimsuit on a date. I forbid it. In fact, I'll phone and tell him you've left the country.'

'Did you not see the delivery I got the other day?'

'What? Since when you do you get deliveries?'

Harriet opened a drawer. 'With so little time to go shopping at present I resorted to online. Is this better?' She held up a sleek dark green one-piece. Not quite game to buy bikinis on the internet, Harriet hadn't been able to resist the colour of this one and loved the high cut on the legs and the little straps.

'Okay, you officially have impressed me. I'll be back with suitable clothing.'

The feel of the fabric against her skin was as pleasing as the perfect fit. She'd never cared a lot about fashion or dressing to impress, other than for special events, but tonight was different.

It had been far too long since she'd enjoyed preparing for a dinner out.

And the first date in about three decades.

With that sobering thought, she frowned at her reflection in the mirror inside the wardrobe door.

'Don't do that because you'll spoil your makeup. And Mum? That was a lovely choice. Fits well. These will fit you for sure and I couldn't have picked better colours.' Olive had brought some of her own clothes. A pair of soft, wide-legged pants in dark green and a sleeveless blouse which was cream with tiny burgundy butterflies.

'Oh, I love these but you only bought them just before we left Melbourne and I've not even seen you wear them yet.'

'They still have the tags.' Olive began removing those. 'I seem to have so many clothes compared to you. Am I selfish to buy so much?'

'Um... no. Selfish is about the last word I'd use in the same sentence as Olive. You've never chased fashion brands but always had your own style and I can't remember the last time I bought you any clothes, because you've had good money sense and saved for what you want.'

Olive still looked a bit uncertain. 'I might go through my stuff another day and donate some. Try those on and I'll start getting myself ready. I'm meeting Kasey in an hour.'

She disappeared and Harriet slipped the blouse and pants on. The mirror agreed with Olive. The style and colours suited her and with a quick breath, Harriet smiled at herself.

'Tonight is a new start. Whatever happens, I'm finding myself again and I like it,' she whispered. And then she slipped off her wedding ring and put it into her jewellery box.

When there was a knock on the door at almost seven, doubt flooded into Harriet. What was she doing going on a date only months after a divorce? What if Brock didn't enjoy her company? Or she, his?

What if I mess something up?

Olive had already left so she had nobody to give her a pep talk.

She could always text Brock and say she was unwell.

Coward.

Before she could change her mind, Harriet slung her bag – with its towel, dry lingerie in case there was somewhere she could discreetly change after a swim, and half the contents of her usual handbag – over a shoulder and opened the door.

Just like that, her fears melted away.

Brock's eyes smiled at her. And his mouth. He wore a linen shirt with the first two buttons undone, his black hair just touching the collar in stark contrast to the natural fibres of the shirt. His pants were the same material and he wore sandals on his feet.

You look like a movie star.

'Hello, Harriet. Do you mind a short walk?'

'Not at all.'

She stepped out, locking the door behind her, and when she turned he took the bag from her and tossed it over his shoulder.

'No car?'

They walked onto the footpath outside the cottage.

'I have a different form of transport tonight.' As if it was the most natural thing in the world, Brock held out his hand and Harriet took it.

They wandered along Temple Road in the direction of the tunnel under the cliff. Was a picnic on the beach in order? The evening was warm and there was still some light although the hues were gradually changing toward sunset. Harriet hadn't been on the beach at night and the idea was a bit exciting. Warm sand and water. Dark skies. Few people.

'Olive and Kasey have gone out tonight as well,' Harriet said. She had a need to fill the silence.

'I'm happy they've become friends. Kasey is lonely despite trying to hide it. Being home helps, but then she'll be back to Sydney in a few weeks for the next semester.'

There was a sadness in Brock's voice which resonated.

'What is she doing?'

'Bachelor of Music. She's a talented musician but lacks confidence. Her university is very focused on developing skills, with tutors who are among the best Australia has to offer when it comes to production and composition and performing, and at times she judges herself unworthy of her place there. She'll be fine, but she has to trust herself more.'

'It is so hard sometimes. Olive has lost her way a bit. Lost her confidence in herself.'

Brock frowned. 'I wondered... she told me she'd dropped out of a law degree but that was the sum of the conversation.'

'She had a dreadful experience. Someone a few years ahead of her and also living on campus. A young man who wasn't anything like she expected when they began dating.'

'He didn't—'

'No. She says not. But he tried to control her every move and it took her a little while to see it.'

'That's terrible. What a strong person she is. Kasey thinks the world of her.'

'I believe it goes both ways.'

What a wonderful thing to have in common. Two smart and gorgeous young women with the world at their feet... if only they could find their way.

'Has Kasey always known the path she wanted?'

Brock laughed. 'Oh yes. Even as a small child she'd roam the garden singing or be scribbling lyrics. Music always was her passion, but it took a while to narrow down the options. We've had a dozen instruments as well as singing lessons, local musical theatre, even being in a band briefly. That's how she knows Billy Webb. He played keyboards and she sang.'

'Are they...'

Brock glanced at her. 'An item? Not even close. Good friends but there's never been a spark there.'

Why did you just squeeze my hand?

They crossed the road and followed the path beside the river through the tunnel beneath the cliff. Had Brock already set up a picnic? He was only carrying her bag. Unless they were going for a walk before dinner.

On the sand they stopped long enough to remove their sandals. Going around the lagoon, Brock guided them toward the old jetty and Harriet's heart skipped in delight.

'A yacht?'

'I didn't ask if you like being on the water.'

'I adore it. Not that I've had many opportunities for years, but my whole family back in New Zealand sail. We lived on Auckland Harbour and most weekends would be out on the water, and even now my parents are retired they still sail. But this one... what a beauty, Brock.'

'Thank you. She's a few years old now, close to twenty, and doesn't get out as often as she'd like. I want to change that now I'm based at home again.'

They stepped onto the jetty.

'I bought her when Kasey was three. Don't laugh at her name.'

As they reached the end of the jetty where the yacht slowly rocked with the tide, Harriet stopped, letting her eyes roam. It was a sloop, long and sleek, white with a burgundy trim. Her name was *Lemon Pie*.

'Fitting. Not that she looks remotely like one, but owned by a chef, it suits.'

'Kasey named her. Meringue was her favourite, but she couldn't say it so it was always shortened.'

'I'm going to admit to loving that particular dessert.'

Brock's smile was oddly sad.

Harriet took his hand in hers. 'Have I said something wrong?'

He lifted her hand to his lips and kissed her fingers before releasing them. 'This is new to me, asking you out. Anyone out. Perhaps before we step onboard you should know that I've been a widower for many, many years. Since my twenties. I may not be well versed in the modern conventions of dating.'

Harriet drew in a sharp breath. It was still hard to imagine losing your partner so young.

What if Jason had died? They'd been so fortunate that his brush with death had been just that.

'The only man I ever dated, I married. We were younger than Olive and we had three or four dates – only one of them in a restaurant because money was so tight. So I guess when it comes to conventions I'm in the same boat.' Harriet glanced at the yacht. 'Well, a bit outside it.'

That brought a chuckle from Brock. 'Shall we fix that?'

He climbed aboard, dropped his sandals on the deck and took Harriet's from her, then placed her bag onto a seat.

'Would you care to join me?' He held out both hands.

'Sure would.'

Harriet grasped his hands and stepped onto the yacht, giving herself a moment to adjust to the rocking motion. And to enjoy the touch of his skin. She smiled up at him, happy that the sadness had left his eyes and was replaced with the gentle humour she knew.

'We have about an hour of light left, so I thought we might sail just past Willow Bay and moor in a quiet inlet for dinner. As long as you don't mind sailing back here in the dark.'

'It sounds perfect.'

'In that case, make yourself comfortable.'

. . .

Being on the open sea, with salty wind in her hair and the creaking of the boat beneath her feet, was bliss. And watching the sun move toward the horizon and change the colour of the ocean from out here was surreal. Harriet might have grown up sailing but almost always it was within the confines of the harbour rather than along the New Zealand coastline.

Wait until I tell them.

'Them' being her parents and older brother, Simon. She hadn't seen them in some time and a sudden yearning for her family was enough to bring tears to her eyes. She made a silent promise to arrange a Zoom call with them and Olive.

'Do you see Willow Bay?' Brock pointed.

In the distance the bushland with its small beach and couple of dozen boats moored was familiar.

'Is that where *Lemon Pie* lives?'

'It is now. When Kasey and I were in Sydney for a while I took her up there and was able to explore the harbour at leisure. I think that's why Kasey chose to attend university there. Such a great city.'

'But you've chosen to move back here.'

'Rivers End is home, Harriet. Over the course of my career I've lived in several countries and many cities, most beautiful and exciting and engaging. But every time I came back to visit my parents, all it took was to reach the top of the driveway to know where I belong.'

Harriet moved a bit so she could better see Brock's face as he navigated the yacht with a gentle touch. 'This is going to sound strange.' She looked away.

'What is?'

'The day Olive and I met you, I saw your house with the trees wrapped protectively around the garden and the flowers and soft grass.' When Harriet looked back, Brock was watching her and she smiled. 'I got out of the car and felt the most incredible sense of...'

'Go on.' His voice was quiet but intense. He wanted to know.

'Serenity. Peacefulness. Sanctuary. Yes, sanctuary.'

He nodded as if satisfied with the answer, then took a small step back from the wheel. 'Would you care to drive?'

'Oh yes please, but she's bigger than anything I've sailed.' She moved to the wheel and touched it. 'Anything I need to know?'

'Trust yourself.' Brock sat on one of the seats along the side and stretched his arms out along the back. He was relaxed.

And so should you be.

Harriet had a fair wind and an open sea.

TWENTY-TWO

There were no other yachts, nor sign of habitation, in the tiny inlet where *Lemon Pie* was anchored. Only a few minutes past Driftwood Cove, a narrow gap between rocks led to heavy bushland going almost to the water which was deep and quite calm.

Harriet had handed the yacht back to Brock as they'd neared, not knowing the coastline nor how the boat would handle once her spinnaker was down. Her senses still tingled from the sheer joy of the last half hour and she promised herself to find a way to start sailing again. And teach Olive to handle a yacht.

'Does this place have a name?' Harriet gazed around in awe at the old forest growth.

'It will but not that I can remember. Somehow it has escaped the interest of most sailors and what you see on land is all protected. We're allowed to go as far as the tree line and no further.'

Once Brock had the yacht stable, he led the way below deck. Fitted out in polished timber, it was more spacious than Harriet had imagined.

'Two double cabins, one at either end. Galley straight ahead.'

He pointed out the bathroom, which was small, before taking some bottled water from the fridge. The galley, as expected, was modern and functional with plenty of storage space, a half-sized oven and full stove top.

'Would you like to swim?' Brock offered Harriet one of the bottles. 'We'll lose the light soon enough.'

'The ocean is calling me.'

He smiled, tiny lines crinkling up around his eyes. 'Harri-et, oh Harri-et, come let us caress your skin with our salty, silken touch.'

Harriet caught her breath.

His eyes mesmerised her. His lips attracted her. There was no point denying that. She wanted to kiss him. Brock's smile changed and the air was electric. It wouldn't take more than a small movement to touch his arm or his chest.

This is happening too fast.

'I might get my bag and bring it down here. So I can change later.'

'And there's plenty of towels if you need any.'

'Oh, um, thanks, I have one. I'll be right back.'

Harriet shot up the steps and once on deck, opened the water and drank some and then grabbed her bag and headed back down.

Brock was in the kitchen, turning the oven on.

He glanced over. 'Feel free to use the front cabin to change in.'

Great idea, except he was between Harriet and the cabin and she wasn't quite ready to get so close to him again just yet. As if sensing her emotions, Brock finished whatever he was doing and moved toward the back cabin. 'Meet you upstairs?'

Stepping into the cabin was to be enveloped in everything Brock. It was obviously his space, with men's clothes hanging in the open robe, a Brock-sized dressing gown on the end of the bed, and the scent of him everywhere. It was a comfortable room with a thick doona and plump pillows on the bed and a handful of books on a shelf. Harriet stepped out of her clothes and draped them near his dressing gown, then pulled the towel from her bag. Remembering Olive's instructions about her hair, Harriet removed the clip and slid it inside the bag then ran her fingers through her hair to loosen it.

Brock was sitting at the stern, his toes almost touching the water, eyes on the bushland. Harriet lowered herself next to him.

'Do you see the roos on the beach?' he asked.

A mob of a dozen or so kangaroos congregated on the sand, some slowly hopping through the shallows while others stood around.

'They can swim, can't they?'

'Sure can.' His eyes turned to her. 'Shall we?'

She didn't move or answer. It was difficult to keep her mind clear this close to him.

His lips turned up. 'Shall we... swim, Harriet?'

That made her laugh and she pushed herself forward and slipped into the warm sea. She paddled close by, not wanting to move too far from the yacht with the light fading. Brock stood and once she was a little distance away from the stern, dived in, going under the water for a moment before emerging near her. With his jet black hair plastered to his skull and droplets of sea-water on his skin glistening from the last rays of the sun, Brock looked younger and almost like a Greek god. He might have called her a sea-goddess but had he looked in a mirror lately?

For a while they swam around the yacht in lazy circles, switching it up between swimming and talking while floating. The kangaroos had stopped to watch them for a while, their heads high as if trying to work out what these strange people were doing, but then they melted back into the bush.

When the sun dipped below the horizon, they climbed aboard and sat for a few minutes in silence, broken only by the chatter of birds as they settled for the night.

Brock got up and stretched. 'You're welcome to take a shower below if you like.'

'I think I will. Do you want to go first?'

'Never. But I will make some final preparations and put dinner in to heat.'

'May I sit here for a moment more and enjoy the evening air?'

He leaned down so that his face was close to hers. 'Don't disappear into the night.'

'If there's food on offer then I'm not going anywhere.'

'So you accepted my invitation for food rather than my company? Don't answer.' With a grin, Brock straightened and disappeared down the steps.

While Harriet showered and then changed back into her clothes, Brock had worked magic both in the kitchen and up on deck. As she'd towel-dried her hair the aromas wafting into the small bathroom made her mouth water.

When she emerged from the cabin there was no sign of Brock so she went up the steps, stopping in surprise at the beautiful table he'd laid. A white cloth covered what was an otherwise plain table between two seats. Silverware and white crockery were complemented by dark red cloth serviettes and a short, fat, red candle flickered. To one side was a second table with drinks, a couple of covered trays, and serving utensils.

'I'll be back in just a minute. Let me wash the salt from my hair. I poured you a glass of sparkling water for now.'

When Brock returned, Harriet was taking some photographs in the small amount of light left. She put the phone away and smiled as he waited by the table.

'Would you care for wine? I won't drink any seeing I'm going to be behind the wheel later. Otherwise there is a lovely crisp non-alcoholic apple cider made by a friend of mine. Or sparkling water.'

'Cider sounds nice. And this looks and smells divine.'

'I'd pull your chair out but they are quite firmly attached to the deck.' Brock gestured for Harriet to sit. He poured cider into two tall glasses and then removed one of the covers. 'Baked gnocchi with a sauce of home-grown garlic, herbs, and pumpkin, gently stirred with locally sourced cream. As well, I've made a salad of rocket, English spinach, baby Roma tomatoes, and cucumber.'

I'm dreaming. Perfect food. Perfect yacht. Perfect man.

'Those are among my favourite foods and I'm so impressed you grew some of the ingredients. Are the potatoes yours as well?'

'They are.' Brock collected her plate and began to scoop gnocchi onto it. 'My mother is responsible for having created the gardens at home. She is a wonderful cook and was part of the local Country Women's Association for decades, winning many prizes at local agricultural shows. Next time you visit you must see the produce gardens.' He laid the plate in front of her and took his. 'Olive and Mum pottered around out there for a while the other day.'

'I know, Olive announced we have to have start growing our own vegetables.'

'Have you ever done so?'

'For a while I did but my ex-husband wanted space for a swimming pool so my little area was sacrificed.' She smiled to make it seem like something that hadn't bothered her. In reality she'd been upset for months but only once argued the point with Jason before backing down. As always. 'Once I buy somewhere I've promised Olive we will have as many veggie gardens as she wants.'

Brock said nothing, putting his own plate down and bringing the salad to the table. He sat at last and gazed at Harriet, the flickering of the candle's flame reflecting in his eyes. 'Was it a nice swimming pool?'

'No,' Harriet laughed shortly. 'Just a little rectangle with horrible tiles and ugly fencing and you know what else? He only ever used it if we had guests for a party. I don't think it turned out as he expected.'

Raising his glass, Brock extended it toward Harriet who lifted hers, then he made a toast. 'To our own swimming pool, the Southern Ocean.'

'Oh I'll drink to that.' Harriet touched the rim of her glass to his. Having an entire ocean as their playground held a lot of appeal. 'And one can grow their own vegetables in it.'

'I love using samphire and nori,' Brock said.

For a minute or two they discussed the merits of different types of seaweed for cooking, then began to eat. Harriet didn't speak again until the final bite was gone. Brock had just finished and topped up their glasses with cider. 'So was the food worth coming on the date?' The corners of his mouth lifted and his eyes were warm.

'Definitely. In fact, I'd go further than that.'

He leaned forward a little.

Harriet did as well. 'If you have that on the menu of a restaurant anywhere in the world, I would go there.'

'Even London?'

'Sounds nice.'

'Amsterdam?'

'Do you have restaurants across the globe?'

'I have interests in a few. But *this* gnocchi? Nowhere else on Earth will you find the exact recipe because' – his hand reached over the table and brushed a strand of her hair back, his touch light and soft and devastatingly electric – 'I made this recipe for tonight. For you, Harriet.'

Her heart thudded and her senses were alive... perhaps for the first time in her life.

What have you done to me?

She couldn't move and had no words worthy of his statement but he didn't seem to mind, letting his fingers trail down her face to finally brush across her lips.

When Brock sat back and picked up his glass, her skin tingled from his touch and she blinked to clear her head. From the moment she'd met Brock, he'd drawn her to him and if he truly felt the same then this might be the start of something... wonderful.

'I promised you an answer the other day,' he said.

Her expression must have been blank because he chuckled in a low, throaty tone which did nothing to help.

'T loves M.'

'Of course. The engraving near the stone steps. I'd love to hear about it.'

'The engraving is decades old, from the nineteen-sixties when a young man declared his true love for the world to see. He was the son of the stationmaster, in fact, the very last stationmaster because the railway station soon closed and he retired. But Thomas was an artist who might have been poor, yet still wooed the youngest daughter of the richest family in the region.'

'Do you mean the Ryans? The Temples were long gone by then, I imagine.'

Brock nodded. 'The story of the Temple family is a whole different one.'

'Did Thomas marry his true love?'

'There is a long story about the two of them and although much of their lives were spent apart, the ending is happy. My mother knew Martha in their teens, and rekindled their friendship a few years ago.'

'Martha?'

'Have you met her?'

'Does her great-niece live here? Christie?' Surely a piece of the puzzle in the diary wasn't living in Rivers End?

'Perhaps. In the past few years I've been away more than home and the town has changed in the blink of an eye. Talk to Mum. She knows most of the town's history and what she doesn't, Bess does.'

Harriet planned to do exactly that. First though she'd brief Olive and they could revisit some of the diary to get their facts straight. If the Martha from Brock's story was M in the diary and she still lived in Rivers End, was it possible she knew who had been involved in the treasure hunt?

'Shall I bring dessert?'

'You are spoiling me, Brock. Nobody has ever...'

'Ever what? Made you a meal?'

'Not exactly. Olive cooks. And Jason did. Now and then. I can't explain properly but yes please. I would love dessert.'

Refusing Harriet's offer of help, Brock deftly removed the evidence of the main meal and disappeared below deck. The few minutes alone were needed. Harriet understood herself better than she'd articulated. By creating a recipe just for them to share, Brock had – in one evening – made her feel something which all those years with Jason never did.

She felt seen.

They talked well into the evening, sitting on the bow of the yacht on a thick blanket. Brock spoke – hesitantly at first, and then with more confidence – about the wife he'd loved so deeply and lost only five years into their marriage. Left with a small child and memories, Brock had drifted aimlessly for a year. That was when he'd bought the yacht.

'I sailed her for weeks at a time, leaving Kasey with my parents. Then I'd come and get her for a few days back on the water. She's as comfortable sailing as I am. Over and over, that was our life until my grief gradually eased to heartache, and heartache turned into a lingering sadness.'

Harriet took his hand and held it between both of hers.

'When Kasey turned five and we celebrated her birthday at my parents' home, without her mum for the second time, something changed. I recall standing outside the house setting up a table for the kids who were invited. I kept changing it because I couldn't get it right, not the way Isla would have done, and the strangest sensation took over my body.' He glanced at Harriet. 'You may reconsider dating me.'

She squeezed his hand and smiled in encouragement.

'For a moment I felt Isla beside me. Her larger-than-life personality and direct way of speaking her mind. And I was certain she spoke to me.'

'What did she say?'

His eyes glistened. 'She told me to start trusting myself. And she said to be bold and have courage both for Kasey's sake and mine.' Brock drew in a long breath and released it. 'And then, she was gone and the sadness was as well.'

'What a powerful message.'

'I've never told anyone about it.'

Harriet's heart, which had been aching for the young man and his child, almost burst with a rush of warmth. 'Thank you for sharing that with me, Brock.'

For a while they sat holding hands, the lapping of the sea against the hull the only sound. Then Harriet spoke about Jason. His diagnosis and subsequent recovery and change of heart. It felt right to let Brock into her own history after he'd so generously trusted her with his. He listened and asked a few questions and she kept to the facts. There was still too much she'd not made peace with to talk openly about her feelings around Jason. And Brock didn't press but he traced her finger where the wedding ring had once been.

An hour later, content and weary, Harriet stepped off *Lemon Pie* onto the jetty at Rivers End beach. The night sky was filled with brilliant stars which she'd admired all the way back. Sailing at night was an experience adding new elements of wonder to being on the open sea. The entire evening had been magical.

They strolled back to her cottage, where the living room light was on.

'Olive's home. Would you like to come in?'

Brock stopped them both just inside the gate. 'Thank you, no. I'm going to sail back to Willow Bay and sleep onboard so might head off before the tide turns.' He wrapped his arms around Harriet and held her against his chest. 'Tonight has been... perfect. I'm not going to ask to kiss you though. Once I do that, I'll be lost forever.'

His heart thudded against Harriet. There was no disappointment. He wasn't going to rush her or himself and that felt good.

TWENTY-THREE

20 January 1961

R brushes off my stern words about putting the clue on a grave. B is on the other side of the road and won't even look at us. But V is already trying to work out the new clue. She is such a determined kid. As cross as I am with R, I try to help V.

'Let's catch up with Bess and she can help as well,' I suggest. I'm not keen to stand around in the car park either and it isn't fair that Bess missed out.

Violet is happy with that and reads as she walks.

My heart sinks when we get close to Bess because she's been crying. Her eyes are puffy and she's trying to dry her cheeks with her hands. I give her a hug.

Violet hasn't noticed because she's puzzling over this clue. It is the hardest one yet and I don't mind helping her because the sooner we finish this, the sooner the day can be a celebration again.

'Read it aloud, Violet.'

She glances at me and begins.

'Where gums are tall
and sometimes fall
Beyond the largest home of all
A place exists
past turns and twists
Above the very highest mists
Inside a rift
Your arm must lift
To find your birthday gift.'

Her arms both drop to her sides and her expression is priceless. This has really stumped her.

Bess has sorted herself out and decides to jump back in. She's probably as over the day as I am. Ruby has looked at her watch a few times and I don't know if it's because we've taken so much longer than our test runs, or she has somewhere to be. Probably meeting the boyfriend again.

'Violet, is there any of the clue you can work out?'

'All I can think of is that the largest home of all is Palmerston House. I've never seen a bigger house anywhere in Rivers End.'

'Shall we start walking in that direction then?'

Bess and Violet head off and I hang back a bit, slipping my arm through Ruby's so she stays near me and we can speak quietly.

'When do your parents expect you both home?' I ask, thinking that is a better approach than bringing her sneaking around into it.

'Just over an hour. By the time we've found the co— the gift, we'll have to go home rather than have the picnic at the sheoak. It's a bit annoying because I wanted to give Violet a chance to use the gift.'

'Do you mean to navigate there?'

'It might have been fun for her to find another way through the forest.'

'Well, what if she navigates home?'

Ruby looks surprised. 'I guess. I mean, it won't be too difficult because we'd still stick to the path but at least she can have a bit of fun with it. Good idea, Nettie.'

'Glad to know I'm useful for stuff apart from planting clues all day,' I mutter.

I feel her arm stiffen and when I glance at Ruby, her face is bright red.

'Don't be angry, Rubes. I'm not really having a go at you.'

'I keep making mistakes,' she says. Her voice is weird. Upset but almost... scared. 'Don't do things like me, Nettie. Stay away from... well, dangerous people.'

My heart lurches. Dangerous? Does she mean the boy? Is she in danger from him?

But then she laughs and takes her arm back. 'I think the heat today is making me say silly things. Ignore that, okay?'

That's the last thing I'm going to do but we're too close to the others to ask more questions. It'll keep for a bit.

We follow the road past houses and cross over another road. There's a few farms here and they all back onto the hills. Bess and Violet turn toward Palmerston House and before we reach the main streets of the town, they stop.

'It says its beyond Palmerston House but that it is above the mist,' Violet says. 'Ruby, do you remember that time when we went riding on a misty morning? We went up and then the track went back and forth and suddenly we were looking down at the top of the mist. Is that where I have to go?'

Ruby lets out a strange squeal which I think is excitement. 'You *do* remember!'

Violet jumps up and down and then grabs her sister's hand. 'Come on! We know the way. Everyone, keep up.'

. . .

'Why did we leave the hardest one for last?' Bess whispers to me. 'That hill has left my legs shaky.'

I know what she means. We could have made the treasure hunt just as much fun for Violet without all the extremes of walking and climbing. But we're here now and there's a sense of satisfaction knowing it was the three of us who made this happen.

'Is this the place, Ruby?' Violet stops in a clearing at the end of the track and gazes around. 'There are lots of tall gums.'

'And some which fall.' Ruby gestures in the direction of a huge old gum which has probably been on the ground for years. The branches at the far end are long dead and there are large cracks along the trunk.

Violet marches up and down its length, her eyes darting around looking for anything which matches the clue. The trunk on its side is as tall as she is and after a minute she turns to us, shoulders slumped.

'I don't know. It says I have to lift my arms but I can't see where to climb up.'

'Is that what it says though?' Bess asks.

'Inside a rift your arm must lift... oh, inside. But I don't know that word.'

'You are so close to finding it, Violet. Don't give up now. Use your reasoning,' Ruby urges. 'If it says that you lift your arm inside something, what might that mean?'

'Is a rift a hole? Because I saw a big gap in the side before.' Violet returns to the spot and peers in. 'Too dark. Is this a rift?'

Bess puts on what I call her 'school teacher' voice. 'A rift might be a few things but in this situation, other words that fit would be breach, crevice, crack, nook, and a few others.'

'So you mean a hole.' Violet grins. 'And I am going to stick my arm in there even if there are spiders or rats or snakes.'

Ruby's eyes widen in horror. 'Snakes! Oh, don't you do it.'

But Violet's arm is already inside, right up to her shoulder, and her faces grimaces as she feels around. And then she beams and steps back and triumphantly holds up the oilskin package. 'I found it! I solved the treasure hunt.'

We all hug Violet and each other and then we find a spot on the grass in the shade so that Violet can finally open her birthday gift.

She can't undo the leather laces but manages to slip them off and then Violet unwraps the oilskin and lifts the pouch up. 'Whatever is this?' She holds it against her ear. 'Not a watch.'

Ruby is so impatient and reaches out as if to take it. Violet giggles and holds it out of the way and then pulls the drawstring open and looks in. Watching her face is the best part. She's worked so hard today to find this and now she doesn't know what it is. But then she empties the pouch onto her hand and gasps.

'A *compass*. Is it real?'

'Sure is. Do you like it?' Ruby asks.

Violet turns it over and then back to the face and her finger traces the gold rim. 'Is it really for me?'

'It really is,' I say. 'We don't know much about its history but we thought that makes it even more interesting. It is a treasure for a treasure.'

Violet looks at us one at a time. 'Thank you, Bess. Thank you, Nettie. And thank you, Ruby. I love and adore this forever. Did it come from a shipwreck? Or pirates? I can't wait to show Mummy and Daddy. Can we go home now?' She jumps to her feet.

'We might need you to navigate the way,' Ruby mentions.

I pick up the oilskin and pouch and leather laces left on the ground and add them to my satchel.

For a minute Violet studies the compass and then glances at Ruby. 'I can navigate. But can you all keep up with me?' With a big smile, she throws her arms around Ruby, then Bess, and then me. 'Best birthday ever. And still the party to go which makes me the luckiest eleven-year-old in the whole of Australia.'

With that big announcement, Violet skips away. 'Keep up!'

She is so happy and all of us are smiling a lot. Our treasure hunt worked out in the end and I still have to finish the map and give it to V later on. I think I might make a second one which is a bit nicer. I took a few photos of V opening her present and they will look nice in a frame. We're all pretty tired. But very happy.

TWENTY-FOUR

NOW

'I feel like we're so far behind now.' Olive flopped onto her chair, diary in hand. 'Do you recall where we finished?'

Harriet sat opposite and glanced at the whiteboard. 'The birthday girl had found the clue at the railway station and they were working on it.'

'Ah, yes. I'll read the clue. The bit before it was just about the writer wishing they'd done this on a cooler day.'

Today was Monday and for once there was little needing Harriet's urgent attention. She'd spent a couple of hours during the morning on the business financials but thanks to their point of sale system, which integrated with their accounting program, it wasn't a difficult task. They'd had a light lunch and gravitated to the dining room.

Olive turned a few pages until she found the new clue. '*Above and below people can go, from near and far with a boat or car. A founding name with a road the same, will be the place in a tiny space.*'

'A founding name? One of the original families?'

'I imagine so, Mum. So there's the Ryans and Temples.

There must be others. Both have stuff named after them. Above and below and boats and cars mentioned.'

'Temple Bridge. Cars on top and boats underneath on the river. And the name is also given to the road and the river. I wonder what the tiny space is though? Do you feel like a walk?'

Olive jumped up with a grin. 'I was hoping we might finish the treasure hunt. Let me put shoes on and get us some water to take.'

Once they were out in the sun Harriet was glad she'd worn a hat. The day was humid and storms were expected for the rest of the week. Olive carried the diary and had brought a photo-copy of the map along.

'I wonder why the map was in the diary,' Olive said. 'Wasn't it supposed to be framed or something to go with the compass?'

'Just one of many unanswered questions. Did you enjoy your evening out with Kasey?'

Olive had been out again most of Sunday and they'd not caught up about their respective Saturday nights.

'Kasey is so nice. We talked and laughed a lot. Had dinner at the wine bar and listened to Billy play piano until he'd finished for the night and then the three of us sat on the beach. We only left when we saw the yacht heading to the jetty so you and Brock wouldn't think we were spying on you both.' Olive gave Harriet a sideways glance. 'That was a bit posh, having dinner on a yacht.'

And I haven't stopped thinking about it since.

'Very posh. Brock turned it into a five-star restaurant with a white tablecloth and silver and candles. Oh, and I saw a mob of kangaroos hopping around in the waves.'

'No way. Can we go there and watch for them?'

'You'll need to ask Brock where we were because I think unless you get permission it's boat access only. Kasey will prob-ably know. She grew up sailing.'

'When you and Brock were almost back to the jetty she was

skiting about how she could sail every bit as well as her father. And she was happy that you've started dating him.'

'It was just one dinner.'

'There'll be more.' Olive sounded both confident and pleased about the prospect.

They reached the bridge and took the narrow footpath on one of its sides. Halfway over they stopped and peered down. The river was slow and beginning to narrow as it approached its final destination.

'I think this is the right place with the above and below thing. We need to look underneath the bridge but which side first?'

'You pick, Olive.'

Olive led them to the end of the bridge and crossed over to the side closest to the beach. Here there was a steep dirt track going to the bank of the river and she ran down it, grabbing a bush to stop herself going straight into the water from the momentum. She gazed back up with a sheepish grin.

'I might walk down.' Harriet watched her footing and joined Olive without any mishaps.

They were on a flat area which disappeared under the bridge but there was no way a person could walk under there. Not an adult.

Olive handed over the diary, knelt down and after turning on her phone's flashlight, looked underneath. 'There are plenty of places here for an envelope. Lots of little ledges and stuff but so low to the ground.'

Harriet opened the diary. 'Okay, so this clue was supposed to be planted by the diary's owner, we're still calling her "N"?'

With a nod, Olive straightened and turned off the flashlight.

'It seems she got in underneath but couldn't bear the enclosed space and made herself feel ill by doing it. When the other girls arrived she was lying on the ground and dizzy.'

'Oh, the poor thing. And she'd been doing all the clues and

running around in the heat so no wonder she wasn't well. What happened next?'

'They all went to get ice creams and take a breather. V then began to work out the next clue and it was a lot harder at first.' Harriet handed the diary to Olive. 'I know you enjoy this part.'

'Toward the mountains, near the fountain. There is a hush within the walls, upon their knees the people fall. There's names and dates, and earthy weight. Tread lightly, dear and feel no fear.' Olive looked up. 'They expected a kid who just turned eleven to work this out?'

'Keep in mind that they lived here and most likely always had, so what we might struggle to understand may very well have had more obvious meaning. I don't know of any fountains other than the one in the driveway of Palmerston House. Do you think that's what they mean?'

They climbed back to the road and gazed in the direction of the stately old home. It was out of sight but not by much.

'The hills rise behind it,' Olive said, 'but I wouldn't call them mountains.'

'What about the second part? A hush within the walls. A library?'

'Nobody is quiet in libraries, Mum. For someone who worked in them you have to know that.'

Harriet sighed dramatically. 'In my day, children were quiet in libraries. Adults as well.'

That made Olive laugh.

'However, I am rethinking it because why would people fall onto their knees in a library? I mean, books are pretty special but even so.'

'A church.'

'Clever. Have you come across any churches in town?' Harriet was certain she'd seen one but couldn't remember where.

'There's one in the street behind Bess's home but that's the

205

only one I'm aware of. Shall we walk and I can do a search. And we can get an ice cream on the way. Purely in the spirit of the diary.'

The ice creams were a good idea and delicious, overfilled in crunchy cones. Olive had discovered that there was a second church but it was built in the seventies so not part of the clue. As they ate, they headed along the road which led, eventually, to the Otway Ranges, passing the street where Bess, Annette, and Marge lived.

'We're going in the direction of the mountains but I have no ideas about a fountain. What do you think?' Harriet wiped her fingers on a wet towelette from the little packet she kept in her bag, along with a heap of other often useless stuff.

'Bit of a long shot, but do you think the clue refers to the font in a church? Like, where they baptise babies and stuff?'

'You really are very good at this, honey. I wonder if there is a career which lets you make or solve puzzles like this? You'd be a superstar.'

'Detective. Professional gamer. Doctors solve puzzles, sort of.' Olive turned the corner. 'It would be fun to run those murder mystery parties, although I would love to do something like it for older people in aged care. Keep their brains active and bring some fun into their lives again.'

You have the sweetest soul, Olive. Always thinking of others.

The church was small and old, with a large car park to one side and a graveyard sprawling behind. Trees – mostly gums – were dotted among the graves and a small garden lined with roses was tucked in a corner closer to the church.

'Isn't it peaceful?' Olive spoke quietly. 'I wonder if the clue about names and dates and earthy weight means the graveyard?'

'It makes sense. But would they really put a clue in a graveyard? Being a small town, the girls might well all have attended church here and there's a line between fun and disrespect which they would have had to cross.'

Rather than going through the grounds around the church itself, they walked through the car park to a gate leading to the graveyard. Treading lightly and feeling no fear made little sense but they'd only read a handful of headstones before finding the answer. A crumbling headstone had only a name and year of death – 1867.

'Are you kidding me? Look at his name, Mum. T. Lightly. I can't really believe they'd use someone's grave that way.' Olive opened the diary and ran her finger past the clue, her eyes widening. 'Oh my goodness. There's a conversation between N and R. R says something about N needing to stay away from dangerous people. This is after she's said she's made mistakes. And N is all worried that R's boyfriend... um, well, that he might be dangerous.'

Was this getting too close to home for Olive?

Harriet put a hand on Olive's arm. 'Would you prefer me to read? Or we can leave this now.'

Olive shook her head. 'I'm fine. Really. Maybe this was Tyler's grandfather and every bit as much a creep.' She managed a smile. 'Does it run in families?'

'Good question.'

'Only the best quality from me, Mum.'

'Speaking of questions, being at the church is making me think about that bible. I know it's nothing to do with the diary, but I would like to know its history. And I wouldn't mind heading home and getting out of this heat.'

'This bible belonged to Annette or, more likely, her deceased husband, and should have been passed on to Brock. He is the oldest son?'

They'd stopped long enough at the bookstore to collect the

bible from the safe and were now home, back at the dining table. The bible sat between them alongside the diary and the poetry book, which Harriet had also picked up.

'He's an only child, but how do you not know this? He's *your* boyfriend.'

'Olive! He is not my boyfriend. For one thing I'm too old for boyfriends and for another I only recently divorced and it is hardly right for me to fall... for me to move on so quickly.'

'Did you just hear yourself protesting too much?' Olive had a faint smile on her lips. 'And have we gone back to the Dark Ages? Dad didn't cark it and leave you wearing black for years. You'd still be married if Dad hadn't turned into a middle-aged hippy or whatever.'

That made Harriet smile.

'Look, you have every right to be happy and Brock makes you laugh. But as important as this conversation about your future is, the bible comes first.' The amusement in Olive's eyes was a dead giveaway of how much she enjoyed teasing her mother. 'You said Annette wasn't interested in having it back. So it mustn't be an heirloom.'

'Not a Salisbury heirloom at least. I admit I've not gone through every page and perhaps we should, although I'm reluctant to handle it a lot.'

'Do you know anyone who could look at it? A valuer or some antiquities dealer?'

'Not personally, although I have some contacts. In which case, I'll get the poetry book evaluated as well.'

'Wouldn't it be funny if they are worth millions! We could buy our own yacht,' Olive said.

'More likely they're of historical interest only. A bit like the diary, and I do wonder if we should just skip ahead. See if there are more photos and make sure it ended well.'

'Are you worried too now?' Olive picked up the diary. 'I've had a feeling all along that R was in a mess of some kind and hope it's just a crush which fades away. But we agreed to follow this adventure as if we were part of the group and I really want to keep to that.'

The pleading look she gave Harriet was a stark reminder that they'd begun this because Olive needed something special to hold on to rather than worrying about her father's whereabouts. But it was more than that. This was also their own adventure as they discovered their new home and learned more about each other. Olive loved every second of their exploration of Rivers End and working on the clues left by teenagers over sixty years ago.

Harriet put her hand on Olive's arm once more and squeezed. 'If you can bear the suspense then I'm going to grit my teeth and go along with you for the ride.'

Relief flooded Olive's face.

This really means a lot to you.

'Thanks, Mum. In that case, shall we keep reading the diary?'

TWENTY-FIVE

'*Where gums are tall and sometimes fall beyond the largest home of all, a place exists past turns and twists above the very highest mists. Inside a rift your arm must lift to find your birthday gift.*'

Olive read it twice then groaned. 'Seriously?'

'Here, let me look at the map for a minute.'

They'd got the original map again and focused on the paper inside the plastic sleeve. 'This missing corner, where it's been torn? I reckon that's where the compass was hidden.' Harriet searched for the tiny Roman numerals. 'Can you go through these and I'll write them up?' She got up and opened a marker then wrote 'clues'.

'How they match up? Okay, number one is... hang on. We've not really considered this because it was too vague, but I wonder if we can narrow down where the treasure hunt commenced? We know it was a clue in a letterbox and think R and V lived at that house.'

Harriet wrote on the board. 'We certainly could circle back to that and try to find who the girls are that way, assuming we don't before then. What's next?'

'Two is the grocery store slash supermarket.' Olive

continued until all the numbers and clues were read and then sat back. 'I like how you've done that.'

The whiteboard was a good place for a puzzle in Harriet's opinion. Easier to see the information and hopefully make connections.

Clue 1. Letterbox at home of R and V?
Clue 2. Grocery store on noticeboard (placed by N)
Clue 3. Cave at the beach (placed by N)
Clue 4. Field's gate near railway line (placed by N)
Clue 5. Temple Bridge (placed by N)
Clue 6. Church/graveyard (placed by B)
Final place. Unknown.

'I think there was a note about R going out in the morning before breakfast to hide the compass. Whoever N was, I feel sorry for her. All that running ahead in the heat and missing out on a lot of the pleasure of seeing V as she searched. This R person really doesn't sound very nice.'

'She does come over as selfish, but it's through the eyes of one person. I guess if she had a boyfriend who nobody could know about, she might have been acting a bit out of character. But that raises the question of why this boy wanted to be kept a secret. The idea of him being dangerous has nothing to back it up, at least not yet, so do you think he was painfully shy, perhaps?'

'I have a theory.' Olive touched the diary. 'Mrs Prentice had this for some reason. We think she's too young to be part of the treasure hunt. But what if she is the daughter of one of them?'

Harriet returned to her chair. 'Go on.'

'There might be things later on in the diary which were upsetting to the owner. Did the girls have a bad argument? Did R get caught with her boyfriend and have to give him up? Was the compass stolen and had to be returned? So Mrs Prentice has bad memories of it because her mother has spoken of troubles or something.'

'Which of the girls do you think might be her mother?'

'R, for sure. I think she married that boy but if he was such a private person he might have been upset about being mentioned in the diary. I just can't work out why R would have ended up with the diary though.'

'Good theory, honey. I'm not going to phone Jan Prentice and ask, but we could take a look at death notices for the past few months and see if we can find her father.'

Olive nodded. 'Okay, but not until we work out where the compass is hidden.' She tapped the map. 'The area from the missing corner includes Palmerston House and there's no bigger home in the region. Well, it would have been a home back then because I believe Elizabeth White, and her husband, who is deceased, purchased the property after it had been empty for several years. They renovated and turned it into the beautiful bed and breakfast place it is today. Bess and I had quite a long discussion about it one day.'

Once again Harriet was in awe of her daughter's local knowledge. It might not extend to the identity of the teens doing the treasure hunt but it was an impressive talent.

'It says beyond the largest house so presumably not on the grounds of Palmerston. That means it could be anywhere up the hills there and if above the mist means really high, then who knows?' Harriet had no desire to go hiking in this humidity.

A long rumble of thunder reinforced her thinking.

'So, no long walks today, Mum?'

The plans to keep working on the treasure hunt came to a halt when Olive's phone rang. After glancing at the caller ID she shrieked and grabbed it.

'Dad? Is that really you?'

So he was somewhere on land and with phone coverage. Harriet waited for the angry butterflies to hit her stomach. Nothing happened.

'Yes, I'm fine. Mum's fine. But what about you?'

Harriet touched her stomach. Still nothing.

She smiled and got to her feet. With a small wave she left Olive to catch up with Jason. They could talk without her being there and she'd get a start on dinner.

'I'm over him,' she whispered.

There would always be a part of her that loved him. He'd been her partner for too long to simply turn the feelings off but now it was more the love built by familiarity and shared experiences. Not the romantic kind.

She tapped a number on her phone which went to Brock's voicemail.

'Hi, it's Harriet. I wondered if you'd like to have dinner with me and Olive sometime? Perhaps on the weekend. Or any night, really. That's if you like homemade fish and chips? Okay... Well... bye for now.'

Her heart was going a bit too fast, which was silly. It was only a phone call. Not even one with a human, but a machine.

From the other room, Olive's voice was happy and she laughed a few times. Harriet looked in the fridge, uninspired. The ringing of her phone was a welcome interruption and she smiled as she answered.

'Hi, Brock.'

'I accept your invitation for dinner. I'm away for most of the week but Saturday or Sunday are perfect.'

A peal of laughter preceded Olive into the kitchen who had the phone against her ear. When she noticed Harriet, she grinned and did an about-turn.

'Olive sounds happy,' Brock said.

'She's speaking with her father for the first time in weeks.

No idea where he is, but at least she'll be relieved to know he's landed somewhere safe.'

'It was always hard on Kasey when I was gone for a while but at least we spoke on the phone most days. I'm glad Olive has heard from him. Would you like me to bring anything for dinner?'

Just your warm eyes and the smile which stops my heart.

'Harriet?'

'Sorry. No, not a thing.'

They spoke for a few more minutes, then Olive came back in, this time without the phone, and Harriet excused herself from the call.

'You're smiling, Mum. Was that Brock, by any chance?'

'Maybe. What do you fancy for dinner?'

'A giant salad including cheese and nuts and apples. Plus a baked potato.'

'Oddly specific.'

Olive grinned. 'I've been wanting to use our big potatoes for a few days and that sounds nice and carb-laden. We can add some cheese on top as well. Do you want me to do the salad?'

As they set about preparing dinner, Olive bubbled over with details of Jason's phone call.

'Can you believe it, Dad is in Bali! He has boat-hopped three times and landed a few days ago. But he had to find somewhere to stay and got a job behind a bar. How funny is that? My father pouring drinks.'

'Hard to imagine.'

'He was going on about how there are a lot of ex-pat Aussies where he's boarding. And at the pub, and a few of them have given him tips on all the best places to eat and visit and stuff.'

Olive was grinning as she deftly sliced tomato.

'You're taking this so well, honey.'

'I just needed to know where he was. I mean I'm an adult and

I was stressed so imagine being Kasey and sometimes your father is in France, other times sailing to places where there is no way to communicate, and other times he might have to work for a month solid setting up a restaurant. And did you know he spent a few years running the restaurants for an entire cruise ship company?'

Harriet slid a tray with two foil-wrapped potatoes into the oven and adjusted the heat higher to speed cooking time.

'Does Kasey resent that? Her dad being away so much when she was growing up?'

Was he a good father? That mattered a great deal.

'Can you grab the walnuts from the cupboard? And no, of course not. She adores Brock and admires him for his success as a chef, but also for being there for her at the important moments. You know, stuff like school concerts. He only missed one ever and was on the other side of the world so had someone attend with a phone camera so he could watch. And she had her grandparents and friends so her life as a kid was good. And Mum?'

Olive had such a serious look on her face that Harriet was afraid to listen.

'She had *horses*. So how could she ever resent him?'

How indeed? A little voice deep inside told Harriet it was okay to go ahead and fall in love now. Stop messing around with reasons of why not and just follow her heart.

Over dinner, Olive returned to the subject of Jason.

'He wanted to know about the bookstore. How the grand opening went. Whether customers are coming in. Whether we like living here.'

'Lots of questions.'

'Yeah, I kinda got the feeling he's missing us.'

Harriet couldn't summon a suitable response. She didn't

doubt he'd miss the life he'd left, where he'd had the world at his feet and a loving family.

I wonder if you've learned how to do laundry?

A silly image popped into Harriet's mind of Jason wearing his clothes until they were unbearably dirty and then buying new ones rather than wash them.

'Anyway, I suggested he visit the shop's Facebook page which will give him a lot to look at rather than me sending endless photos. I mentioned our treasure hunt and he didn't really understand what we're doing. He said it is probably a breach of privacy.'

'Did he now. Good thing we don't know the identities of anyone from the diary then.'

Olive gave her an odd look. She must be sounding snarky.

'Do you have anything on this Sunday night, honey?'

'Not as yet. Why?'

'Brock's coming over for dinner and I would love for you to be here. And we could invite Kasey as well if you wanted.'

'I'll ask her. She's only here for a bit longer before going back to Sydney, so it would be nice having her over. But sure, I'll be here as long as you actually want me to be. Otherwise I can make myself scarce. Roam the streets at night. Take shelter in the cave on the beach.'

'The one with big cracks in the wall? Guess it is better than pouring beers in a Bali bar.'

Olive laughed. 'It does sound like pretty awful. Considering Dad sees himself as an adventurer, I'd have expected him to relish these new experiences.'

The storm was all but gone when Harriet took a glass of wine outside and sat on the verandah. Olive was playing music quite loudly while doing the dishes and shooed her mother out to relax for a bit. Salty air mixed with rain was a powerful combination and for a while she held the glass, her eyes closed, using her other senses.

When her phone rang, her first thought was that it was Brock. Hopefully not cancelling dinner, but instead, wanting to talk again.

But it wasn't Brock and she almost rejected the call. Whatever Jason wanted, he could message. Her mood was too good to spoil. Except, he'd call back or phone Olive. And what if something was wrong? She put the glass on the table and tapped the screen.

'Hello, Jason.'

There was a pause. Perhaps he'd already hung up.

'Are you there?'

'You didn't waste much time, Harry.'

His voice was calm. Conversational. But the words put a chill down her spine.

'Olive told me you are working in a bar in Bali. That must be a bit different.'

'I didn't phone to talk about me. When I purchased that building and gifted it to you, the idea was for you to open the bookstore of your dreams. To sell books. A way to support yourself without my ongoing help. Get some friends. Have coffee at the café. Join a club.'

'Sorry, did you actually say support myself without your help?'

Don't raise your voice to him. Don't buy into whatever he's doing.

'Come on, Harry. I've always contributed the lion's share financially. It was thanks to my income that you have that bookstore of yours and yet the ink is barely dry on the divorce papers and you've already found someone else.'

Harriet's hands were shaking so hard she had to use both to hold the phone. Jason's voice held a whine in it she'd forgotten but now it all came back with a vengeance. Any time she'd begun doing something for herself he'd used it. Did he really want to open this particular can of worms?

'No response? Do you think you're being a good example to our daughter?'

'How dare you. I'm not the one who walked away from their family. I'm not thousands of kilometres off and barely keeping in touch which makes Olive worried about what might befall her parent. And let's just circle back to your earlier comment.'

'I dare because—'

'My turn to speak, Jason. The only true thing you've said is that you gifted the building to me. I never asked you to buy it, let alone to drop it on me as a way of easing your guilt. I'm no longer beholden to you other than our connection through Olive. Oh, sorry. You did say something else true. The ink *is* dry on our divorce papers, barely or not.'

Go on. Hang up on me now.

The silence dragged and all Harriet could hear was the thudding of her heart and Olive singing somewhere in the cottage.

'I'm going to say goodnight now, Jason.'

'No. Please don't, not while you're upset. I didn't think about my new lifestyle scaring Olive. And I didn't mean to sound so... Anyway, sorry.'

Harriet took a quick breath. 'Fine. But I don't know what you expected, Jason. Divorced people find love again all the time.'

'Are you saying you love that caterer? Of all things.'

'Goodnight, Jason. I'm hanging up.'

A bubble of hysterical laughter burst out before she could hit the 'end call' button and knowing Jason had most likely heard it made her laugh harder.

'Caterer. Oh my goodness.'

She logged into the bookstore's Facebook page and scrolled

through the photographs until she found the one of Brock and herself. Among dozens of likes and loves was a single 'angry face' reaction. Jason had put it there.

Harriet placed the phone face down on the table and then picking up her wine, gulped a mouthful. He'd had no right to speak to her like that. No right to put a horrible angry face response on the bookstore's page. On Olive's photograph.

Turning her gaze toward the cliffs, she let the tears come.

TWENTY-SIX

20 January 1961

Writing this feels selfish but putting my thoughts and memories and fears down in this diary is the only way I can get through this. Because something terrible has happened.

'Bess, can you follow Violet please! Don't go too far though.' Ruby raises her voice. 'Violet, hold on a minute for Bess to catch up.'

'Aren't you both coming?' Bess looks confused.

I have the same question.

Violet is already almost out of sight, compass held in front of her, but she stops and waves.

'We'll be right along but wait for us where the road forks,' Ruby says.

Bess shrugs and runs after Violet.

'What's wrong?' I sling the satchel over a shoulder. I think we've got everything we brought with us.

'Why do you keeping asking what's wrong?'

'I don't always ask,' I say.

Something's got up her nose today. She folds her arms and glares at me as if I'm in the wrong and it makes me mad.

'If you're missing being with your stupid boyfriend then go and see him. Violet will understand. Not like today is her birthday or anything.'

Ruby's face is pale. I've been too mean. 'Sorry. Don't let's fight.' I hate things not being right.

She won't look me in the eye. 'My boyfriend? He came with me this morning to hide the compass.'

Now I'm getting really cross. No wonder she was late for the birthday breakfast and got the day off to a bad start.

'But why today of all days? You can't *not* see him just once?' I turn to go and she grabs my arm. 'Ruby, what on earth is going on? Tell me now. And tell me who he is.'

'No. No, you don't need to know his name because I told him it's over. He's not as nice as I thought. He's mean.' She touches her cheek and whispers, 'He slapped me when I told him.'

My hand goes to my mouth.

There's tears in her eyes and now she does look at me properly. She's so upset, so hurt and even angry.

'We need to tell someone. Your mother. And your father because he'll take care of whoever this scum of a boy is.'

She's shaking her head. 'I can't. I really can't because he'll tell them about us. We... kinda did stuff. I didn't really want to but he talked me into it and I didn't like it at all and that's why I broke up with him.'

I feel horrible. And furious with this nameless person who has hurt my best friend. But she's trying not to cry so I put my arms around her and hug her.

'Let's go and find the others and get you and Violet home. You need to tell your mum at the very least. Even if she's upset with you. No boy should get away with any of that, Ruby. Any of it.'

I make her drink some water and as we start walking, Ruby spins around.

'What was that?'

'What?'

She holds her finger to her mouth to shush me, her eyes darting around the bushes behind the fallen log.

I can't hear or see anything out of the ordinary but this spooks me. Is that boy somewhere out of sight? Waiting for Ruby to be alone again?

'Sorry. Probably a rabbit or something. Let's go though.'

We hurry away from the clearing and I glance back a couple of times.

But at the fork in the road there's no sign of either of them.

'Oh for goodness' sake!' Ruby cups her mouth with her hands and yells their names.

'Violet probably wanted to get home to show off her gift,' I say. 'Poor Bess might not have been able to persuade her to stay here.'

'Then she should have called for us. Which way did they go?'

Before we can take a step Bess appears along the other road. She's waving her hands and out of breath when we meet her.

'Where's Violet?'

Bess is doubled over trying to suck in air.

'Give her a sec.'

'Violet doesn't know this area. Bess, please, which way did my sister go?'

Arm pointed out, Bess gasps, 'Wrong way. Couldn't catch up.'

Ruby and I stare along the road. It isn't the one we all walked up so recently and is narrow and winding.

Where on earth has Violet gone to?

· · ·

I feel like all I do is make people drink water, but once Bess has had some and is breathing more normally, she is a bit more coherent.

'So I ran down to here to meet her and while I was coming down the hill she was standing where we are now, looking at the compass. And then she said something about no arguments today and before I knew it she'd sprinted off down the other road. The wrong one.'

'She heard us arguing?' Ruby looks like she's going to be sick.

Bess nods.

'But she couldn't have been far ahead of you, Bess,' I say as gently as I can. 'Can you take us to where you last saw her?'

Without answering, Bess tears off again. All that training for swimming competitions must be good for recovery after running.

Ruby and I jog behind. I'm really worried about Ruby. She had a dreadful start to her day and has been trekking all over town the same as Bess and me. I'm tired. Almost exhausted. So she must be beyond tired.

Bess waits for us, peering into the bushes. Surely Violet wouldn't just dive into the forest without one of us?

There's the faintest of tracks and we follow it for a while until there's nothing left to follow. The trees are so tall here and make it a bit dark and gloomy. There are bushes everywhere and they scratch my legs as we try to find a way through.

We've been calling for Violet for a while.

'Everyone, stop for a minute.' Bess puts her hands up. 'One of us call and then listen.'

Ruby looks spent so I take the deepest breath and scream for Violet.

We listen. We wait.

There's no reply.

'We have to find her. It's her birthday, she can't get lost. A girl was lost a few years ago and never found. We have to get help.' Ruby is beside herself, wringing her hands and tears flowing down her cheeks.

'Okay, okay. Ruby, can you find your way back to the road we walked along?' I grasp her shoulders and she nods. 'Are you sure? You go back and find help. You know where we are now so bring people back to here if you don't find Violet at home.'

'What will you do?'

'Bess and I will split up but stay close enough to each other to see or hear. If I call, Bess has to answer. Same with Bess calling for me. That way we can work our way forward.'

'We'll find her, Ruby. She's probably already made it home and won't even realise she's frightened us.'

I have a terrible thought. 'Ruby, go fast. Don't stop for anyone, not even... you know.'

Her mouth drops open and her eyes tell me she knows what I mean. If the boy is hanging around, she needs to avoid running into him.

'I'll be careful.'

Bess and I wait while Ruby works her way back up toward the road. I hadn't realised how far down we've walked but that's a good thing. It means we're heading back toward town. Once we can't see her anymore, Bess and I agree on a direction each and promise to call to each other every minute.

I'm heading to the left. It is very dense with low bushes snapping at my legs and tree ferns to duck under and around. I hear Bess and call back. There's a clearing. I look around and scream out for Violet again but only the birds answer.

At the edge of the clearing there's a small break in the forest and I can just see a bit of Rivers End below.

I step forward and there's nothing beneath my feet and I'm falling and rolling and grabbing at anything to stop me screaming out and then there's pain. A terrible pain in my leg. I smash against a tree.

. . .

Everything is a blur and I think I might have hit my head somewhere. I can see but everything is fuzzy.

Someone is yelling my name but there's not enough breath in me to answer. My ribs and lungs hurt. And my leg... I have the worst pain in my knee that I've ever felt in my life. This is dreadful. I'm meant to be finding Violet.

'Nettie! Nettie, oh no.'

Bess is here. She tries to help me up and I cry out in pain.

'I'm so sorry, Nettie, what will I do? I need to find Violet but I have to go and get help for you.'

My vision is getting better. Her face is close to mine and her eyes are red and tears pour down her cheeks.

'I can't walk but I can stay here while you find her.' My voice is raspy and it is hard to talk. 'Make sure you know where I am.'

'I don't want to leave you.'

I don't want to be left. As the shock from falling fades I am thinking more clearly and know I'm injured enough to need medical attention. How will I get out of here though if I can't walk? When I try to move a bit I gasp and Bess gives me a long, serious look then her tears dry up and she's on her feet.

'I know exactly where you are. There's another path past those bushes leading down and I can see the very top of Palmerston House. I'll take note of where I walk and in no time I'll be back with some help for you. Nettie, are you okay for a little while? I can't see blood apart from some scratches.' She takes her water canteen out and loosens the top and puts it close to me. 'Keep drinking.'

'But what about Violet?'

'She's either already home or else Ruby and I will tell a heap of people and get a search party. Just stay here. Don't wander.'

Before I can tell Bess that I don't think I can stand, let alone walk, she is carefully moving through the bushes toward the path she's seen. She's out of sight in a moment and I'm all alone in the bushland.

Now I'm in Green Bay Hospital. Mum and Dad left a while ago and I wrote as much as I can remember in the diary. I need to sleep. The nurse gave me something for the pain and I'm drowsy. I still haven't found out if V is home. I'm so desperately worried.

TWENTY-SEVEN

NOW

Harriet stood in the second-hand section of the bookstore, staring at the books. It wasn't the first time this week she'd found herself there, unsure what she was looking for. Today she had a purpose.

There were around two hundred books in this section and she was keen to get them sold and begin looking for others to replace them. That's what their purpose was. In the three months since the bookstore opened her focus had been on new books and it had paid off, with a strong clientele and lots of return business for such a fledgling shop.

'What are you thinking, Mum?'

Harriet jumped and Olive offered a half-smile.

'Sorry. Shall I stomp as I approach?'

'Maybe. I was miles away.'

Olive's smile widened. 'Thinking about Brock?'

Even as she felt the heat rise in her face, Harriet turned away, taking a book off the shelf. 'Brock? No. But his mother... a whole different story.'

'Do you mean about the bible and poetry book?'

'I am curious about them. Did she RSVP for tonight?'

'The BAMs are all coming along to the inaugural old and bold club.'

Harriet almost spluttered at both descriptions.

'You know what I mean, Mum. Book club focusing on the old books. Second-hand books. Does second-hand clubbers sound better? I don't think it does.'

'Do you have a name for Kasey?'

'Sure. Bestie. Sweet and simple. And Brock is Super Chef.'

'Your father referred to him as a caterer.'

Olive giggled. 'Brock might not like being demoted that way. Hang on, when did he say that?'

Mentally kicking herself for mentioning that, Harriet headed back to the counter. 'Can you run over to Sylvia's and pick up some goodies for tonight?'

'Didn't you want to choose them? I was just going to upload some special offers to Facebook while the shop's quiet.' Olive pulled a stool in front of the computer she used the most.

Good idea. A bit of sunshine sounds good.

Today the weather again had high humidity, making her skin feel a bit sticky. With only an hour or so until the café closed, Harriet had left it a bit late but had only just thought about providing refreshments for their inaugural book club meeting. There were ten or so people attending, all of whom had shown interest in the second-hand books. The hope was that those people would talk to their friends about the range available and then word-of-mouth would kick in.

As happened every time she stepped foot in the shop, Harriet's senses went into overload. There was still a good selection of cupcakes, mini pastries, and some little quiches and those, along with tea and coffee, would do nicely.

'This is for a book club?' Sylvia asked as she packed goodies into several cake boxes. 'I'd like to join one for more contemporary books.'

'We intend to run several each month, including one for

kids and another for teens. I believe in keeping young minds busy with books and have had quite a bit of interest already. I'll put you down to contact once we work out the details for a contemporary club. I imagine it will be popular.'

'Lots of keen readers in this town, but you'd know that by now. I see a constant procession of customers through your door. We're all very happy to have our own bookstore at last.'

As Harriet waited on the kerb for traffic to pass she thought about that. Sylvia wasn't the first person to say how much the bookstore meant to Rivers End and in some ways it took a bit of the sting out of her conversation with Jason the other night. Her knee-jerk reaction had been to put it on the market. Sell what she'd created and move. But there was no logic in thinking that way and it gave Jason power over her she no longer tolerated.

It didn't matter how she came to own this building and although her income over their marriage was a mere blip compared to his, there was no way to measure the value of everything she'd done as his wife. Not in dollar terms.

Olive was in the kitchen making hot chocolate.

'I'll keep these in the fridge until later,' Harriet said. 'Did I miss a huge run of customers? Orders for a hundred books?' She made space in the fridge and straightened.

'I uploaded the specials. And I figured Dad must have found that picture with you and Brock looking so happy because how else would he even know about him?' Olive's face was serious. 'I hope you don't mind but I've banned him from the page. He can no longer find it, let alone act like a spoiled child with his misuse of emoticons.'

Harriet didn't know what to say, so got a cup to make coffee.

'Mum, you did nothing wrong. Dad needs to get over himself, because he can't be a single, world adventurer but also expect you to live some chaste life which he approves of. Was he cross with you?'

'Nothing I couldn't handle, honey. Did you really ban him from our page?'

'I really did.'

That's my girl.

The group which gathered at seven that evening was small but noisy. Quite loud, at times.

Even Pam, who owned the inn, and her friend Rebecca, both who'd been almost shy the previous times Harriet had met them, were embroiled in an intense debate with the others about which century produced the most interesting authors. Nobody agreed but they were all having the time of their lives putting forward arguments.

They sat in a circle with a selection of the old titles on a low table between them. Olive changed the subject every ten minutes or so and occasionally jumped up to pull a book off a shelf to include in a conversation.

Harriet said little. Watching the group was giving her lots of ideas for future meetings, and she was content to sit back and allow the attendees to form a bond over books.

This reminded her of being a librarian and running book clubs for teens at the different schools she'd worked at. The subject matter was different and the age and life experiences were poles apart, yet a love of reading and the nature of books reached across the generations.

It binds so many of us together.

The refreshments went down well and people drifted to different parts of the bookstore to browse and chat. Annette sat alone so Harriet brought her a fresh cup of tea and second plate of food.

'May I sit with you for a while?'

'I would like that. This is going to be an excellent book club.

At least it will if you can tell Marge to quieten down,' Annette said.

'What do you like most about it so far?'

'Being able to express an opinion without anyone taking offence. Not every book suits every reader and I found it refreshing to listen and speak about that. I did wish to ask you about something, Harriet.'

'Of course.'

'I can't see the poetry book nor the bible, not that I've had a close look thanks to this leg of mine doing its worst to stop me walking. But did you sell them?'

Harriet glanced around. Nobody was close. 'They are at my house, actually. In the safe.'

'The safe? Are they so valuable?'

'Unsure. I haven't yet had them assessed but value can be other than monetary. The historical significance, for example. The poetry book was owned by the Temple family. The bible... can you help me with its history? There's a line at the back about it being handed to the oldest son in each generation and I was unsure if I should return it.'

Annette fidgeted in her seat. 'Return it?'

'Brock is the oldest of his generation, isn't he? But he wasn't the least bit interested in it on the day Olive and I were buying books at your family home.'

With a snort, Annette shook her head. 'It is far from an heirloom.' Her face was set and her eyes were distant. 'Would you round up Bess and Marge so we can go home please? It will take a while to walk and I'm quite weary.'

Rounding up the other women wasn't as easy as Harriet expected and before she'd tried, she'd got Olive to run home and bring the car. Once she had all three ladies together, she asked if they minded waiting a few more minutes and she'd drive them home. Instead of the argument she'd half-expected, Bess and

Marge exchanged a glance and agreed. Annette didn't say a word.

I've upset you somehow.

Once Olive had parked out the front, she offered to stay with the remaining attendees so that Harriet could drive the ladies home.

On the way to Bess's house, Marge was the chatty one, heartily approving of the new book club and making suggestions for next month's gathering. Harriet parked as close to the gate as she could and came around to help Annette out. Marge waved goodbye and went to open the front door.

It took a moment for Annette to straighten and she did so with a faint smile. 'I'm seeing my physio tomorrow and that always helps.' She accepted her cane from Harriet. 'The bible is ancient history, dear. Not valuable. I should have thrown it away decades ago.' She hobbled after Marge.

Bess waited with Harriet until Annette was inside the house.

'I hate seeing her in so much pain. The day she was injured was the worst day in all our lives.' After a deep sigh, Bess kissed Harriet's cheek. 'Goodnight. You are a wonderful woman. You and Olive both, she reminds me of someone but I just cannot remember who.'

On that peculiar note Bess followed her friends into her house.

The bible, the poetry book, and the diary were on the dining-room table.

Harriet and Olive carried plates in from the kitchen, where they'd unpacked a couple of takeaway meals after finally closing up the bookstore. It was after nine and as tired and hungry as Harriet was, her need to revisit what they knew so far was more pressing.

'Who do you think I remind Bess of?' Olive had been delighted when Harriet repeated the conversation. 'What if she's Dad's auntie?'

'Then you would have a gorgeous woman as a relative. Next time you talk to your father, ask him for more details. A name, for example.'

'I will. *If* I talk to him again.' Olive heavily emphasised the 'if'.

'Of course you will and I would hate to see you change your relationship with him because of me. We all need to work through this, honey.'

Eyebrows raised, Olive shoved a mouthful of noodles into her mouth.

'Olive, I mean it. Dad and I both love you to bits and that is something which will never change. Things will settle down in time.'

It has to. Jason has his life and now I have mine.

'Annette has strong feelings about the bible and no matter what she ended up saying about it having no value and being ancient history, I'm convinced there's a story there. As much as I want to find out where it came from and how Annette ended up with it in her library, we can't really keep asking her. Not when she's made it clear she's wiped her hands of it.'

'Maybe Brock knows,' Olive said. 'Gives you a reason to phone him.'

'Brock is away until the weekend.'

'And?' Olive grinned.

'And nothing. We can ask him when he's here for dinner but if his mother has an issue with the bible, so may he.' Harriet reached for the bible and the poetry book. 'I'm curious whether there is anything connecting these.'

Olive's forehead creased. 'I don't see how. The bible is from England in 1830 and the poetry book published in Australia in 1852. What are you thinking?'

'We haven't done much to track down anything on the poems... who the poets were and why the book was put together in the first place if not to be widely available. Is it possible Eleanor Temple commissioned the work as a unique gift for her husband?'

Harriet got up to write on the whiteboard.

Research poetry book

'Oh!'

'Oh, what?' Harriet turned back to Olive.

'This is going to sound weird but what if it is *all* connected? The bible, the poetry book, the compass. Didn't our narrator have concerns the compass was stolen?'

'Go on,' Harriet said.

'Do you remember me talking about the poetry book? Where it came from?'

'How could I forget? It was a gift to Annette's husband from a patient who she disliked.'

'And who was *from a family of thieves*. Those words, Mum. What if the compass was stolen and that same family pawned it off, and those unsuspecting girls bought it. Has Annette ever said where the bible originated?'

'Sadly, no. Only that it is of no value and that alone has my senses tingling. While it is a bit battered, the book is close to two hundred years old and quite beautiful. Whatever it is worth to a collector is one thing but why does Annette dismiss it?' Harriet returned to the whiteboard.

Uncover history of the bible.

Search for reports of stolen compasses and books.

'We could always visit Palmerston House,' Olive said. Her

234

eyes were shining with enthusiasm. 'Mrs White might have old records there of the history of the Temple family when they owned it.'

'Good idea. We might phone and ask first.'

'Cool. And then tomorrow night shall we read some more? I'm dying to know whether V used the compass to take them all home and what her party was like. This is better than any streaming service.'

Harriet finally sat again and began to eat. She was just as keen as Olive to discover more of the adventures of the treasure hunt. How much fun those teens and V must have had. Even though they'd had some difficult moments, they'd accomplished something amazing and hopefully had been proud of themselves.

And what of their adult lives? Was Annette the narrator, using a shortening of her name? If so, did that make Bess the 'B' in the group? It didn't matter. 'N' had used initials for a reason and if it was to maintain privacy for the group then it needed to be respected.

Olive was gazing up at the whiteboard.

The diary had come into their lives at a good time. A distraction for Olive and an interest they shared. Not a lot of younger people would be so fascinated by an old treasure hunt but Olive was enthralled, and more than that, was committed to keeping to the original plan of working their way through the diary in the right order rather than jumping forward. And it was hard sometimes not to flick through the rest of it. Look for more photographs. Have the clues laid out rather than solve them.

Harriet said a silent 'thank you' to whoever the narrator was and for the good fortune of the diary coming into their hands.

TWENTY-EIGHT

The opportunity to visit Palmerston House came earlier than planned and unexpectedly it was through the bookstore. During the afternoon Olive took a phone call and spent a good fifteen minutes running back and forward to the counter, placing books in several piles. Harriet tried to get her attention to find out what was going on but Olive was off again, chatting the whole time.

'Yes, I'm certain that we can deliver these, so is today suitable after the bookstore closes?'

Olive finally returned – carrying three more books – and this time she grinned at Harriet.

'We'll bring an invoice for you and can put you onto seven-day terms.'

I beg your pardon?

'Lovely. We look forward to meeting you, Mrs White.'

Doing a little happy dance, Olive put the phone down. 'I'll need a box. Two perhaps.'

'Would you care to enlighten me?'

'You agreed it was a good idea to go to Palmerston House, Mum.'

'What about the seven-day terms for an invoice?'

Olive's face dropped. 'Oh, I should have asked you. I'm sorry. I just thought because it is Mrs White and this will be an ongoing arrangement, that you'd treat her like you would the book club in Forrest.'

'How about you tell me what just happened? Sit for a minute, honey. And I'm not cross with you but it just surprised me.'

Olive gestured at the fourteen books she'd piled up. 'Mrs White is updating the library room at Palmerston House. She said everything she has in there is more than five years old and it was time to add new books for her guests to read. Both she and her husband are avid readers, plus they have a couple of long-term boarders there. I suggested most of these and she also had a couple of requests.'

'That is wonderful!'

'She said she'll want to buy around five books each month with a mix of new titles and some from local authors and hopes we are willing to help her.'

Harriet couldn't stop smiling. A regular customer like this was valuable. 'Your offer of seven days was perfect, Olive. We might set up the invoice with a discount attached for orders of five or more books. And we're delivering them?'

Now, Olive offered a smile. 'Might have been my idea. She was talking as though she'd drop in for them but I've always wanted to see inside Palmerston House and we can ask her about the history stuff as well. I'll go and find a box.'

'And I'll run the books through the system and print out an invoice.'

The books were a great mix of genres and authors. Olive was fast becoming an expert not only at selling books but recommending them. Both of them read a lot and Olive loved jotting down notes. She was even writing a weekly round-up for

the Facebook page which was being noticed by readers who
came in specifically looking for those titles.

'Alone again? Is this daughter of yours a fabrication?'

Ah, the strange police officer.

Harriet had time to plant a smile on before looking up.
'How are you today, Senior Constable?'

'Just call me Mick.'

'Very well, Mick. How are your plans for an online store
going?'

Mick's eyebrows rose. 'You remembered. Usually people
are polite enough to my face but don't even want to make small
talk. The badge and all. Everyone has something to hide.'

'Do they? I don't believe there's anything in my past which
is worth hiding. How about yours?'

He scowled. More than that, there was a flash of anger in
his eyes and... shame. Harriet was certain she was right.

But the look vanished as Olive emerged from the back
room, carrying a box and humming to herself. She abruptly
stopped humming when she noticed Mick but continued to the
back of the counter where she began packing the books. She
glanced at Mick with a friendly, 'Hello.'

'You must be Olive.'

'I certainly am.'

'I'm Senior Constable Mick Hammond. Call me Mick.' He
thrust his hand out and Olive shook it.

'Nice to meet you. I recognised you.'

This time there was obvious suspicion on his face. 'Where
from?'

'Photos online.'

Harriet jumped in. 'Olive and I are trying to get to know
our new town so we spend a bit of time researching all kinds of
things including the people who hold important positions. Local
councillors, police.' She smiled. 'We share a love of history and
Rivers End is rich with it.'

Mick had visibly brightened at the words 'important positions' and he nodded. 'If you ever need the lowdown on the area or on people, then just ask. Told you I was born and bred here.'

'I read that someone called Desmond Hammond helped build Palmerston House. Was he a relative?' Olive asked.

'Right-hand man of Henry Temple, and my ancestor. There's secret tunnels and rooms there that were his doing.' Mick's phone rang. 'I'll fill you in another time.'

He answered his phone as he lumbered out.

Close up, Palmerston House was even more impressive than Harriet had imagined.

Through open timber gates, the wide driveway led to a multi-level fountain in the centre of a large turning circle. On either side of the driveway, gorgeous beds of flowers lined a deep green lawn and further away oaks, and maples, and ashes offered shade.

The house was built from limestone blocks with locally grown timber – mostly mountain ash – for the wide, wrap-around verandah. Several steps took Olive and Harriet to the front door which was double width. To one side was a sign:

Palmerston House Bed & Breakfast. Please ring and enter.

Harriet did so, opening the door for Olive, who carried the box of books.

They stepped into a lobby with polished timber floors, luxurious rugs, a grandfather clock, and a sweeping staircase.

'Oh, hello! I'm Elizabeth White.'

The speaker was a woman in her late sixties who Harriet could only describe as elegant. She was slender, with short silver hair, tailored dark-grey pants, and a white blouse. Her makeup was perfect and she wore several silver rings, including a wedding band. She emerged from a hallway beside the bottom of the stairs, carrying a folder, which she dropped onto a small desk.

'So nice to meet you. I'm Harriet Main and this is my daughter, Olive.'

'We had such a nice chat earlier, Olive. Thank you for your patience with me.' Elizabeth gestured to a doorway to one side. 'Do you mind bringing those in?'

She led the way into a room with bookshelves and a fireplace and several comfortable sofas and armchairs. Olive lowered the box onto a long side table and gazed around.

'This is all for your guests?'

'Certainly. There are only a few rooms we keep for ourselves and we encourage our guests to make good use of the amenities. With several guests coming this week, one who plans to stay a month, I'm quite thrilled to have these new books to add to the collection.'

Imagining herself curled up on the sofa closest to the fireplace in winter with a book in hand and a dog at her side was easy to do. The appearance of a black kelpie in the doorway, its coat glossy and tail wagging, was a bit surreal.

Did I just dream you into reality?

'Do you mind dogs?' Elizabeth asked. 'This is Jag. He isn't ours but we occasionally have the pleasure of him staying with us while his people are away.'

'May I pet him?'

Olive didn't wait for an answer and was at the door before Elizabeth nodded. She knelt, and the dog snuggling against her elicited little words of delight.

'We are planning on adding a dog to our family once we have our own home again.'

'You should talk to my husband. He found Jag a few years ago after the poor creature's owner passed away. Quite the story and with a lovely outcome. Sometimes dogs find you.'

Olive had given Jag one last pat and rejoined the conversation. 'Is it true there are hidden rooms and passages?'

Elizabeth smiled. 'There is one that we're aware of which leads from under the house all the way to a cave in the cliff closest to us. It was done at the time the house was built so that Henry Temple could keep contraband and hide some of his valuables and even move illegal goods to a boat. It was kept secret until quite recently.'

'Mick Hammond told us his ancestor helped build secret tunnels and rooms.'

'I'm afraid, Olive, that Mick is exaggerating. His ancestor did indeed appear on the employee manifest but given the nature of Desmond Hammond, it's more likely to be a lot of tall tales handed down through the family.'

'The nature of Desmond Hammond?' Harriet asked.

'Reputed to be a petty thief.' Going to a bookcase, Elizabeth selected a small, leather-bound book. 'If you'd care to borrow this you may find it of interest. There's a lot of local history recorded here, including a few facts about the Hammond clan.' She held it out to Olive, who glanced at Harriet.

'May we, Mum?'

'That is so generous, Elizabeth. As long as you're sure?'

'You deal in books so I imagine you know how to look after one. Take your time with it.'

They wandered back to the foyer, Jag following before his ears pricked at some sound. He padded away down the hall.

'My husband is starting dinner, I would say from that reaction.'

'Olive and I would love to know more about Palmerston House,' Harriet said. She had a long list of questions in mind.

Elizabeth's attention shifted to the front of the house. 'I might just check outside as I think that is the first of this week's guests driving in.' She opened the door as a car approached, pulling up behind Harriet's.

'Ah yes. Please do come another day and we can have tea and I'll show you around.' Elizabeth stood on the top step as Harriet and Olive went down them. 'Thank you again for the books. I saw the invoice is there so will pay it when I do the accounts in the morning.'

'No hurry, and please let us know when you want some more books. I can send you through a list of upcoming releases if you'd like?' Harriet asked. 'And our thanks for loaning us the book. We'll take good care of it.'

'Have a lovely evening,' Elizabeth said with a wave.

Olive was almost bursting with excitement. 'Mum, this is called *The Lives and Times of Rivers End* and was written fifty years ago by someone called Walter Bell. There might be more in here to help with the diary! Let's hurry home and read the next entry.'

'Oh honey, don't cry. We don't know what "terrible" equates to for a young teen. It might well be misplacing the compass or turning an ankle. How about we read on?' Harriet pushed a box of tissues in her daughter's direction. They'd got no further than the opening line of the new entry before tears had sprung into Olive's eyes and she'd put the diary down.

'I'm not crying. I'm shocked. And worried.'

Olive grabbed a handful of tissues and quickly removed any signs of tearing up.

'Would you like me to read this one?'

'Okay. But if there is something awful, don't leave it out.'

'I won't. Shall I start?'

It was harder to keep to her promise to read on than Harriet expected. She faltered on the description of R's distressing admission about the boyfriend and it took a steadying breath to read it aloud. Expecting more tears from Olive, she glanced up to a face filled with fury.

'How dare he. How dare that boy slap a young woman for breaking up with him! And what does she mean he made her "do things"? Sex?'

'I get the feeling that's what she referred to. And she's all of fifteen,' Harriet said.

'No wonder she'd been acting weird with her friends if there was so much happening in the background. Poor R. Whoever she is, I hope she got some help.' Olive said the last bit quietly. 'At least from her mum. Would there have been therapists for teens back then?'

'I'd think so. But in a small town, who knows?'

Please take that on board.

Olive gave Harriet a long look. 'What about now? Would it be hard to find someone? Not that I'm saying for me or anything but if someone wanted to... talk?'

Breathing a small sigh of relief, Harriet nodded. 'I'm sure it is much easier now.' She returned to the diary, hoping R's boyfriend was the extent of the 'terrible' thing which happened.

But when the girls lost sight of V, her throat constricted and she had to get a glass of water for both of them. When she picked up the diary again it was with a sense of doom.

Keeping her voice as even as she could, Harriet read about the decision to send R home to check for V and for the others to keep searching separately, and then the catastrophic fall which left the narrator injured to the degree of being unable to walk out of the bushland. And her bravery at being left alone.

'B must have been terrified about making the wrong choice,' Olive said. 'On one hand, the child she was currently responsible for was potentially lost in the area and on the other, her dear friend was in agony and couldn't even stand. Can you imagine being in that position?'

'No mobile phones back then. No online map or way to call for help other than by physically finding it.'

'And that is the end of the entry?'

'Not quite. There's a bit on this next page as well,' Harriet said. '*Now I'm in Green Bay Hospital. I need to sleep. The nurse gave me something for the pain and I'm drowsy. I still haven't found out if V is home. I'm so desperately worried.*'

'No!' Olive jumped up and paced around the table. 'This is more terrible than I imagined. Poor N and poor little V. Can we keep reading, Mum? Please. I have to know what happened.'

TWENTY-NINE

22 January 1961

None of this feels real. I can't remember much of yesterday because I had an operation. But Mum and Dad just left again to go home for the night and I want to finish writing this because I fell asleep too early last time. I want to see R and B but Mum said they can't come and visit yet. It might be they don't want to visit. I don't know. Everything is like a nightmare but I can't wake from it.

After Bess is out of sight, going to get help for me, I cry for a while. I cry in pain and shock and I cry for Ruby's awful experiences with her boyfriend and mostly I cry because Violet has just had the best day ever and now is missing. She must be so scared and confused.

The tears dry up and I look around. Where Bess left looks steep but a few feet away from me on the other side of the tree is a sheer drop. I would have been killed if I hadn't hit the tree trunk. My hand touches the bark and I whisper 'thank you'. But what if Violet had come this way?

I lurch upright and let out a long yowl as red-hot pain shoots all the way along my leg.

Why didn't I pay attention to where I walked? I am helpless here.

Useless.

If Violet fell she might also be somewhere in agony.

Or worse.

I refuse to think that way.

I pray.

'Please God, if you are there, please help Violet. She's only eleven years old and just starting her life. She is a good person who cares about others and I know for a fact she prays to you and goes to the church every Sunday. Please guide her to safety. Please keep her safe. Amen.'

I think it helped to pray. My mind is more peaceful and I lean my head against the tree and close my eyes.

I wake up with a shock. I didn't mean to sleep and the sky is almost dark. Someone is shouting my name. And someone else. Taking a breath I call out but my voice barely makes a sound. I lick my lips and try harder.

'She's near the tree. Yes, that one.'

Bess is here. I heard her. But it is my dad who is coming closer and closer until he is on his knees beside me. I have never seen him cry but his eyes are shining and red-rimmed and he keeps saying my name over and over.

There are other people and one has a medical bag and talks to me in a friendly and calm way, asking about what hurts and how I fell and am I dizzy. When I say I was asleep for a long time, he tells my dad that they need to get me to hospital quickly. A lot happens and I cry a lot because moving me onto a stretcher hurts so much.

'Where's Violet?' I grab at Bess as two men begin to carry the stretcher. 'Did you find her?

Her head shakes.

And then the pain is too much and I close my eyes again.

The medical man makes me stay awake. When I close my eyes he talks to me and he tells me there are many people searching for Violet. He is certain she will be found very soon. And that people will take turns searching all night until she is home safe.

Dad is with me until we get to the ambulance. He kisses me very gently and says he is going to run to our house for the car and to get Mum.

I've never been inside an ambulance. It is amazing with all the supplies and medical equipment and the medical man sits in the back with me. The sirens come on which makes me laugh but the laughing changes to little sobs because if it is so urgent to get me to hospital I am probably going to die.

At the hospital a doctor and some nurses prod at my leg and arms and head and shine lights in my eyes but they also give me some medicine and my body doesn't hurt as much and I feel a bit silly. As if I am floating.

Later I am put into a ward with three other beds but no other people. Just me in that whole big room alone except when the nurse checks me. Then Mum is running in and she is trying not to cry and she asks if she can kiss me. I want her to hug me but she is very careful and then Dad brings two chairs and they sit with me for a long time. They look so sad and worried and I feel awful because it is my fault. When it is really late the nurse comes in and says I need to rest and they can return in the morning. After they go, she gives me more medicine and I ask her for my diary.

I have to have an operation to fix my leg. The knee is dislocated too badly to avoid the surgery. My toes have all swollen right up and the doctor told my parents I will need more work on it as I grow. My back still hurts and I have concussion from hitting my head. I don't remember a lot of what happens but when I wake up my leg won't move and I keep going back to sleep.

It is night before I properly wake up and my parents are there again. They brought my old teddy bear and a new sketchpad and pencils and a book to read.

When I ask again about Violet they look at each other a funny way and Dad says I need to get some rest tonight and we will talk tomorrow. They kiss me before I can argue about it and say they will see me after breakfast and they love me very much.

I have my night medicine and the lights go down low and it is quieter so when two of the nurses stop outside the door, I can hear them talking. It is about Violet.

They say it is such a pity.

Nobody comes to check on me or tell me the truth. My whole body feels frozen and all I can see in my mind, over and over, is Violet waving on the path.

THIRTY

NOW

The diary was closed on the table.

Olive was in Harriet's arms, weeping uncontrollably, her chair fallen after she'd pushed herself up in shock and distress. Harriet rocked her daughter side to side, uttering sounds of comfort which were just as much for herself.

This was not the outcome she expected. Not even close. The wonderful journey they'd followed was meant to end happily. Wasn't it?

I should have read it first.

Regret about doing this together came from her need to protect her child from pain but Harriet pushed the feeling away. Life wasn't kind and in time Olive would come to terms with this sad story from the past.

'Her name... the little girl.' Olive drew in a long, shuddering breath and straightened. Her eyes were heavy with grief. 'Her name was Violet.'

'I know. We finally found out.' Harriet took Olive's hand. 'Let's sit outside and have some fresh air.'

It was dark now but the temperature was pleasant and for a while, Olive and Harriet were deep in their own thoughts.

Occasionally someone would walk by and cars went back and forth. In between, the crash of waves on the beach was a distant but soothing backdrop.

'Do you think she really did... die?'

'I hope not, honey. I hope it is just the way it is worded. If N overheard a comment when under the influence of painkillers or sleeping pills she may well have misunderstood. The nurses might have meant it was a pity Violet had gone missing.'

'It sounded so final.'

'Because she used Violet's name instead of V?'

Olive nodded. 'And the bit at the end. We've seen a photograph of Violet and I can imagine her standing on a dirt road waiting for the other girls, waving.' A tear slid down her face and she brushed it away. 'I feel sick about it.'

'Me too. We've become attached to people through the words of a teenager from the past. We've lived through her eyes for a while.'

'She was stuck in a hospital unable to help find Violet. How frustrating and probably scary would that have been for her?' Olive turned in the chair to look at Harriet. 'She was fourteen, injured, and alone. It is like the diary was the only way she had to express her thoughts.'

'You always think of how other people feel, honey. I'm so proud of you.'

'I think I feel too much.' There was resolve in her eyes. 'This is nothing to do with the diary, or maybe everything, but I want to see a therapist. And if you can help me find out how, I want to make sure Tyler has to explain himself to the board when he applies for the bar. They only admit people with a fit and proper standing in the community. Their words.'

Harriet got up and reached out her arms for Olive, holding her tightly against herself. 'Anything you need. Anything at all.'

You brave, wonderful woman.

It was like coming out of a long stint in the shadows to bright light and Harriet wanted to sing with joy and relief.

Olive finally stepped back. 'I don't want to feel like this any longer.'

'You have a sensitive soul. Look how easily you relate to people. Even Mick Hammond didn't faze you, yet a couple of our customers have mentioned him to me in less than glowing terms and he got my back up the first time I met him.'

Olive frowned. 'He is troubled, I think. Do you remember what Elizabeth said about Desmond Hammond, his ancestor?'

'Something about being a thief. A petty thief.'

'Oh, that's the word. Yet Mick sounded proud of him. Or at least proud of his association with Henry Temple. But he could be proud of that aspect yet ashamed of the reputation which followed.'

'Have you considered psychiatry?'

'As a career or to become a patient?' Olive finally smiled. 'I wonder if we can find out a bit more about the Hammonds.'

It might be a distraction for Olive but it was one Harriet was happy to encourage. Whether they ever returned to the diary was a discussion for another time but at least Olive was still keen to uncover the history of the town. Harriet headed for the kitchen to make tea and find some dessert because there was nothing like something sweet to comfort hurt hearts and celebrate small steps forward. Olive wasn't far behind and after washing her face and collecting the little book Elizabeth had loaned them, she joined Harriet at the table.

'I thought we'd eaten all of these!'

'There were two tucked at the back of the freezer and although I imagine Brock would shudder to see me defrosting them in the microwave, I don't care.' Harriet grinned as she poured fresh cream into two bowls, each containing one of the lemon tarts from the grand opening. 'They are hot.'

'And they smell so good.'

When they both had eaten and sipped some tea, Olive opened the book. 'As I mentioned, this was published fifty years ago by Walter Bell, who it seems was involved with the local historical society. I don't think that exists now because I was searching for something the other day and although the society name came up there was no website.'

It was a slim paperback more in the style of a leather-bound notebook. Olive glanced at the table of contents.

'We can go by decade. That might take a while.'

'Go to the back, honey. There may be an index.'

'Oh, there is! Good work, Mum. Anyone would think you'd been a librarian.'

Harriet drank the rest of her tea as Olive ran her finger down one page and the next. What Olive had said about feeling too much was true. She'd always been attuned to other people's moods and body language and sometimes would be overwhelmed... as with the diary. It made her into a beautiful, caring human but also one at great risk of being hurt.

'Well this is helpful. There is a whole section on the founding families and their subsequent contribution to Rivers End and the Hammonds are included.'

After turning to the relevant page, Olive began to read.

'Desmond Hammond, date of birth and death, parents' names and so on. In the employ of Henry Temple until 1853 which was when Palmerston House changed ownership to Eoin Ryan. Temple died in that year as well.' Olive glanced up. 'You don't mind me paraphrasing?'

'Go ahead. We can revisit anything of real interest.'

'Okay. In 1857 Desmond was arrested for theft. Items were recovered including several valuable pieces originally belonging to Henry Temple. He claimed and produced evidence that these had been given to him by Temple. The charges were dropped.'

'Just as well or he'd have been in terrible trouble back then.'

'His son Raymond appears to have been free of scandal. But Raymond's son Ralph, grandson Bert, and great-grandson – who is not named – both faced court on several occasions and did jail time. All for theft, including receiving stolen goods.'

'Quite a family history! Is there a year of the most recent conviction or arrest?'

'Um... there is: 1968 for the unnamed Hammond. This was published a few years afterwards, so that is the extent of the information. So Mick was born into a family of thieves and has gone in the opposite direction by becoming a police officer,' Olive said. 'I wonder if that caused a rift with his family?'

'I imagine it would. Circling back to the unnamed Hammond, is there anything else mentioned about him?'

Olive's eyes flicked over the page. 'The arrest in 1968 was for assault. He was twenty-five years old. What are you thinking?'

'The timing is close to that of the diary. This man would have been around seventeen in 1961. I don't know, Olive, but after Mick mentioned stolen books to me I've had in the back of my mind that he knew something about them. There's no way he'd know we have the bible and poetry book, not unless Annette or Brock told him, so seeing all the books might just have sparked off some memory of his family history.'

Olive closed the book and leaned forward, her eyes bright. 'Or Mick might be related to the boy in the diary. And maybe that boy was responsible for the compass and fob watch appearing in the fabric shop. So how do we find out his name and whether he's still alive?'

Kasey dropped in at lunchtime the next day to see if Olive was free for lunch. Harriet shooed them out with instructions to take as long as they wanted.

Although Olive had felt more settled last night after their

investigation into the Hammond family – which they'd eventually run into a dead end with – she'd been quiet all morning, only showing glimpses of her normal bubbly side when customers came in.

Harriet began work on a new window display featuring books connected to the region. Surf Coast, Shipwreck Coast, Great Ocean Road – all had a wonderful selection of non-fiction and fiction titles and she had a dual purpose to showcase them. The first was purely to highlight how many books were available which had local flavour. The second was the hope of beginning some conversations about the area.

She loved making displays. So did Olive, but for once, Harriet really wanted to do this one. She had something in mind. The window she chose was the one closest to the door and she moved a long, low table to the front, then added a second one which was higher and not as wide, behind it to make a second level. The lower table had more depth and that was perfect. After covering it with a dark blue tablecloth, Harriet opened a beautiful picture book to a two-page painting of a shipwreck and laid it in the middle.

Around it she placed a selection of items she'd collected over the years as well as a few she'd recently purchased online.

There was a mini anchor. A ship in a bottle, which she'd given Jason for a birthday and he'd decided wasn't one of the things he wanted to take when he left. A small painting of a tall ship foundering on rocks. An old-style telescope on a stand. And a compass.

Is it too obvious?

She ducked outside to take a look.

It was missing something.

Back inside she collected a couple of the oldest books in the second-hand section and added those. Still not enough. She'd need Olive's opinion – and help.

Turning her attention to the second table she placed the

remaining books at angles in a row. That caught the eye and all she needed was to complete the lower table and then wait. Hopefully.

On their way back in, Olive and Kasey stopped to look at the new display. Harriet had just finished with some customers and wandered outside.

'Very nice, Mum. Needs a bit more, though.'

'I like it,' Kasey added.

'What in particular?' Harriet asked.

'The telescope and compass and the old books. It reminds me of tall ships and treasure.'

That's what it needs. A map.

'Are you coming over for dinner on the weekend, Kasey?'

'I can't, Mrs Main. It's on Sunday, isn't it?'

Harriet nodded.

'I'll be in Warrnambool with Nan. We try to go there for a girls' weekend with dinner and a movie when I visit. We'll be back Monday.'

'Oh that sounds nice. I'm sure Annette loves doing that. Are you staying over as well?'

'Yes, we go to the same little cottage every time. It overlooks the sea and Nan enjoys sitting in the garden and watching the waves. Not quite in the town but close enough.'

Some customers went through the door with a smile at Harriet and she left the young women to finish their conversation. Olive had been lucky to find such a good friend. So was Kasey. Some friendships really did last a lifetime and hopefully theirs would be one of them.

Olive rearranged some of the display to make space for a map. Not just any map, but one she'd found in one of the picture books of the area. She'd made a photocopy then scanned that to her computer where she'd adjusted the saturation of the colour, giving it a sepia look. The next step was to print it in four sections then connect them as seamlessly as possible to make it bigger. After adding some 'X' markings to a random selection of landmarks, Olive carefully burned a few edges over the kitchen sink.

'I remember you making something similar in primary school for a project. But this is outstanding.'

Harriet helped Olive place the map and then they used the compass, base of the telescope, and a couple of handfuls of gold coins to weigh down the corners. In front of the drop of the tablecloth was a sign.

Find your treasure in local books

'Do you think that's okay or should it read, *No time for a treasure hunt? Read a book instead?*'

'Leave it for now. It can be changed every day if you want.' Olive stretched. 'Today I'm going for a run because I've missed a few.'

'I might come and have a swim if you're going to the beach.'

'I'm thinking of learning to surf. Kasey loves it and she's good, too. She says the only thing missing from Rivers End is a surf shop. But there's a few people who do private lessons.'

Harriet returned to the counter. 'You should learn. And we can go to wherever there is a surf shop. I imagine Green Bay. Warrnambool for sure. But I can think of a few things which would make the town perfect.'

'A library?' Olive grinned as she began to tidy the top of the counter, straightening brochures and bookmarks and tending to a vase of flowers. 'A dog shop. Oh, I know. A heated indoor pool for winter swimming.'

'How about a garden centre?'

'Okay. You definitely win.'

During the afternoon the window was the centre of attention for people passing by and a few came in to browse. A couple of the locally written books sold and Harriet was pleased that part of her plan was working.

Marge, who was walking with James Regal, stopped for a look.

She peered close to the glass for a while and then scooped her little dog under an arm and marched into the bookstore and straight to the counter.

'Hello, Marge.' Harriet was already halfway around the counter to greet her. 'And James Regal, welcome.'

'Why do you have a treasure map in the window?'

'To fit in with the theme of the Shipwreck Coast.'

'What about the compass? Why is that there?'

Harriet and Olive exchanged a quick glance.

'Same reason. Just to attract attention.'

Marge's chin lifted. 'Well it certainly does do that. But treasure maps are better suited to pirates and it isn't a game for the inexperienced or young.'

With that peculiar statement, Marge marched back outside and crossed the road without even looking, resulting in a car screeching to a stop and a horn blast. She didn't seem to notice and in a minute was out of sight.

'Mum?'

'Quite a reaction. I wonder...'

'Whether she is the narrator?'

'I'd been thinking it must be Annette because of her leg injury but for all we know, it might have been Marge. I don't recall Annette ever saying it was her knee...'

Perhaps they had this completely wrong.

THIRTY-ONE

'You look gorgeous, Mum. Stop fussing.'

'I'm not sure about my hair.'

'If you keep screwing your face up like that you'll create lines in your makeup. Not to mention adding lines to your face. Your hair is lovely. Just don't go outside into the humidity because it will make it frizzy. I wish this next storm would hurry up and clear the air! All we've had lately is one after another.'

Harriet had been fine until she'd slipped into a yellow maxi dress. She'd never worn yellow but the colour suited her skin and it was a bit daring and different. The top had thin straps, the waist accentuated her figure, and the skirt swirled around her ankles when she walked. It felt wonderful.

Olive had done her makeup again and insisted on putting Harriet's hair into a fancy knot on the top of her head, with strands softening the look around her face.

'I don't remember ever being so nervous about having a friend visit for dinner.' Harriet's half laugh was unconvincing to herself. There was no 'friend' about Brock. Not *just* a friend, anyway.

'Are you sure you want me here? I can find somewhere to go for a few hours. Or the whole night.'

Harriet swung away from the mirror about to tell Olive she had completely the wrong idea, then she recognised the mischief on her face.

'Okay.'

With suddenly wide eyes, Olive didn't have a response for once.

'What if I give you some money and you go and play some arcade games? There's bound to be somewhere in town you can hang out.'

Olive burst into laughter.

There was no more time to check her appearance. Brock would arrive soon and there was still a lot to do. Harriet did a final twirl and then headed for the kitchen with Olive right behind.

'Put me to work, Mum. I'm not just here to look great and be a chaperone.'

Rather than letting Olive bait her any further, Harriet grabbed a notepad. 'Here's what needs doing and we can split the tasks.' She scribbled a list. 'I'll cook once Brock arrives. What do you want to do?'

'Where's that money, Mum? For the arcade games?'

'Very funny, young lady. Can you check the table, please. And light the candles. Oh, and make sure the flowers are floating in their bowl, not sinking.'

Harriet opened the fridge door. She'd prepped as much as she could and was happy with the whiting which was ready to be dipped into batter. Thick chips had been parboiled and would go into the deep fryer to finish off. Coleslaw just needed its creamy dressing, which was made and ready to mix in. And three glasses were chilling the chocolate mousse made earlier today.

'Beautiful.' She closed the door, ready to find her apron.

'Very beautiful.'

Harriet jumped.

Brock stood in the doorway, holding flowers. 'I didn't mean to startle you, Harriet.'

'Goodness, I didn't hear the door. Please come in.'

'Olive saw me walking by the window and had the front door open. These are for you.'

Brock held out the flowers and when Harriet accepted them, he leaned down and touched his lips to her cheek.

'They are gorgeous. I love peonies but thought their season was over.' Harriet drew in their sweet scent. 'Would you hold them while I get a vase?'

'At home we have two large greenhouses, one for vegetables and the other for flowers. Well, it was for flowers for a long time but once Mum decided to move, she gave away what wouldn't plant well in the garden and now there are only peonies and orchids still growing.'

Harriet chose a vase she'd only ever used once. It was a glazed ceramic one in the shape of a pitcher in a cheerful yellow colour. She'd bought it on a whim years ago and Jason hated it.

Makes it even more perfect.

After filling it with water she retrieved the flowers from Brock and loosely arranged them.

'These can go here for now.' She placed the vase in the middle of the table. 'So pretty.'

'I love the pitcher. And I love it being the colour of your dress.'

She glanced down. 'So it is.'

'Is it safe for me to come in?' Olive called.

Brock stepped close to Harriet and whispered, 'Should we shock her?'

As tempting as that was, Harriet had no intention of beginning dinner with a kiss. Not the kind she wanted. There'd be no way she could concentrate on handling hot oil.

All she could manage was a quick smile and his own broadened.

'Fine, don't answer. I'll come in anyway.'

'You're already in here, honey. Brock, what would you like to drink? We have white and red wine, beer, spirits, sparkling water, and some of the apple cider you introduced me to.' Harriet put an apron on to protect her dress.

'Happy to have a white wine. I'm staying at Palmerston House tonight, thanks to a very early meeting tomorrow, so I'll walk back.'

'I'll do the drinks.' Olive collected three wine glasses. 'Brock, would you prefer to sit here or go to the living room?'

Brock pulled out a chair and sat. 'I like kitchens.'

While Harriet cooked they talked about the week just gone. Brock had been in Sydney having meetings with the owners and board behind the new assisted living communities.

'Rivers End is due for completion in spring and the first residents will move in about one month later. Before that, the final fit-out will happen and staff will undergo training. Three more will open by summer, so our community will host new staff being trained for the others. I continue to be impressed by the ethics and passion of the owners.'

'Will Annette be one of the first to move in?' Harriet asked, testing the heat of the oil.

'She will, along with Bess and Marge. And as much as I know she loves living at Bess's house, I feel Mum will do well with access to more facilities. Kasey told me Mum's feeling a bit of pain at the moment.'

'Her leg?' Olive asked.

He nodded. 'She's looking forward to using the heated pool and having a bit more physical therapy than at present.'

Olive was persistent. 'Did she hurt herself a long time ago?'

'Many decades past.'

Harriet glanced at Olive.

'Did she fall? Or have an accident?'

Brock regarded Olive with some humour. 'Why is my mother's knee so interesting?'

'Knee? So it *was* her knee.'

'Olive, do you mind dressing the coleslaw?'

Of all times to be having this conversation! Harriet's hands were more than full between finishing the batter process and watching the oil. Annoying Brock with personal questions about his mother was a terrible idea.

'Sure thing.' Once Olive got to the fridge she gave Harriet a frustrated glance but she got the two bowls out without an argument.

'Any other help required?'

'Not a thing, Brock. You are the guest.' Olive spoke with authority. 'Mum, where's the tartare sauce?'

Whoops.

Over fish and chips, coleslaw, and a tartare sauce Brock insisting on whipping up using mayonnaise, lemon, and finely diced gherkins, conversation flowed. Olive chatted about some of the interests she shared with Kasey and then Brock spoke about his meeting in the morning. It was at the construction site and involved final kitchen designs for both the main building and the dozen or so individual cottages also being built.

'Dan Harrington is a talented builder. Have you met him?'

'I've seen the name on a vehicle and it's plastered across the assisted living site, but I don't think we've come across him yet,' Harriet said.

'He's one of the people at the meeting in the morning, which is before the work begins for the day.'

Olive helped herself to more coleslaw. 'I told Mum the other day I'd love to create and run interactive games for older people. It would be interesting working with people who have a lot of life experience and could draw on their knowledge to compete.'

Brock looked impressed. 'It *would* be interesting. What do you have in mind?'

'Could be anything as long as it means people working toward a goal. Some might be individual games, or else teams. I thought the murder-mystery types... whodunits with lots of clues. Not a board game but one where the players might need to find places or items.'

'Like a treasure hunt?'

Olive's eyes shot to Harriet's.

'Fascinating response. Care to fill me in?' Brock dipped his last chip into tartare sauce.

'About my ideas for games?'

'Nope. About that sudden look you two shared. I'm good with secrets.'

But what if, like Jason, you think what we're doing is wrong?

Harriet couldn't bear for Brock to think badly of her and Olive. Yet somehow, deep inside, she felt he wouldn't. Not for something like this. And being open with him meant a great deal. As his warm gaze held hers, she knew she wanted more than what she'd had with Jason so the only way forward was with honesty.

'The day we first met you, Olive and I were on a book-buying spree. Our last stop resulted in a box of mixed books but the owner wasn't home and left them outside with a note to either take the lot, or none. It wasn't until we unpacked the box to itemise it that we found an old diary. I phoned the seller but she told me it no longer belonged to anyone and we were welcome to either throw it away or read it. She wiped her hands of it.'

'I thought we should see if there was a name inside,' Olive said. 'There wasn't, but a map fell out.'

Brock leaned forward, curiosity in his eyes. 'A map?'

'Of Rivers End. Part of it is missing but when we started reading the diary we realised it had been drawn by the person who wrote the entries.'

Through the window behind Brock, which looked out to the street, a car crawled by. It was almost dark outside and the light tapping of rain on the roof had just begun. When the car continued on, Harriet put it down to the driver looking for a house number.

'Mum, what if we show Brock the whiteboard?'

They'd moved it onto the back verandah earlier to make space in the dining room. Harriet racked her brain, trying to visualise what was on there. Had she written anything about suspecting Annette and Bess might have been involved?

'I do love a whiteboard.' Brock stood and began to collect the plates.

'Okay, if you two don't mind clearing the table I'll go and get it.'

'Don't you need a hand, Mum?'

Harriet was already in the hallway. 'I'll be fine.'

It only took a minute to check the notes on the whiteboard. There was nothing to identify anyone but she thought twice about where she'd written about researching the bible and poetry book and quickly rubbed that out.

Brock and Olive were busy washing up when she wheeled it in. Her glass of wine was full again and she took a sip, watching them work. The banter between them made her smile, with an exchange of comments about Brock having to wash dishes to pay for his meal.

'Shall I get dessert ready?'

'More washing up?' Brock grinned at her. For some reason he was wearing her apron and it didn't completely fit him which made it every bit as silly as the fact it was purple with white teapots all over.

She shook her head at him and transferred the glasses of

mousse from the fridge to the table. 'I am fussy how about how these are washed, so you'll need to do your best.'

Brock blew a handful of bubbles in her direction and she squealed and moved out of range. Olive had a fit of giggles and began blowing bubbles at Brock.

Right in the middle of this there was a knock on the front door.

'I'll go. You two can clean the wet floor.'

Harriet was smiling when she opened the door.

The man in front of her wasn't smiling. He held a bouquet of flowers and there was a duffel bag at his feet.

Her stomach dropped.

'Hello, Harry. No kiss for your husband?'

THIRTY-TWO

30 January 1961

With everything in my heart I wish there was a way to undo this. I have prayed and begged God to make this right. If one of us had to be taken that day then it should have been me. I wish it had been me.

I've only been out of hospital for a day. I'm not allowed to walk yet and have the use of a wheelchair for a while, until I start physical therapy. It makes everything hard. Dad has to carry me in and out of the car and Mum has to help me dress and wash. I hate every minute of being unable to walk and do for myself.

But I'm the lucky one.

Everyone keeps telling me so. Doctors and nurses and my family. The neighbours as well who have come to bring me sweet things they've baked because nobody knows how to talk to me properly.

There's nothing to say.

Violet's body was found at the bottom of the sheer drop. The one near the tree which saved my life. It was instant. They tell me that anyway. She was out there alone for almost two days until a searcher found the compass and then Violet. When we had begun to look for her, she would already have fallen.

And it wasn't our fault. Mum and Dad tell me so over and over. Nobody is to blame for this tragedy.

Except I know different. The signs were there but we weren't looking. We made mistakes from almost the beginning by not having planned properly. Ruby forced Bess into being in the graveyard and that moment changed things. Bess was afraid and upset and Violet noticed and it stopped us all from working together as well as usual. And then Ruby and I argued before I learned the truth about the boyfriend.

I think Violet wanted to be alone with her compass to have a break from us.

Nobody has been to see me. My friends, I mean. I guess I understand that Ruby is grieving even more than me but Bess hasn't come. She knows I'm home. Mum let everyone know. Bess will have blamed herself. I know her. She is sensitive and caring and was the last person to see Violet. Ruby had asked her to watch Violet. Take care of her.

If only Ruby hadn't let the others go on ahead.

If only Ruby hadn't been involved with a cruel boy and needed to talk to me right then.

Violet would still be alive.

I was still in hospital when the funeral happened.

Mum and Dad attended. They said it was sad but beautiful words were spoken by many people.

She's buried in the church graveyard and today I am allowed to visit.

I can manage the wheelchair okay and although Mum pushes me as far as the car park, she lets me go the rest of the way alone like I want. I look back and she's standing watching me and I think there are tears on her face. I don't want to see anyone crying because it only makes me feel colder inside. Since after that night when I heard the nurses talk I haven't shed even a single tear.

Inside I feel nothing.

On my lap I have a posy of purple daisies. I push the wheels around and around, bumping over the grass until I can see Violet's grave in the spot Mum told me to look.

I stop.

There's no headstone and the ground is dirt instead of grass. It is a bare and barren place with nothing of Violet.

I've never been to a funeral and I've never noticed anything but grass on graves but of course there has to be a hole dug first. Something hurts in my heart. I push forward until I'm there. So many flowers are gathered in the middle. Big wreaths and small bunches and everything in between. And underneath them all is Violet.

Being careful not to fall out I lean down enough to place the posy on a spot of bare dirt.

'Those were her favourites.'

Bess is here. She holds more flowers and something else. An envelope.

'Everyone brings her roses and lilies and stuff but you know she loved purple daisies,' Bess says. 'I'm so sorry you're hurt, Nettie. I wasn't allowed to come to the hospital or I would have.'

'Why not? I needed to see you so much.'

'My parents. They think you and Ruby... that you left me to look after Violet and it was dangerous what we did with the treasure hunt. I'm so sorry.' The last bit she whispered.

We did leave Bess to manage. It wasn't on purpose. We didn't know what would happen.

'I understand.'

After putting her flowers on the grave Bess walks around to

me and kneels beside the wheelchair. 'Did I do okay? Getting help for you?'

A sudden rush of tears want to spill over and the pain is coming again. Not in my leg. But my heart and soul have a hole which is getting bigger.

'You saved my life, Bess.'

'But I let Violet die.'

'No. No, you didn't.' I grasp her hand. 'Ruby made some dreadful mistakes with that boy and she was all mixed up and upset and needed to tell me stuff. That held us up. You did good, Bess.'

She is trying to believe me. I can see it in her eyes. Bess offers me the envelope.

'What is it?'

'The photos, Nettie. Every photo except one. Ruby put the one from the cave in her pocket.'

There are goosebumps all over my arms.

'These belong to her parents. To Ruby.'

Bess shakes her head. 'Ruby won't talk to me. I think if you look after them, then in time she might forgive us and then you give them to her. You took almost all of them.' She gets to her feet. 'I have to go. I love you, Nettie. You are my best and dearest friend in the world and the only friend now.'

She runs away. I watch her race between headstones until she is out of sight.

I open the envelope. There are ten photographs.

I lift my head and scream at God. I shout that he is evil and that I hate him and will never forgive him. And when I can't scream another word I put the photos back in the envelope and into my pocket.

30 March 1961. I have to go and see Ruby. I have to give her the photos now before it is too late and she makes the worst mistake of her life.

THIRTY-THREE

NOW

Harriet knew she had to move. Or speak. Or something.

Jason was on her doorstep.

He lifted the flowers a bit. 'I came prepared.'

'I'm not. How... actually, why are you here, Jason?' The last time they'd spoken was over a week ago and he'd been angry and then remorseful for being angry. 'And why do you have flowers? Are they for Olive?'

'No, silly. They're for you.'

Without asking if he could, Jason stepped forward and tried to plant a kiss on Harriet's lips. Her hand instinctively shot out onto his chest and stopped him.

'Sorry. Sorry, I've been looking forward to seeing you so much and you must be a bit surprised.'

'Surprised? I thought you were on another continent.' She dropped her hand.

'Mum? Who's at the door?'

Harriet moved to one side as Olive's head appeared around the kitchen door.

Her mouth dropped open and then she flew up the hallway with a squeal. 'Daddy!' And then she was in his arms, crushing the flowers against him. He grinned over her head at Harriet.

She turned and walked back to the kitchen.

Brock was leaning back against one of the counters, ankles crossed, holding his glass of wine, and still wearing the apron. He looked completely at home and relaxed but he raised his eyebrows. 'Daddy?'

'My ex has decided to visit without warning. At this time of night. I'm sorry.'

He smiled and held out a hand and when Harriet took it, he drew her close so that when he spoke, only she would hear. 'Sorry is not your word to say on this occasion. Tell me if you need me to leave, otherwise I'll hang around. For dessert, of course.'

'Of course.' That made her smile and dampened a ridiculous feeling of needing to protect... who, exactly? Brock was an adult. Olive was delighted.

Me. I need to protect me.

Harriet released Brock's hand. 'I'll keep working on dessert.'

'Have some more wine.'

'Excellent idea.' Harriet collected the glass, sipping rather a large mouthful on her way to the fridge. From there she extracted a bowl of fresh cherries she'd pitted earlier. Deciding that carrying the wine was slowing her down, she put it onto the counter near Brock.

'And the kitchen is just through here.'

Olive appeared first and rolled her eyes at Harriet and Brock.

Jason was close behind and he stopped and dropped his duffel bag onto the floor. He glanced at the kitchen, at Harriet, and then stared at Brock. Brock stared back. The silence dragged and then Jason extended his hand and walked around the table.

'Jason Main.'

'Brock Salisbury.'

'Nice apron.'

'Nice flowers.'

Jason still held the bouquet but it was a bit worse for wear. He handed it to Olive and the men shook hands.

Olive glanced at Harriet with a slightly worried expression then slipped the flowers into the sink. 'Sit down, Dad. Would you like a drink?'

He pulled out a chair and sat at the table. 'Yes, thanks.'

'Water, apple cider, beer, wine, orange juice. Actually, not the beer or wine if you're driving tonight.'

Jason made a small snorting noise. 'A beer or two wouldn't hurt even if I was driving tonight.'

Harriet's head shot up. 'What do you mean?'

'I haven't booked anywhere to stay, Harry.'

'And there's no room here, Jason. You'll need to find a place.'

Of all the nerve to turn up unannounced in the middle of the evening and expect to stay.

'We can discuss it later.'

'If you mean once Brock leaves, I think you are assuming a lot.' Harriet kept her voice steady. 'As I said, there's no room here for a guest I'm afraid.'

Olive plonked a beer in front of her father and reached for her phone. 'I'll see where we can get you a room for tonight.' She began to search. 'The inn doesn't take guests after nine and it is past that now. Brock, do you think Mrs White has space?'

'I took the last room.'

'Oh, so you're not staying?' Jason opened the beer and raised it in Brock's direction. 'Cheers, mate.'

As much as Harriet wanted to have it out with Jason right there and then, one look at Olive's face kept her quiet. All Olive had longed for was to know her father was safe and even though she would feel the tension in the room, she kept stealing glances at Jason as if not quite believing he was real.

Brock finally straightened and brought Harriet's wine glass to her. 'Sit for a while. Let me convert these into dessert for four people.'

Her mouth opened to say no, that she wasn't in the mood to share food with her ex. But there was such warmth and caring in Brock's eyes that she found herself doing precisely what he said.

While Harriet had been answering the door, Olive had wheeled the whiteboard into the kitchen and pushed it against a wall. With dessert finished – and barely noticeable that it was stretched thanks to Brock's clever replating and addition of more cherries – Jason suddenly noticed the whiteboard.

'You're not still doing this?' He frowned at Harriet. 'Pretty intrusive to someone's privacy.'

'Dad, the diary has no names in it. Well, it has one. But only referring to someone else, not the person who owned it. You can see all the initials up there which is how the narrator referred to her friends.'

'Her? So you know that much.' He shook his head and got to his feet. 'Which way to the bathroom?'

Olive jumped up and showed him. When she returned, she flopped onto her seat. 'Oh boy.'

Under the table, Brock squeezed Harriet's hand. 'I have many questions about this diary. You mentioned a map earlier.'

'Yes.' Olive brightened. 'Drawn by hand by the narrator. She was really talented even though only fourteen. It appears to have been a draft and she intended to create a second one as part of the treasure hunt prize.'

'And what was the purpose of the treasure hunt? Do you know?'

'We do.' Olive got up and poured herself a glass of water.

Harriet took over, well aware of Olive's feelings about Violet.

'It was a birthday gift for another girl, a younger sister of one of the friends, who loved shipwrecks and pirates. We've been reading one entry at a time and following along with their adventure. We don't know who the narrator is, nor the other girls. Well, apart from one who was named. But we've learned a lot about Rivers End and being so new here, getting the chance to explore was wonderful.'

Jason had returned to his chair while Harriet was talking. He had a glass of something with him.

'Is that my whisky?'

'Our whisky. The bottle I was given when I left the firm. Seeing as you hadn't opened it I thought I might.' He'd been generous with the amount in the glass and tapped the side with a finger. 'The glasses were also a gift to me.'

Then why didn't you take them when you left us?

It wasn't worth debating.

'Olive and I turned this into our own treasure hunt... at least in the respect of following the clues.'

'I still think this is wrong, Harry.'

'So, Harriet, where did the clues lead?' Brock's expression hadn't changed but he emphasised her name ever so slightly.

She'd always hated Jason's shortening of her name but like so much in their marriage had given up trying to change the things which didn't work. That was her fault. She'd been compliant and complacent in order to make for a peaceful home and for the first time since the divorce, Harriet understood this completely. And she no longer had to be the nice and endlessly polite one.

'They began at the home of the birthday girl. Her sister was one of the teens involved and we have no idea where they lived. Instead, we began at the next clue which was the supermarket.'

Olive nodded. 'Back then it was called a grocery store and was smaller, but we worked that one out and moved to the next, which was inside the cave on the beach. Do you know the one, Brock?'

'I do. What was next?'

His genuine interest and encouragement of Olive touched Harriet. Her instincts were right to trust him with this.

'The old railway station. Actually, not the station but a place they called the "field's gate".'

'I've heard the term. Is it at the end of the shunting area?'

'It is, and from there we went to Temple Bridge. I don't think the narrator liked that clue because it was meant to be put under the bridge where it is very enclosed and she had the job of doing so. It made her feel dizzy and unwell.'

'My mother has that response in small spaces,' Brock said.

Interesting.

'You both actually followed clues from an anonymous diary around the whole town?' Jason asked. 'Clever. Good way to get to know the place.'

For the first time tonight, Jason sounded like the man Harriet had married. The edge had left his tone and his face showed some interest instead of suspicion. Probably the whisky was dropping his barriers a bit.

'It was a lot of walking,' Olive said. 'After the bridge was the church. The old one up past the BAMs' place.'

She covered her mouth with a hand as all eyes turned to her.

'Sweet child of mine.' Harriet smiled at Olive. 'Up past where your mother is living, Brock.'

He chuckled. 'It isn't the first time I've heard that. And my mother thinks it funny.'

'What does BAM mean?' Jason looked from one to another. 'This is one of your memory shortcuts, Olive?'

'Okay, okay, I'll stop doing it. So, we went to the graveyard which was incredibly interesting with some very old graves. The clue was clever saying to tread lightly and we are pretty sure it referred to the grave of someone named T. Lightly.'

'And the next clue?'

'Actually, Dad, why don't we go and talk in the living room because I want to hear all about your travels and tell you about my new friends and stuff.' Olive gave Jason no time to refuse, picking up his glass as she got to her feet and disappearing through the door.

Jason didn't look like a man who wanted to move.

'Come on, Dad.'

'She's missed you, Jason. And she has your drink.'

And Olive would not want to talk further about the diary. Not until they knew what happened after N overheard the nurses talking.

Jason got to his feet with a grunt. On his way out he scooped up his duffel bag.

Harriet dropped her head into her arms. How had this happened the first time Brock came to visit? His chair moved and then his hands rubbed her shoulders and she realised he was behind her, gently massaging the stress away.

'That feels good.'

He continued for a moment or two and then his lips touched her neck. He worked his way to her ear leaving a trail of butterfly kisses which tingled her skin and shot fire into her veins.

'I might say goodnight,' he said.

'No.'

'No?' There was a smile in his voice.

She sighed and slowly straightened. 'You have an early start.'

'And you have an unexpected house guest.'

Harriet stood and leaned against Brock, whose arms came

around her. She listened to his heartbeat and felt his warmth and strength and it was enough for now.

Olive had collected an armful of blankets and a pillow and left them on the sofa. She'd said goodnight to Jason and while he was setting up the makeshift bed, hugged Harriet in the kitchen.

'Dad asked me if you and Brock are serious.' She kept her voice low. 'I said that isn't my business.'

'Good answer, honey. Sleep well.'

'You too. Don't stay up too late.'

All Harriet wanted was to crawl into bed and think but she went to the living room where Jason was unpacking clothes from his duffel bag.

'How long are you staying, Jason?'

'You want an honest answer?' He perched on the arm of the sofa. 'I might stay for good.'

Harriet sank onto a chair. That wasn't what she expected.

'Hear me out, Harry. I was hasty going off alone like that. Being so ill messed up my perspective and my judgement and I'm sorry I bailed on you and Olive but that's in the past. I can set up an accounting practice here and we'll buy a decent house and get you that vegetable garden you want and Olive can have a dog. No cats though.'

He was serious. His expression was earnest, his body language open and his voice almost excited.

'If you don't want to keep working we'll hire someone to run the shop and you can live a good life again.'

'I'm sorry? A good life *again*? I am living a good life now, Jason.'

'How? Working non-stop? And this place is tiny. We can find somewhere with a pool and big grounds and go travelling. Together though. Wherever you want to go.'

Deciding the whisky was talking, Harriet got to her feet.

'Tomorrow I'll find you a motel room. Live in Rivers End if you wish and I know Olive would be thrilled if you were closer but don't imagine for one minute that we are getting back together.'

He smiled. 'Of course we are. But sure, I'll get accommodation and give you a bit of space. Sleep on it. Think about how good our lives used to be. I still love you.'

There wasn't any answer Harriet could come up with which wouldn't result in an argument. She turned off the light on her way out.

THIRTY-FOUR

The promised storm had failed to appear and the light rain overnight had stopped, leaving the air muggy and ominous clouds looming. But Harriet let herself out of the cottage before the others woke, longing to walk along the beach before the weather finally became stormy again. She needed to plan her approach to the problem at hand. The biggest problem, anyway.

Jason had been snoring in the living room when she left. How he slept on a sofa which was too short for his height was beyond her, but then again, any discomfort was entirely of his own making.

He wasn't going to stay another night under any circumstances. If there was no accommodation to be had in Rivers End then there were other towns within an easy drive. The further away the better. His belief that he could front up here and move in with her and Olive, effectively picking up where they'd left off, was ludicrous.

She walked along the jetty to the end. The sploshing of the water beneath the old timber boards was oddly soothing and a hopeful, early-rising seagull joined her.

'What would you do, birdie? I'm done with trying to look after everyone's feelings but my own.'

A hot breeze blew her hair over her eyes and she brushed it back and then her fingers touched the side of her neck where Brock had kissed it. Last night he'd been an anchor in a storm-of-sorts. His quiet support hadn't wavered even when Jason had been out of line.

I want to be with you, Brock.

How strange it was to be standing here, at the end of the jetty over the Southern Ocean, with a life which only a year ago she would never have dreamed of. A beautiful bookstore which she and Olive created themselves through sheer hard work and commitment. A closeness they'd never enjoyed so much. A whole town filled with people who welcomed them as friends. And a man with laughter in his eyes and kindness in his heart.

Had Jason not divorced her, she'd have missed this completely.

Not so long ago she would have taken him back in a heartbeat. She'd been frightened to lose him. Terrified to start over at almost fifty years of age. Except being thrown in the deep end showed her how strong and resilient she really was.

'Mum!'

Harriet swung around. Olive jogged along the jetty, her face glistening with perspiration and her chest heaving.

'Good morning. I didn't notice you on the beach.'

Olive came to a stop and took a few deep breaths, then opened the water bottle she always carried and swigged a mouthful. The seagull ventured closer, beak open, but when no food appeared it flew away.

'Ran... up the hill... and down the stone steps for a change.'

'Goodness, that's a lot in this heat. Was your father awake when you left?'

Another swig and Olive was almost back to normal.

'I woke him up and told him to help himself to coffee. I said we would help him find a motel or something.'

'Are you okay with that, honey? I might start walking back if you want to walk with me.'

They left the jetty and headed toward the lagoon.

'The thing is that Dad can't stay with us and not just because there isn't a spare room.' Olive glanced at Harriet. 'The way he just arrived was weird. As if our lives were fine to put on hold for his plans. He can't just walk in and... and change things!'

'He went through a lot when he was ill.'

Olive stopped dead and put her hands on her hips. She looked furious.

Is it with me?

'Did I say something wrong?'

'Mum, you never say anything wrong. You keep the peace and make excuses for everyone and I want you to stop. I know you made Dad phone me that night when we were out for dinner and I was feeling a bit sad, and it was good to talk to him but I would have coped. I really would have.'

The words had poured out of Olive and her eyes had filled with tears.

'You can't fix everything and you don't need to, Mum. Dad's always been a bit selfish... okay, a lot selfish, and I think you just got used to it. So even though it is up to you about whether you go back to Dad or not, I have to tell you what I think.'

'I'm listening.'

Olive's arms dropped to her sides and Harriet took one of her hands.

'I really am listening.'

With a quick nod, Olive continued. 'I think Dad should go back to travelling. I think you and Brock should keep dating. He makes you laugh and be silly and get nervous and dress up and it suits you. The minute Dad arrived last night you stopped all of that and started trying to make everyone else feel good again. I love you but I *like* the new you much more than the old one.'

Olive threw her arms around Harriet as if she'd never let go. 'Honey?'

Releasing Harriet, Olive shook her head. 'I'm so angry with him for what he's done. So angry.' And then she took off, pounding the sand in long strides.

Outside the cottage, Harriet took a moment to compose herself. Olive's insights had both hurt and resonated and she had a lot to think about. She couldn't just walk in and tell Jason to leave. It wasn't as simple as Olive made it sound. Decades of being married had shaped Harriet.

Being divorced, being away from him had given her the chance to see him with new eyes and although a part of her would always love him, it was no longer the part which wanted to be with him.

She let herself in and left her shoes near the door, walking barefoot to the kitchen as the aroma of fresh coffee drew her in.

The fridge door was wide open. Two burners on the stove were lit. On the table was an open egg carton and scattered beside it half a dozen empty shells. The toaster popped. But Jason was nowhere to be seen. And nor was the whiteboard.

Returning the eggs to the fridge, Harriet closed the door then turned off the stove. Beside it was a bowl with cream and eggs waiting to be whisked. Three plates were piled on top of each other. A half-empty cup of coffee was still steaming.

And this is what happens when Jason decides to cook.

The back door swung open and Jason stepped inside carrying a wet dish cloth.

'Oh. You're back.' He headed for the sink and began to clean the cloth under the tap. 'Good, good. Breakfast is minutes away.'

'I saw Olive on the beach.'

'You did? She told me about her new friends. Country life suits her, don't you think?'

'She told me she woke you, suggested you have some coffee, and that we can then find you accommodation. Or you could drive back to Melbourne.'

He wasn't happy with the cloth and tossed it into the bin and then dried his hands on a tea towel. 'There's nothing for me in Melbourne these days. I've already booked a room at the inn and will stay there in the short term while I look for a house to buy and office to lease. We'll be all back together under one roof before you know it.'

Harriet only half-listened, her attention on the dish cloth in the bin. It was streaked with black. 'Did you move the whiteboard?'

He shrugged and began whisking the eggs.

'Jason? What did you do?'

Not waiting for an answer, Harriet went outside.

The whiteboard was pushed back against the wall on the verandah and it was completely empty. All the clues and notes she and Olive had written up were wiped off. Her hands clenched. He'd gone too far.

'Shall we wait for Olive to have breakfast?' Jason called.

Harriet stepped inside, closing the door quietly although she had a rare urge to slam it.

'The toast already popped, the stove was blazing, and you've whisked the eggs. All should have waited until she was back if you wanted to serve three people at the same time.'

Jason was about to light the stove again and his hand paused as he looked at Harriet with the most comical of expressions. He wasn't used to her being critical.

'Why did you clean the whiteboard?'

'Darned thing took three goes to completely get the marker off.' He stepped away from the stove and crossed his arms. 'I've told you twice it isn't a good idea to poke around in someone else's life.'

She couldn't stop the frustrated laughter which only served to intensify her irritation. 'Yet that is precisely what you are doing right now. You are poking around in my life, in Olive's, and telling us how to live. Scolding us for something which we've treated with respect. And do you want to know why we began reading this diary?' She took a quick breath. 'Because Olive needed something to keep her mind busy instead of worrying about where her globe-trotting father was. She embraced the treasure hunt, set up rules at the beginning, and we keep to them. I think it was much healthier for her than stressing over when or if she'd ever hear from you again.'

'Of course she would. I knew I was safe.'

'Well whoopty-do, Jason. As long as *you* knew that *you* were safe. Did it ever occur to you that Olive and I cannot read minds?' Harriet's hands were shaking. 'Does Olive know you cleaned off the whiteboard?'

'I'd done the first clean and she said something about a run. But why would it—'

'Jason! I just saw her on the beach and she's so angry and upset and now I know why. Do you have no idea what she's been through in the last year? None?'

'I know I failed her and you. Both of you have hammered that into me. Okay? I know the divorce unsettled her.'

Harriet gripped the back of a chair as her heart pounded in her ears. Her throat was dry and closed and she had to swallow hard to speak and when she did, her voice was unnaturally high.

'Unsettled enough for her to get into a relationship with a control freak. Unsettled? No, Jason. Devastated and shocked and disillusioned. She thought he was nice. Protective. Safe. Someone she could tell her sorrows to and she felt she had plenty. But he used them to control her. Make her believe she was at fault for you leaving.'

'Oh, Harriet...' Jason's face had paled.

'She lost trust in her judgement and he made sure she would only depend upon him and that meant making sure she missed enough classes to fail her exams. He wanted her with him and made her feel guilty if she wasn't.'

Jason sank onto a chair. All the bravado and over-confidence had gone and his eyes glistened with tears. And seeing him so suddenly vulnerable, Harriet's fury drained away.

'But you know what? Our girl is strong and failing those exams woke her up to what he was doing. That and finally talking to me, not that she said much but enough to let me be there for her.'

'And he's gone? He's out of Olive's life?'

'Long gone.'

'I had no idea.'

There was a long silence. Harriet's stomach fluttered in panic from the scene she'd caused and she searched for the right words to make things better. But what had Olive told her only a short while ago on the beach?

You can't fix everything and you don't need to, Mum.

'I need to apologise to Olive.' Jason got to his feet. 'And I need to find a spot to think for a bit. Go for a walk and then check in at the inn. Can I come back later and just... talk? To you both?'

'I'll phone you. Or Olive will. Once we've all had time to think.'

Jason nodded and walked past her, touching her shoulder briefly. In a moment, the front door opened and then closed.

THIRTY-FIVE

Harriet finished stuffing sheets into the dryer, imagining it was her ex-husband she was pummelling.

She wanted all evidence of him out of the cottage and had thrown the sheets in the washing machine first. The blankets she shoved into the bottom of a clothes hamper for another day because there was no way they'd dry today. Not according to the recent weather alert of an imminent and potentially damaging storm.

While the sheets washed she'd cleaned every surface he might have touched but when it came to throwing away the flowers he'd bought, she couldn't. They didn't deserve that. Instead, she moved the vase into the laundry.

Back in the kitchen she smelled the peonies and closed her eyes for a moment. They were welcome here, as was the man who'd gifted them. By now his meeting would be over and most likely, Brock would be heading home. Harriet glanced at the oven clock and frowned.

Where was Olive?

She probably believed Jason was still here and was too cross to deal with him.

I should have let you know he'd gone.

Harriet dialled Olive's phone, which went to voicemail. She left a message and then went out to the front gate to see if she was almost home.

The air was buzzing with electricity and above her, the sky was almost black as angry clouds sullenly sat above. There was lightning moving inside them and a chill swept through Harriet. Surely Olive wouldn't stay out in this?

Stepping back inside, Harriet picked up car keys then replaced them.

Olive wouldn't want her mother driving around town looking for her. Maybe she'd gone to meet up with Kasey because wasn't she back today with Annette? Or was that tomorrow?

Thunder boomed overhead, rattling the windows and making Harriet jump. An instant later, the rain began. Heavy, driving rain.

After dialling again, Harriet stood at the open front door. The gutters on the edge of the roof were overfilled, water cascading down in a sheet. Olive would be soaking wet when she got back unless she'd found some shelter. Or was with Kasey somewhere.

Voicemail again.

'Honey, I'm worried about you in this awful weather. Just let me know that you're okay and if you need a lift, I can come and get you.'

Heart racing, Harriet checked the app on her phone to find Olive's phone.

It popped straight up, somewhere in the area. The beach showed up and the town and there was a radius of several hundred metres.

'Not much help.'

Then it refreshed as it tried to pinpoint more accurately and the little icon, which was meant to represent Olive's phone, appeared near the graveyard at the end of the beach.

Toward the beach, the sky lit up as lightning streaked across it like an arrow and there was a crash and then a boom of thunder. It must have hit a tree or something. Harriet looked back at the phone.

The icon had disappeared.

'No you don't.'

She exited the app and went back in.

Nothing.

'Olive...'

Harriet raced around the house, throwing on shoes and a raincoat, and collecting her bag. She checked again outside the front door, after closing it behind herself and when there was no icon despite there being a signal, she rang Brock.

Thunder clapped as he answered and it was all she could do not to burst into tears.

'Good morning—'

'Olive's missing.'

'Where are you?'

'Just leaving home to look for her. The phone finder thing showed she's somewhere around the clifftop graveyard.'

'In this weather?'

'She's been out running. I didn't notice the time. I have to find her.'

'The cave is at the bottom of the cliff so she's probably taken shelter. I'll come and get you.'

'No. I'll meet you there.'

Before he could say otherwise, she hung up. He was probably right. Olive had sheltered in there before.

Harriet shoved the house key into the door and flung it open. In a minute she'd got the blankets from the hamper and although it made no sense, all she could feel was Olive calling out for her.

. . .

Driving in the storm was horrendous as the wipers worked overtime to clear the rain. Visibility was reduced to only a few metres ahead. The headlights made no difference as day became a bizarre version of twilight.

She'd driven with the expectation of parking near the shortcut to the beach through the cliffs but a glance down as she crossed Temple Bridge changed her mind. The normally lazy river was swelling fast and choppy so it might not be a safe route. Harriet followed the road up the hill and turned into the car park on the cliff.

Brock wasn't here yet and why should he be? He was probably coming from home and that alone sent another shiver through Harriet. His road was difficult under normal circumstances and today it would be treacherous.

The trees and bushes dotting the graveyard wildly thrashed in the wind. Olive wasn't up here.

Before climbing out, Harriet rang Jason. It immediately went to voicemail so either his phone was off or he'd rejected the call.

'Olive hasn't come home from her run, Jason. The last known signal from her phone was near a cave on the beach. From the car park at the top of the cliff there are some stone steps to the beach and at the bottom is a shallow cave. I think that's where she is. I'll call you when I find her.'

He could do with that information whatever he wanted.

She checked the finder app and almost dropped the phone as Olive's icon appeared again. It was only metres away.

After shoving her phone into a pocket, Harriet got out and was immediately hit with the wind and rain. The raincoat was useless, its hood detaching and flying away and the so-called waterproof material already drenched, so she dragged the whole thing off. All she wore was a T-shirt and shorts and they gave no protection from the downpour. Her hair whipped about in the wind as she ran to the top of the steps.

Only a short time ago she'd wondered what it would be like on the beach in a storm.

From up here the full extent of the weather was terrifying. The ocean churned, huge waves slamming onto the beach. The jetty was almost under water. There was no horizon as heavy low clouds, filled with rain and lightning, might have come straight from a horror movie. And Harriet, who was afraid of storms, was out in the middle of it.

Olive was all that mattered.

Harriet took her time down the steps. Every instinct was to run but the stone was slippery and she was buffeted by the gusts coming off the sea. The most ridiculous image was in her mind. The narrator of the diary standing on the cliff, seeing the beauty but filled with a sense of foreboding. Harriet cried out to send the thought away but nobody could possibly hear her over the thunder.

She slipped, only staying semi-upright after a heart-stopping slide which left her on her behind. She pushed herself up and staying close to one side of the rock, made it to the sand without another incident.

Down here was a bit more protected and she leaned against the limestone where the engraving was. T loves M.

I wonder if I can use a chisel? H loves B.

The adrenaline was making her hysterical.

She caught her breath, her hands pushing the hair from her eyes to search the beach for Olive. One fear on the way down was that her daughter had slipped as well. But she was nowhere in sight.

Lightning snaked from the sky and hit the end of the jetty with an explosion of timber. Pieces flew into the air and were lost among the waves.

Harriet inched her way along the cliff face.

The cave was close.

And she would find Olive inside. Wet, upset – probably, but safe.

She reached the entry to the cave.

It didn't make sense.

The entrance was gone.

A thousand rocks filled the place where it had been.

Harriet screamed.

Harriet dropped onto the sand and pounded it until her hands hurt. She wanted to die. Olive was inside the cave. Crushed beneath a thousand tons of limestone. But even as her brain processed the terrible information, a glimmer shone through.

What if she's alive?

As she stood she saw something close to the bottom of the rocks. Her eyes barely made sense of it. Olive's phone. Harriet snatched it up and opened the cover. It worked. And as soon as it lit up, there was a flashing message repeating over and over.

In the cave. Find me, Mum.

In the cave. Find me, Mum.

But how?

Harriet scrambled to her feet and returned to the wall of rocks. There were gaps large enough for the phone so Olive must have pushed it through one.

'Olive! Olive, can you hear me?'

If Olive answered there was no way to hear her. The storm wasn't giving up yet and between it and the ocean it was almost deafening.

'I'm here! I'm here, honey. Hang on.'

Harriet began to pull at the rocks. Small at first. Throwing them aside. But the larger ones were too heavy and looked unstable and she stopped.

'Harriet!'

Brock ran across the sand from the direction of the lagoon, flanked by another man.

'Hurry! Olive's in the cave and it's blocked.'

While Brock stopped long enough to grab Harriet's hand for a second, the other man began sizing up the rocks.

'I think more will fall, so please be careful,' Harriet called.

'That's Dan Harrington. He'll assess it and I've called for the SES to come. Are you sure she's in there?'

Harriet showed him the phone with its flashing message. 'She'd pushed it through a gap. She mustn't have had signal in there but the phone finder came on again.'

Dan was on the move, working his way around the base of the cliff and perilously close to the waves as he gazed up at the top. Then he ran to meet them. 'Looks like lightning hit the edge up there and sent rocks down so with a bit of luck the cave itself is intact. Hi, I'm Dan.'

Harriet couldn't muster a smile in return.

'Can you phone the SES and tell them exactly where we are and what has happened? Brock, we can keep moving some of the rocks.'

Retreating to the spot against the wall with the love heart, Harriet searched for the number of the local State Emergency Service and after a short delay, spoke to someone to relay the extra information. When she returned her phone to a pocket, she stayed where she was. Although she wanted to help, she stayed out of the way. Brock and Dan worked together to shift a few large rocks without causing further falls. She didn't have the physical strength to move bigger rocks.

The rain was easing but the wind still buffeted the beach in regular gusts strong enough to lift the sand.

A shout from above came from a man dressed in SES gear standing on the edge directly above the cave. He and Dan yelled back and forth and then he vanished. Harriet went to Brock.

'What was that about?'

'Barry says there's no sign of imminent collapse but to get a move on. Here's more help. Do you want to tell Olive to move right back?'

'You've spoken to her?'

'Gap on the right about half your height.'

As a stream of people, all SES, hurried down the steps, Harriet found the small gap and dropped to her knees.

'Honey? Olive, its Mum.'

'My plan worked.'

Harriet laughed, hearing Olive's voice.

'It did, you clever girl. Now you have to get as far from the entry as you can. The SES are here and it might get noisy and messy for a bit.'

'Okay. But... just tell them to hurry.'

'They are. I'll see you very soon.'

Tears began to fall as she stood and made room for the experts. She found a spot a few metres away where she wasn't in the way but could see everything, not caring that she was drenched to the skin and pushed by the wind.

Half a dozen men got to work on removing the rocks, stopping often to check they weren't creating more hazard. Apart from Brock and Dan, Harriet knew Barry by sight as he was Sylvia's husband, and another man was the surfer who owned the golden retriever she'd made friends with. And with a jolt, Harriet realised Jason was there, lugging chunks of limestone with his bare hands until someone tossed him a pair of gloves.

A young woman came to her, another member of the SES. She carried an oilskin jacket and gently placed it over Harriet's shoulders.

'Christie?'

'They'll get her out. I heard her talking to her father just then.'

'I can't thank you enough. All of you.'

Christie grinned. 'Trust me, this town knows how to help when it needs to. They saved my life once. Martin and I love being able to pay it forward.'

'Martin?'

'Over there. The most handsome of the men.'

The surfer.

Harriet's eyes drifted to Brock as he and Jason worked together to lift a particularly large piece of rock.

'It won't be long. We've got some blankets and a stretcher if she needs one. There's an ambulance on the way. Even just to check her over.' Christie put an arm around Harriet. 'You did great finding her.'

Work suddenly stopped and Dan climbed through a cleared space and disappeared.

Harriet began to run as first one, then the other of Olive's arms appeared and then Jason lifted her through. He held her like a baby and she wrapped her arms around his neck and then Harriet threw her arms around them both.

Olive was safe.

THIRTY-SIX

30 March 1961

Ruby is going to marry Donny because she is pregnant. She isn't even sixteen yet and he is horrible and I have to help her find another way. If only she will listen to me.

I watch Ruby's house for a while until her mother goes down the road. Her parents still won't let me visit and she won't leave the house unless she has to. I was going to ask Bess to come with me but I don't want her being in trouble if we get caught.

I'm walking okay enough now although I have a brace on my knee. The doctor says if I do all the physical therapy and take my time strengthening it then I should regain full use in a while. I'm not allowed to ride a horse or bicycle for ages. So I walk to Ruby's house and all the way I practise the things I need to say to her.

She mustn't marry Donny. If I'd known he was her boyfriend I would have told her parents because he and all his family are mean and awful. No wonder he wouldn't let her tell anyone they were dating. And I know she is pregnant with his baby but there has to be another way. We don't live in the fifties. Women can raise a child without a father and we will all help her. She can go back to school and Bess and I will take turns with the baby even if her mother doesn't help.

On the street outside her house I falter. The letterbox where Violet found her first clue is still there. I guess the grocery store is still in the same place and the cave and bridge and all the spots we left clues but this one was the first.

Nobody answers the door when I tap so I go around the house and Ruby is sitting on the back steps reading a book. She doesn't see me at first and I quickly check the envelope and the new version of the map on nicer paper are still inside the diary so I can show her the ideas I've written down. I care so much for Ruby and will do anything if I can be her friend again.

*　*　*

How dare Nettie come here and expect me to listen to her nonsense!

She is just a child. Fourteen. How can she know how I feel? Or what I want?

It doesn't even matter what I want. I made my bed and now I have to lie in it. Forever. My mother might have wept but my father yelled and called me names I had to look up and then I found out what a bad person I am. I hope he never finds out I took money from his wallet to buy the compass.

Donny says things will go alright as long as I am good. And I will be. My baby will never be treated badly and Nettie doesn't understand how cruel it would be to only have one parent.

I told her to go away. I don't ever want to see her or Bess again. They are as much to blame for Violet dying as I am. But then Nettie pulls out her stupid diary and an envelope with the polaroids from that dreadful day and she even made the final map. She is crying when she shows me and I stand up and try to go into the house. She follows and is on the top step and I scream for her to leave.

Her face turns a funny colour, all kind of pale, and she stops crying and puts the envelope into the diary and then she is folding the map and I grab the diary from her. She tries to get it back and there's a ripping sound and she is left holding part of the map and I have everything else. And I don't mean for this to happen but I push her and she tumbles off the top step onto her injured knee. And she is shrieking in pain and my mother arrives home and I hide the diary and the map and the photographs because Nettie wants them and I just want her to hurt as much as I do.

This diary is never seeing the light of day again. My mother hid it for me until we moved into our own cottage this week and I found a good place to keep it where Donny won't ever find it. He can't ever see what was written about him. Nettie and Bess know never to come near me again. Or near my baby. She's so beautiful and tiny and even Donny is all soft and kind to her. We named her Jannelle after his grandma. Jannelle Violet Hammond.

THIRTY-SEVEN

NOW

The whiteboard was back in the dining room and the diary was on the table.

'I still can't believe Dad thought he had the right to erase all of our work.' Olive took a marker and wrote across the top of the board DO NOT ERASE. 'But I'm proud of you, Mum. You were calm and controlled and fierce.'

'Fierce? I like that.'

And I love that you are here and uninjured and safe.

Almost a week had passed since the storm. How Olive had avoided being hit by any rocks when lightning had struck the cliff and cause the slide was a miracle. She'd been given a clean bill of health by the paramedics and then once at home had slept for hours, waking with a huge appetite and feeling a bit ashamed for worrying everyone. Jason had been hard to get back out of the house and Harriet understood. She couldn't bear having Olive out of her sight and would be eternally grateful to the SES as well as Brock.

Harriet had insisted she take time off work and over the days, her daughter had spent time with Jason and their relationship appeared to be healing. Today was sunny and perfect to be out outside but Olive wanted to return to the diary.

She took the marker from Olive and wrote *Violet*. 'Am I reading?'

Olive sat and opened the diary. 'I don't mind.' She found the new entry. *'With everything in my heart I wish there was a way to undo this. I have prayed and begged God to make this right. If one of us had to be taken that day then it should have been me. I wish it had been me.'*

'How sad. Poor little Violet gone and our narrator taking it all on her young shoulders.'

Olive gulped and nodded.

'Still okay to read?'

'I think, yes.'

It was the saddest of stories and by the time Olive stopped to drink some water, Harriet had wiped more than one tear away.

'It would have been devastating to be blamed for this tragedy when it was a day motivated by love,' Harriet said. 'The injury sounds bad. The kind which might affect someone for their entire life.'

'Do you think the narrator is Annette?'

'There are some compelling reasons why it might be.' On her feet again Harriet wrote on the whiteboard.

Annette

Teenager in 1961
Raised in Rivers End
Lifelong leg injury
Claustrophobic

Narrator

Teenager in 1961
Raised in Rivers End

Injured knee as a teenager
Claustrophobic

'I'm not sure how we would even go about asking Annette now we know about the tragedy. What I am curious about is how on earth the diary ended up with Jan Prentice? There's no "J" who is mentioned and we are pretty certain she is closer to my age than the teens would be now,' Harriet said.

'And the photo. We have one photo in the diary and at the end of the entry N said she was taking the photos to R. Last time we talked about why Mrs Prentice might have it we were going to look for an obituary for her father and see if it helps us work out if her mother was one of the girls.'

Olive turned the page and gasped.

'What's wrong?'

'Look at this. It starts with the same handwriting and then it changes and is in red. Oh, Mum. We need to read on.'

There were no words between them for a while after Olive read the entry written first by N and then finished by R. Neither of them was crying but it wouldn't take much for that to change. Harriet noticed she was gripping the top of her legs with her hands and when she released them, there were marks from her fingers.

Harriet's phone began to ring in another room.

'Want me to get it?'

'Let it go to voicemail, honey.' Harriet stood and picked up a marker. 'I don't know about you but I'm struggling to comprehend what just happened.'

'A lot. I'm shocked, Mum. Really shocked.'

'We have names now.' Harriet began to write on the whiteboard.

N is Nettie. Short for Annette
B is Bess
R is Ruby
Donny Hammond was the boyfriend
Jannelle Violet Hammond is likely to be Jan Prentice, and is
probably Mick's aunt.

'Jan Prentice got rid of her mother's diary. Except it really
belongs to Annette so why didn't she return it to her?' Olive's
eyes narrowed as she read the whiteboard. 'I wonder if there
was ever reconciliation between the friends. Violet's death was
a tragic accident but even Ruby acknowledges all three of them
were responsible for the events of the day and her part made the
most difference. Not only because she let Violet go ahead and
the argument, but by putting her friends in positions which
were stressful.'

'Guilt maybe. Ruby not only lost her little sister but also her
friends and her youth. Jan Prentice told me the diary can't hurt
anyone again, among other things. If Donny ever found and
read it, oh it would have been bad.' It didn't bear thinking about.

'How do we find out whether it was Donny who went to jail
in 1968 for assault?' Olive got to her feet and leaned against
Harriet, her head on her mother's shoulder. 'Would he have
hurt Ruby if he found it? He'd already slapped her for trying to
break up with him and back then I guess it was brushed under
the rug. Even these days.'

Harriet's phone rang again and Olive kissed her cheek and
shot out of the room. Her voice was bright as she chatted to the
caller. It must be Jason.

Dropping onto her seat, Harriet opened the diary to the last
entry. Throughout this entire treasure hunt they'd only turned a
page when there was a new clue. That had amounted to a
quarter of the diary, if that. But the remains of the diary felt

bulkier than if they were simply pages and Harriet began to flick through.

There were no more entries but a whole lot of pages were missing. Two were taped together, holding something within. Something square and thick.

Olive reappeared, holding out the phone and mouthing 'Brock'. Her eyes shot to the diary and widened and then she disappeared again.

'Hi there.'

'Are you doing anything important today?'

There was an odd tone to Brock's voice. A hesitancy.

'Olive and I are working on the diary. Why is that?'

'The diary is why I'm calling.'

'The diary?'

He didn't immediately answer. Harriet's mind raced. What had changed since last week? He'd been intrigued, encouraging. And when Jason had been negative and cutting, Brock had been the opposite.

'Brock, have I crossed a line?'

'You? Impossible, Harriet.'

Olive was back with a thin knife.

'I'm not too busy for you. Never,' Harriet said.

'Would you and Olive come up to the house? Any time today. And can you bring the diary and if you still have it, the bible Mum sold you?'

'Of course. Can you tell me why?'

Olive was about to slice through the tape and Harriet put her hand out to stop her.

'Mum wants to speak with you. She saw your window display earlier. Now she wants to talk.'

'We can be there in an hour?'

'Lunch will be ready.' Brock hung up.

Olive had questions in her eyes.

'Annette saw the window display and wants to see us at Brock's house. With the diary and the bible.'

'I guess I shouldn't slice this open then.'

'I guess not.'

'Do you think Annette will understand what we've been doing? Like, that it was never intended to hurt her?' Olive looked anxious, which mirrored Harriet's feelings.

'I honestly don't know, honey. But what I do know is that you and I may have a missing piece of Annette's life, which matters. And good or bad, we're getting a rare chance to reunite something important with a woman who has suffered greatly.'

Olive drove to Brock's property, more confident on the twisty climb after several visits to see Kasey. They'd collected the bible, poetry book, and the diary along with the map.

'Kinda weird Kasey not being here.'

'She's become a good friend, hasn't she?'

Olive nodded. 'She invited me to spend a week with her in Sydney next term break. Would you mind?'

Seeing you happy?

'I think you should go. Sydney is a beautiful city and if you can spend time near the harbour, you'll love it.'

'Cool. I'll tell her.'

The car reached the top of the hill and Brock's house was ahead, with its backdrop of trees and beautiful surrounding gardens. Although she'd only been here once, it felt like coming home.

'Why are you smiling, Mum?'

'No reason.'

By the time Olive parked the car, Brock had wandered out to meet them.

'Thank you both. Mum's in a bit of an odd mood and I'm at

a loss at how to help. Do you think this diary has anything to do with her?'

Brock looked worried and Harriet longed to touch his face and tell him things would be okay. But would they?

'This morning we've read more and some of it is a bit distressing. Do you want us to talk to you about it first? Because we do feel your mother was one of the teenagers in the diary, if not the narrator.'

'I thought as much. Mum is incredibly guarded about her childhood and I've always felt something dreadful happened. Something too painful to tell me. Let's go and see where this takes us.' He reached for Harriet's hand. 'Lunch is ready in the gazebo.'

The gazebo was a spacious covered structure filled with light and greenery from potted and hanging plants and it was close to the most beautiful swimming pool Harriet had ever seen. It was fresh water and exactly as she imagined a secluded rock pool might be somewhere deep in a valley. It even had a low waterfall.

It took all of her restraint not to take a photo and send it to Jason to show him what a real swimming pool was like.

Annette was seated at a long table and she smiled a welcome and gestured for everyone to sit. 'Have you been out here before, Harriet?'

'No. The only time I've visited was to buy books and I saw the reading room and kitchen.'

'Then Brock must show you around after lunch.'

Sitting here with the sound of the water and occasional chatter, Harriet's heart was happy. Between the surroundings, the company, and the food – slices of quiche, salads, and sourdough – her earlier feeling of being home was amplified. Wherever she ended up buying a house, Harriet intended to create the same sense of welcome and harmony.

Lunch eaten, plates all to one side, Annette leaned her arms on the table and gazed at Harriet.

'I had a somewhat cryptic message from Marge last weekend telling me to look at the display in the bookstore window, so on the way home, Kasey and I stopped there. And I've been back for another look. I'm wondering what prompted you to have certain items? A map, for one.'

Annette's eyes didn't waver from Harriet's but her hands clasped and unclasped each other over and over.

'The map? I hoped it might start a conversation.'

'With whom? And why?'

'Why? Because Olive and I have been following a story from the past. One which began as a wonderful adventure but sadly turned into a tragedy. And we hoped someone who had knowledge of those events might see my display.'

'But for what purpose? Dredging up the past is a dangerous game, Harriet.'

There was no anger in Annette's voice. No accusation. Only a quiet sadness which tugged at Harriet. If she'd made a mistake by looking for the owner of the diary then she would try to make amends. Olive's eyes darted between Annette and Harriet.

'I can see that now and if I've caused you any pain then I sincerely apologise. What we stumbled upon appeared, on the surface, as nothing more than a teenager's record of a few weeks in 1961. Before we read a single word I tried to locate the author... the person we've referred to as the narrator because we had no idea who it was until recently. But I was told it belonged to nobody now and should be thrown away if we didn't wish to read it.'

'You have the diary?' Annette's voice was little more than a whisper and Brock moved from where he sat to pull up a chair beside her.

Olive opened her bag and slid it out.

Annette gasped and then covered her mouth with a hand.

'We found it at the bottom of a box of books we purchased. It was actually the same day we bought the poetry book and bible from Brock,' Harriet said, rushing her words. 'I contacted the seller who wasn't very friendly and wanted nothing to do with it. And it was by sheer accident that we found the treasure map inside.'

'Oh my dear lord. I think you had better tell me everything.' Annette grabbed hold of Brock's hand. 'Olive, dear. Would you run into the kitchen? There's a box of tissues on the counter and I have a feeling they might come in handy.'

Olive and Harriet took turns telling how they'd read the diary and followed the clues as though they were part of the treasure hunt. That they'd deliberated about the connections between the people and places. How they had becoming immersed in the world of three teens and life in the early 1960s. The speculation about the origin of the compass and bible. Their admiration for Nettie. Sympathy for the sensitive Bess. Heartbreak over Violet.

'And Ruby, what did you feel for her?' Annette asked.

'At first we felt she was a bit self-centred.'

'A bit?' Annette laughed aloud. 'She always was selfish but it didn't stop me loving her because she was also intelligent and could be very kind.' The smile vanished. 'How she got herself into trouble with Donny Hammond is still a mystery. I wonder sometimes if she was just so bored with her small-town life that he was a bit of a thrill. All it led to was a lifetime of sadness. Poor Ruby.'

Every so often, Annette would look at the diary but she hadn't made a move toward it. Brock still had her hand in his. He'd said nothing throughout the conversation but his feelings showed on his face. Sadness, a lot of the time.

'In the diary, you wrote about suspecting the compass had been stolen,' Olive said. 'Did you ever learn anything else about it?'

'Not for a long time. After I fell at Ruby's house, I was in and out of hospital for months and even spent time in Melbourne, at the Children's Hospital. I had more surgery and healing took time. Not just my leg, but my heart. For the longest time Bess and I blamed ourselves for Violet's death and then seeing Ruby married to that awful man and her turning her back on us... anyway, I pushed a lot of that out of my mind. But the compass was indeed stolen.'

Olive's eyes widened and she leaned forward. 'Was it by Donny? And did it come from the Mahogany Ship?'

Another chuckle from Annette and she released Brock's hand. 'Oh, I loved that theory of mine about a shipwreck which to this day cannot be located even with modern technology. I even deciphered a couple of words which turned out to be part of a dedication of sorts. The strength of a tree, the freedom of the sea.' Her face became sombre. 'After Violet died, the compass was recovered and was scrutinised by local historians and even sent to one in Melbourne for a period. Ruby and her parents refused to have anything to do with it, of course. Eventually, decades later, it was returned to Palmerston House. Elizabeth keeps a glass cabinet with a small collection of items which belonged to the Temple family. The original Temple family. Although nobody is certain of the origin of the compass, it was stolen from Henry, along with a fob watch. There may also have been two books.'

'The poetry book and the bible,' Harriet said.

'Yes. They were gifted to my husband by Donny Hammond, who was his patient for a while and knew of his love of books. Ruby had passed away and I think he wanted the bible, in particular, gone from his house. Unlike Ruby, Donny wasn't a churchgoer.'

'Are you saying the bible belonged to Ruby?' Olive asked with a gasp. 'And he gave it to your husband, knowing the history between you and Ruby?'

'I'm sure it gave him some twisted pleasure. Now I have no evidence it was stolen, any more than I do the poetry book but I've always felt that if one came from the Temples' then probably so did the other. But Donny's parents gave the bible to Ruby as a wedding gift. And we all know the reputation of the family as thieves.'

Olive took out the bible and placed it beside the diary.

After a brief hesitation, Annette reached for the bible and picked it up. She turned the bible onto its front and opened it to the last page. 'You will think me a heathen but would one of you hand me a sharp knife?'

Brock found an unused one among the plates and handed it to his mother with a raised eyebrow.

'Ruby and I used to hide notes in books. School books, anyway, but it was a bit of fun and probably led to our interest in doing the treasure hunt.' Annette carefully slid the end of the knife along the inside of the back cover until a gap appeared beneath the top layer of paper. She put the knife down and slipped a fragment out.

'Oh my goodness!' Olive found the map in her bag, still in a plastic sleeve. 'Is that what I think it is?'

'You really do have the rest of my map, child. Thank you.' Annette unfolded the fragment as Olive gently removed the map from the sleeve and laid it close to the older woman. The fragment was a perfect fit. 'I never thought to see it again.'

Brock pored over the map, his arm around Annette's shoulders. 'You drew this when you were just fourteen? But you always told me you can't draw... oh. I'm sorry.' He dropped a kiss on her hair. 'You stopped drawing.'

Annette nodded. 'My life changed. A tragedy will do that. But I met your father and he loved me despite my sadness and self-blame and over the years I forgave myself and Ruby. I'd never blamed Bess for any of it but she still sees it differently. There's only one thing I wish I could have back because those photos we took that day were all we had together.'

Without a word, Olive opened the diary to the taped pages.

THIRTY-EIGHT

Hand in hand, Brock and Harriet had wandered around his property. He'd shown her the vegetable gardens and orchard as well as the greenhouses. They'd said hello to the horses. Wound their way through the trees to a large flat rock at the top of a slope facing Rivers End. They'd stood there for a while deep in their own thoughts, a breeze blowing in from the sea which was just visible behind the distant cliffs.

Now they sat on the edge of the swimming pool, bare feet dangling in the water. Harriet longed to sink into the cool depths and swim beneath the waterfall but that would have to wait for another day when she had swimwear with her.

Over in the gazebo, Annette and Olive were still talking and it looked as if they were going through photo albums. At one point, Olive burst into laughter which subsided to a giggle when she caught Brock's eye.

'I fear my mother is showing Olive my childhood photos. This may be traumatic.'

'For Olive?'

'For me.'

He sounded so woeful that Harriet had to look twice to see

the telltale flicker of his lips. She dropped her hand into the pool and quickly splashed a scoop of water up. Straight into his face.

Brock gasped and his mouth stayed open as water dripped from his hair to his chin.

What is wrong with you, Harriet?

'Oh I am so—'

Before the word sorry could come out, Brock had somehow got to his feet and lifted her into his arms in one movement. 'Sorry? Is that what you were about to say? Are you sorry?'

She glanced down at the water which wasn't far beneath her. 'Sure. Yes, Brock. I am sorry.'

He took a few steps further in and the water appeared to rise.

'Splashing your host isn't very socially acceptable.'

'Carrying your guest into the middle of a swimming pool is even worse.'

Brock grinned. 'Then tell the truth, Lady Harriet.'

'Lady Harriet?'

'Perhaps I want to be your knight in shining armour.' He shifted his weight a bit to better balance.

'Except I don't require rescuing.'

He chuckled. 'You are aware of your current predicament?'

Her eyes darted to the surface of the pool which was only inches away. If he dropped her she'd be fully submerged in a millisecond. But the ensuing splash would probably saturate him which was a satisfying thought.

'Okay, I'll tell you the truth.'

His face was so close that she could have lifted her chin and kissed him. Instead, she whispered, 'I'm not sorry I splashed you and would do it again in a heartbeat.'

'Take a breath.'

A heartbeat. Two.

Cold water engulfed Harriet as she was unceremoniously

dropped. She touched bottom and kicked herself upright. Brock hadn't moved and now, even as he threw his head back and laughed, he steadied her with firm hands. Her top and shorts stuck to her and water poured off her hair and down her neck.

'Mum? Are you okay?' Olive was halfway to the pool and suddenly stopped. 'Oh. You two are playing around. See, I told you. Brock makes you happy. Good.'

With that she turned and jogged back to the gazebo.

'Do I make you happy?'

'Do I *look* happy?'

Harriet wiggled out of his hold and swam to the waterfall. She ducked under it. It was secluded in here, with soft lighting under the water. Brock followed her in and there was a question in his eyes that she wasn't quite ready to answer. She found the bottom of the pool and stood in the water, which stopped just under her arms.

'Is Annette going to be okay?'

Although the change of subject seemed to throw Brock, he gave it a moment and then nodded. 'Mum has never given even a hint of what happened all those years ago but I remember Bess once mentioning a terrible accident with a young girl. A couple of children have gone missing over the years and one was never found. I don't know what my father knew but they were so close. They had a marriage of the heart, body, and mind.'

I like the sound of that.

'When Annette cut open the tape and those photos were there... I had shivers down my spine and then she began to cry,' Harriet said.

'I've rarely seen her weep. This might have brought back a lot of bad memories but also good ones. Better times with friends, who will now forever remain that age in her mind, thanks to being caught on film.'

Brock moved closer although he didn't touch Harriet. 'Are you taking Jason back?'

'Why would you think that?'

'He still loves you.'

'And I still love him, but as Olive's father. As someone I shared most of my life with. He knows our marriage is behind us.'

'Mum? Assuming you are both behind that waterfall then I'm just letting you know Annette and I are going to go make something for afternoon tea. And there are towels here.'

'Should I answer?' Harriet whispered.

'You did.'

'You've lost me, Brock.'

He touched Harriet's face, ever so gently. 'Do you remember when we said goodnight outside your cottage? The night we went out on the yacht?'

The air tingled with electricity. She nodded, unable to speak.

'I told you I wasn't ready to ask if I could kiss you because once I do, I'll be lost.'

One arm slipped around her waist and with his other hand he brushed strands of wet hair from her face.

'The thing is, even if we never kiss, I am lost.'

'Then we are lost together,' Harriet whispered. 'And I would like you to kiss me. Please.'

For an instant Harriet thought there were tears in his eyes but then she closed hers and their lips found each other.

It took Annette a few days before she was ready to speak about the past with anyone else other than Bess and Marge. Harriet and Olive had been regular visitors to Bess's home, witnessing an outpouring of grief as well as powerful healing and love between the friends.

She'd asked Harriet to come with her today. Olive was watching the bookstore and Brock came with them. When they reached the police station, Harriet asked – for possibly the third time – if this was what Annette really wanted.

'He's Donny's grandson. Doesn't that worry you?'

Annette shook her head. 'The point is, dear, that he is Donny's grandson. He isn't Donny and although young Mick has his share of hangups, at heart I feel he is a good man.'

Mick Hammond was expecting them although he only knew Annette wanted to report possible stolen goods. His eyes narrowed when the three of them appeared at the front desk but he ushered them in and found extra seats.

'You know everyone who is here, Michael, and I wanted to speak to you personally because it may affect you.'

'No idea what you mean. What are you reporting?'

Annette cut to the heart of the matter.

'Your grandfather was a patient of my husband and on his retirement, Donny gave him a book. From the start I wondered about its origin and there is now a second book which once belonged to Donny requiring attention. Perhaps of the police, although this is an historic offence. Not new.'

Mick sat back, arms crossed, a scowl on his face. Harriet could see why some locals avoided him.

'What are these books and what makes you think they were ever stolen?'

'A poetry book and a bible. The former includes a hand-written note from Eleanor Temple to her husband, Henry. Now, we've done some research and it appears the bible, or one very like it, was mentioned in a list of items stolen from Henry not long before his untimely death in 1853. Actually, both books were, along with a compass and a fob watch.'

His face turning bright red, Mick's hand went to his top pocket and he uttered an oath.

'What's wrong?' Harriet asked. 'Do you have a fob watch? One from your grandfather?'

'Thieving, lying, evil excuse for a man.' Mick dragged a gold fob watch from his pocket and dropped it on the desk. 'He left that to me. In the will and all. My aunt got the house and she sold it real quick and left the minute she could.' He thumped the desk and moaned. 'He hated me being a cop and now he's got me good.'

'Hang on, if he left it in a will then you are not culpable, Mick,' Harriet said. 'You need a lawyer to talk you through it but what he did is nothing to do with you.'

Mick didn't look convinced but he straightened and opened a notebook. 'Let's get some details about these books.'

By the time they left the police station, Mick was in a better frame of mind. Brock had phoned his own solicitor, Mr Appleby, and Mick had an appointment to see him. At the door Mick had thanked Annette and Harriet and shaken Brock's hand.

'This might be a turning point for that young man,' Annette said as they headed for the bookstore. 'Carrying around shame and guilt, particularly when not of your own making, is a dreadful thing.' She suddenly stopped and hugged Harriet. 'Thank you.'

The bookstore was busy and Olive was running between customers when Harriet returned. The phone was ringing and Harriet took care of that before anything else. Once she and Olive had served almost everyone, Harriet rushed to the bathroom and then got a glass of orange juice to take back to the counter.

'Did it go alright?' Olive pounced on her the minute she sat. 'Are we in trouble with the law?'

'Doubt it. Poor Mick discovered that he may be in possession of stolen goods himself.'

'No!'

'Turns out Donny left Mick a fob watch. One which

315

Annette recognised from the fabric shop all those years ago. Poor man is a bit in shock.'

'See, I told you he was troubled. So are we going to set up a side-hustle?'

'Doing?'

'Healing. You know, people healing. We can discover the truth about their past and help them find peace again.'

Harriet got to her feet and cuddled Olive so tightly her daughter protested. But she didn't let go at first. 'You are the kindest person in the world. The most incredibly caring soul I've ever met.'

'And the most squashed human ever. Well, I might have been if you hadn't found me on the phone app.'

Olive freed herself but was grinning.

'And you are never to scare your mother and me that way again.'

Heart dropping, Harriet noticed Jason at the end of a stand, holding a couple of paperbacks.

'Oh, and Mum? Dad's been taking a look around. Sorry. Forgot to mention it.'

'I like the range you have,' he said.

'You do? Thanks.'

'It suits you.' Jason gazed around the shop. 'The two of you have created something wonderful and I'm proud of you both.'

Unsure how to respond, having never heard the word 'proud' come out of his mouth, Harriet looked down.

'Harry? Harriet.'

She raised her eyes. Jason was smiling. The old Jason who'd been there through good and bad times and helped raise their daughter.

'I'm going to buy a few books and then head back to Melbourne. What happened on the beach... I've done a lot of thinking. And although I'm not ready to make plans, I might look at finding a place to live around Geelong or Torquay where it isn't such a hike to see Olive.'

'She'll like that.'

'Like what?' Olive joined them. 'Dad, have you remembered anything about your auntie? I've asked you at least three times this week!' She crossed her arms and tried to look stern.

Jason grinned and ruffled her hair like she was a little kid. 'It finally came back to me. Auntie Beebee.'

'Beebee?'

'You know that thing you do to remember names? B for Bess and B for Barrett. My Mum's sister.'

'No way.' Olive ran behind the counter and began flicking through the orders book. 'Mum, do you know her last name? Our Bess? I took an order for her last week and I'm sure I wrote a surname...' Olive squealed. 'It is her! Bess is my great-aunt!'

'So you know her?'

This was wonderful. Harriet hugged Olive as she ran back.

'Mum, may I have the rest of the afternoon off? I'd like to reintroduce Dad to his aunt. She is, after all, the reason we have this bookstore.'

At one minute to closing time, Brock wandered into the bookstore.

'Unless you know exactly what you want, I'll be locking the door in seconds.' Harriet smiled as she rounded the corner with her keys.

'Good thing I know exactly what I want.'

A little shiver of delight went up Harriet's spine from the way he delivered the words and she locked the door.

'Where's Olive?'

Harriet brushed past him slowly. 'Visiting her great-aunt.'

'You found who it is! That is lovely news.'

'Bess.'

'Our Bess?'

'The very one. Yet another unexpected joy from our move here.'

'Another?'

Harriet just smiled and began to close the register. While she cashed up, Brock told her he would be away next week again. 'I still travel a lot, Harriet. Sometimes for weeks at a time.'

'Good thing there are inventions such at telephones. Even Zoom calls. And as a self-employed businesswoman I can hire an assistant if Olive is off following her own dreams, and take holidays now and again.'

'Did she tell you I sent her some links to read?' Brock asked. 'Chef schools.'

'She did. And she's also researching aged care options. Her future is bright.'

It truly is. And she is truly happy again.

Harriett took the takings to the safe and Brock turned off the lights. They met in the kitchen.

'Would you like to have dinner with me tonight?' Brock loosely wrapped his arms around her waist.

'I would. Do you like going to other people's restaurants?'

'Yes. There's always something new to learn.' He dropped a kiss on Harriet's lips. 'I want to keep learning about you.'

She kissed him back. 'I like doing this.'

He grinned and then stepped back and ran a hand through his hair.

Why are you nervous?

Her heart began to race.

'We can talk more at dinner but I've been wondering for a while... my place. My home. Could you ever... in the future, see yourself living there?'

'Where the air is pure and the trees are a sanctuary and the gardens are beautiful and the swimming pool is wet?'

They both laughed, easing the tension a bit.

'Yes. I could live there.'

His smile grew wider.

'Are you going to sell it to me?'

'Sell it... oh.' He swept her back into his arms. 'Sorry, this is a package deal.'

'You and the house? But you'll cook so I guess that's—'

His lips smothered whatever silly thing she was saying. Her arms came up around his neck and when he lifted his head, all she could see was her reflection in his eyes.

'I love you, Brock. House. No house. I love you.'

'And that kind of answer means you won't be dropped in the pool again. Unless you want to be. I love you, my dear lady.'

Tears rolled down her cheeks and Brock kissed them away.

As they left, she stopped near the window overlooking the intersection. If she tried hard enough she could imagine a time long ago. But she only had to look around to know that her present and future were right here, right now.

A LETTER FROM THE AUTHOR

Huge thanks for reading *The Bookstore at Rivers End*. I hope you were hooked on Harriet and Olive's journey. If you want to join other readers in hearing all about my new releases and bonus content, you can sign up for my newsletter!

www.stormpublishing.co/phillipa-nefri-clark

If you enjoyed this book and could spare a few moments to leave a review, that would be hugely appreciated. Even a short review can make all the difference in encouraging a reader to discover my books for the first time. Thank you so much!

Years ago I heard about a shipwreck which became known as the Mahogany Ship and it sparked so many questions. Although the wreck may have been the figment of someone's imagination or misinterpretation of what they saw one dark night, there are many people who believe it is real and so far, undiscovered. When I began to brainstorm ideas for this book, the Mahogany Ship came up again. I loved the concept of a relic from a mysterious wreck being imagined as part of that history.

What could be more fun than a treasure hunt, with the relic as a prize?

Two treasure hunts!

Because Harriet and Olive are at very different places in their lives – although connected by so much – I wanted them to rediscover their unique strengths through an adventure. This would test them and ultimately bring them closer to each other, and to themselves but along the way they would face risks and fears and ultimately find a place of happiness.

Thanks again for being part of this amazing journey with me and I hope you'll stay in touch – I have so many more stories and ideas to entertain you with! From my heart to yours.

Phillipa

www.phillipaclark.com

facebook.com/PhillipaNefriClark

instagram.com/phillipanefriclark

tiktok.com/@PhillipaNefriClark

linkedin.com/in/phillipa-nefri-clark-4a126814b

AUTHOR'S NOTE

Research is such an integral part of writing a novel, particularly one with historical aspects. In Australia we have a fantastic resource called Trove. It is run by the National Library of Australia alongside many research partners and freely available to anyone. It is wonderful having access to a broad range of information from the past. I'd like to acknowledge the SES (State Emergency Services), highly trained volunteers who truly are there to help no matter how severe the weather. Writing a book is just the beginning and I am so thankful to the team at Storm Publishing for the tireless work behind the scenes. And a special mention to my gorgeous editor, Emily Gowers, who asked me to give her more drama. I hope I have succeeded with this story.

GLOSSARY OF AUSTRALIAN TERMS

Brumby: Australian wild horse

Doona: duvet, comforter or quilt

Esky: cool box, cooler, chilly bin

Op-shop: thrift shop, charity shop

Sheoak: a family of trees native to Australia

Skiting: boasting or bragging

Tarax: Australian soft drink company originally based in Melbourne

Printed in Great Britain
by Amazon

41180015R10189